WEBS
OF
POWER

Published by Emerald Book Company
P.O. Box 91869, Austin, TX 78709

For ordering information or special discounts for bulk purchases, please contact Emerald Book Company at: P.O. Box 91869, Austin, TX 78709, (512) 891-6100.

Design and composition by Greenleaf Book Group LLC

Publisher's Cataloging-In-Publication Data
(Prepared by The Donohue Group, Inc.)

Quinn, Darlene.
   Webs of power : a novel / Darlene Quinn. -- 1st ed.

   p. ; cm.

   ISBN: 978-1-934572-23-8

1. Upper class women--United States--Fiction. 2. Consolidation and merger of corporations--United States--Fiction. 3. Retail trade--Unites States--Fiction. 4. Rich people--United States--Fiction. I. Title.

PS3617.U366 W4 2008
813/.6
                                    2009929667

Printed in the United States of America on acid-free paper

12 11 10 09   10 9 8 7 6 5 4 3 2 1

First Edition

WEBS
OF
POWER

A NOVEL

DARLENE QUINN

EMERALD
BOOK CO.
A Division of Greenleaf Book Group LLC

DEDICATION

To my mother, Evelyn Stafford, and my loving aunt and friend, Lorraine Leabo, for their belief in me and for reading each and every word of my first attempts at writing fiction. My mother passed away on March 8, 1994, before the publication of either of my novels. My aunt passed away on October 18, 2007.

And to my husband, Jack, the loving man who is always there for me.

ACKNOWLEDGMENTS

This story could not have been conveyed without the generosity, wisdom, and guidance of the following individuals: Allen Questrom—master of merchandising, retail, and company turnarounds, who led Federated Department Stores out of bankruptcy and on to the acquisition of The Broadway/Emporium Stores and R. H. Macy & Company, Inc.; Terry Lundgren—chairman, president, and CEO of Macy's, Inc. (formerly known as Federated Department Stores), and a true believer in "a balanced life." Others to whom I owe my firsthand retail education and the ring of authenticity throughout this work of fiction are the former executive and the sales and sales-support associates of Bullock's/Bullocks Wilshire. My questions regarding financial ramifications of hostile takeovers were capably answered by Gary Olson, first vice president of wealth management with Smith Barney, and Bob Hughes, MDRT with American General.

I also owe a great deal of gratitude to Margaret Thompson Davis, best-selling Scottish author and mentor, Frank Gaspar (Pulitzer Prize nominee), award-winning author Elizabeth George, and multi-genre author Maralys Wills, who introduced me to the art of writing fiction through their workshops and their critiques of my early work. I would also like to express my appreciation to Laura Taylor, my perceptive editor, and to my manuscript readers, Carol Hess, Barbara McClaskey, and Sally Sopking. Thank you to members of my writer's group—Evelyn Marshall, Wesla Kerr, Lori Newman, and Susan Posner, and to fellow authors Tom Kirkbride (*Word of Honor*–Gamadin Series), Kathy Porter (*Gray/Guardians*), and Robert S. Telford (*Handbook for Theatrical Production Managers*), who gave encouragement and guidance through the many drafts of this novel.

And a very special thanks to my savvy publicist, Peg Booth, and to all the wonderful professionals at the Greenleaf Book Group whose enthusiasm and dedication not only greatly enhanced this work of fiction but also made the journey to publication an exciting and enjoyable adventure: Justin Branch—Senior Consultant; Alan Grimes—Production Manager; Linda O'Doughda—copy editor with an excellent eye for detail; Neil Gonzalez—Cover Designer; Ryan Wheeler—Marketing Manager; Ashley Marion—Marketing Associate; Kristen Sears—Distribution Manager.

Finally, special thanks to my father, Charles Stafford, for his constant support and belief in me, and most of all to my supportive husband, Jack Quinn, who puts up with my unorthodox hours and makes everything possible.

Hollywood Hills, California

Paige Toddman woke on the morning of January 25, 1988, drenched in sweat, the damp sheets plastered to her body. The nightmare she thought she'd put to rest was back. She feared closing her eyes. She feared Mark would awaken to find her, once again, thrashing about. Most of all, she feared talking in her sleep. Without thinking, Paige traced the thin scars that circled her wrists with her fingers. Faded now and barely visible, they reminded her of deeper scars that she had concealed through a lifetime of lies. They were raw and permanent.

She slowly turned her head and prayed she hadn't awakened her husband. But he wasn't beside her. She shook off the tangled sheet and climbed out of bed, her course of action clear.

She took a steadying breath, anxious about the new secret she kept. Her news had the power to tear her marriage apart, but she couldn't let one more day slip by. She must tell Mark today.

Paige hurried through her morning routine then slipped into her leotard. "Mark?" she called out. She paused. Then, hearing his raised voice echoing through the open doorway, she sped down the tiled corridor and rounded the doorway into his study.

Clad in his usual Armani sweat suit, Mark gripped the phone receiver so tightly that his knuckles looked white. "An isolated case of poor judgment I might forgive, but never a bold-faced lie. There's no place in my organization for lies or liars. You're through . . ."

Paige stood paralyzed as Mark slammed down the receiver, whipped his body around, and filled her in on the seemingly minor transgression of the general manager he'd just fired. She listened without comment.

His words echoed in her head. As he had done so many times before, Mark turned into a whirlwind of rage when confronted by dishonesty.

"Lying bastard. Screws up his life, then tries to screw up mine. Thought he was the type of man I could count on . . ." Mark continued his diatribe as he followed Paige into the exercise room. He flipped on the TV, grabbed a glass of orange juice, and gulped it down.

She drank hers slowly. As he began his daily routine, she hit the record button on the VCR and gestured to the TV. "Mind if we listen to this later? I have something important to tell you."

Mark pushed a sandy-colored strand of hair off his forehead, leaned forward, and tilted Paige's chin up. "About time. When there's no sparkle in your eyes and that quirky sense of humor fails to surface, I know something's bugging you," he teased. He glanced at the TV as CNN's Lynne Russell came into focus. "Just give me a few minutes to get rid of these kinks." He stretched his arms above his head and paused. Flashing that boyish grin she usually found hard to resist, he raised his right hand as if under oath. "Ten minutes, then I'm all ears."

Paige set the remote control on the floor beside him and tried to ignore the churning in the pit of her stomach. As Mark launched into his first set of sit-ups, she theatrically raised her wristwatch to eye level.

She made no move to begin her own warm-ups. Instead, she jammed her arms into the vivid blue terry-cloth robe she found draped over the ballet barre.

Mark finished his last set of push-ups.

Paige nodded toward an exercise bench. "Sit down. I have to get this all out at once, so please, just listen. And don't interrupt."

"Sounds ominous." Mark pointed the remote at the screen. He leaned forward, about to rise, but stopped short. She saw his body stiffen and followed his gaze. A familiar face appeared in the window above the newscaster's head.

What now? Paige wondered.

Australian land developer Philip Sloane has made a hostile offer of $47 per share, or an approximate $4.2 billion, for the Consolidated retail empire . . .

Mark blinked at the screen. The nerve in his left eyelid flickered. Paige dropped down to the floor beside him, her eyes too now fixed on the TV, her hand gently squeezing his.

"Everything we've worked for is about to go straight down the toilet." Mark punched out each word, his voice guttural—sounding nothing like his own.

There'll be no good time for my news, Paige thought, as her hand moved slowly across her belly. Distracted by Mark's pain, the urgency of her problem faded—but only for the moment.

Boston, Massachusetts

Alone in the home of her fiancé's parents, Ashleigh McDowell roamed aimlessly from room to room, aware of each unfamiliar groan as the stately Victorian home settled into twilight.

She thumbed through the well-worn pages of her organizer as if she might regain a degree of control over her immediate future. But no amount of planning, no matter how meticulous or detailed, could alter it.

She had not heard from Conrad since he'd rushed his father to the hospital three hours earlier. She stared at the telephone, willing it to ring. Once again, she flipped through her organizer, dwelling on the worst-case scenario.

When she and Conrad had slipped into bed the night before, their world seemed full of promise. Now, Ashleigh felt it all coming unhinged.

Conrad's parents, eager to meet her, had instantly made her feel a part of their family. She enjoyed the subdued elegance of their home—so like the one of her own childhood.

Memories of the previous night filled her thoughts. Conrad's father, Bradford Taylor, had appeared to be in excellent health—a man in control of his destiny. If disappointed that his only son had chosen not to follow in his footsteps, he revealed no sign of it. His own commitment to the "hands-on" leadership of his empire, Taylor Commercial Investments, remained crystal clear.

The first blow had come early that morning as they sat around the breakfast table, listening to news of Philip Sloane's hostile offer for the Consolidated department stores. Conrad's expression had changed from astonishment to incredulity. But before anyone had fully taken it in or discussed the impact a takeover might have on their careers, Bradford Taylor had doubled over and gasped in pain.

An eternity passed before the color returned to his face. Yet, he waved off their concern. "Just a bout of indigestion," he'd said, and shifted the focus back to Sloane's attempted takeover. "But there must have been some foreshadowing."

"Incredible as it seems, there wasn't," Conrad replied. "The stock is obviously undervalued. We were vulnerable. Unfortunately, the board dragged their feet in approving our plan to combat the downward trend." He paused, about to switch to the impact Sloane's unexpected bid might have on his and Ashleigh's careers at Bentley's, a prestigious West Coast division of Consolidated. But Conrad was cut short when his father began to rub the bridge of his nose, murmuring something about blurred vision.

Instantly taking charge, Conrad said, "Dad, I'm driving you to the hospital right now."

The phone rang, jarring Ashleigh back to the present. She leaped to her feet and snapped up the receiver. "Yes?"

"On the way to the hospital, Dad's speech became slurred . . ." Conrad's voice broke, then he continued, "He's had a stroke."

An hour later, Conrad returned to the house. He dropped down on the sofa beside her, his dark hair disheveled, a light stubble shadowing his jaw. "Mom is staying at the hospital."

Ashleigh nodded and reached for his hand.

"The doctor said Dad's chances for recovery are excellent, but he could retain a slight weakness on his left side."

Conrad sounded far from convinced. Glancing out the window, Ashleigh saw tree branches, covered with new-fallen snow, glistening in the sunlight. Their beauty the day before had delighted her. Now, she felt only the cold.

"Until Dad is on his feet, I'll have to take over his company."

"Of course you will."

Conrad went on as if she hadn't spoken. "Taylor Commercial Investments is more than Dad's legacy—it's his life." He paused, his gaze unblinking. "It's Dad's life, not mine, but what else can I do?" Not waiting for Ashleigh to respond, he said, "And now with Sloane spinning Consolidated into play, there couldn't be a worse time to bail out on Bentley's."

Ashleigh swallowed hard. With a voice she prayed would remain steady, she said, "You don't have a choice, love. Besides, it won't be forever." As she spoke, her positive spirit kicked in. "I know how hard it is to put your career on hold, but your dad's a young fifty-nine. He'll want to return to the company as soon as he's able." Circling his neck with her arms, Ashleigh kissed her fiancé lightly on the lips.

After returning her kiss, Conrad said, "I can't predict how long I'll need to stay in Boston, but I can face anything as long as you're by my side."

Ashleigh gently pulled away. "I love you more than ever, Conrad." Her voice faltered. "Somehow we'll work things out," she said softly, willing it to be true. Then thoughts of her own obligations in Southern California filled her head, and she felt their future begin to crumble.

Greenwich, Connecticut

In Philip Sloane's spacious master bathroom, Viviana De Mornay stared at her reflection. She no longer looked as she had in her prime—she looked better. In her youth, she had lacked a keen sense of style and sensuality, precious assets that can be mastered only with maturity.

No one would believe she was pushing forty. She turned her head to study her profile. The skin at her jawline was a bit tighter than she would have liked, but that would ease with time. Leaning closer to the mirror, she confirmed that the swelling was gone and that her makeup concealed the bruising.

She swung her blunt-cut, dyed-auburn hair back and forth then smoothed it into place. Philip had been away on business while she had sequestered herself in his country estate to recuperate. She could hardly wait for him to see her. No doubt about it, Philip's personal cosmetic surgeon was the best.

Viviana wore a simple, black cashmere, mid-calf gown that hugged her slim figure. Her only accessory was a pair of three-inch heels. At five-eight in stocking feet, she preferred not to add to her height, but without high heels, her ankles appeared too thick. *Better to be a tad taller than Philip than to have unattractive legs.* She took one last look at her silhouette in the full-length mirror. Satisfied, she headed for the living room.

Philip wouldn't arrive for another half hour, giving her time to select a couple of their favorite Sinatra CDs to play soft and low.

Placing Philip's glass in the freezer to chill, she poured herself some vintage cabernet sauvignon. She picked up the *New York Times* and arranged herself on the couch in front of the bay window to await his arrival.

Viviana reread the front-page article about Philip's takeover bid for Consolidated and felt a glow of pride. She savored his power. Now her peers and other loyal coworkers of Bentleys Royale would see that power. They'd give her a bit of flak, perhaps, but when they discovered that she, their own fashion authority, would be the next Mrs. Philip Sloane, wife of Consolidated's new owner, they'd change their tune.

Enjoying that image, Viviana refilled her wine glass. Midway through the article, however, she froze as her gaze fell on a photograph of Philip. He had attended Saturday night's black-tie extravaganza at Carlingdon's, the Consolidated store that had captured Philip's heart and imagination. An unfamiliar woman, displaying a generous cleavage, hung on his arm.

The caption under the four-inch picture read: "Philip Sloane and his enchanting wife, Helga, take time out to celebrate before the corporate raider becomes fully immersed in an all-out battle for Consolidated."

Red wine spilled down the arm of the white sofa. Struggling to catch her breath, Viviana tried to take in what she'd just read. Philip had not been away from New York this past weekend. He'd been less than fifty miles from her. He had not left Helga behind in Australia. Had he even begun divorce proceedings? Had everything been a lie?

Her emotions ranged from denial to hurt and then to anger. Viviana grabbed the Steuben bowl from the coffee table and raised it high above her head. Her hands shook. But before she hurled it into the fireplace, her mind snapped into focus. She lowered the bowl, carefully returning it to the table.

Thankfully, Philip had not walked in. His vanity equaled hers. If she attacked him, she would lose him. Venting her anger would shatter her future. It was definitely not worth the risk.

Viviana hastily gathered the pages of the newspaper and shoved them out of sight under the sofa. She dashed to the kitchen for a cloth to clean the wine stains from the sofa. Then she freshened up her makeup in the powder room and steadied her nerves by downing another Valium. Strolling back into the living room, she began to plan for the performance of her life.

Tonight would be one Philip would remember—a night free of conflict, a night for love. She would fill his head with words of admiration, the kind of validation that a wife of many years would surely fail to offer.

At the sound of gravel under tires, Viviana peered out the window. She saw Philip's Jaguar round the circular drive. In less time than it took him to mount the front steps, she met him at the door with a seductive smile and a frosted tumbler of eighteen-year-old Chivas Regal on the rocks.

CHAPTER

2

Paige stood on the front steps, unconsciously rubbing her arms as she watched Mark's Porsche disappear down the winding road. When she glanced up at the leaden clouds darkening the sky, she felt an oppressive heaviness settle inside her. Even before Sloane's unconscionable bid had hit the news, the sensation of losing control over her destiny had been driving her mad. Now, temporarily immobilized by the announcement, an even deeper sense of vulnerability washed over her.

Don't dwell on it, Paige admonished herself. Heading back to the exercise room, she tossed her terry-cloth robe on the bench and raised an unsteady leg to the ballet barre. Moving through her stretches and exercises like an automaton, she flashed back nearly twenty-two years. Paige swallowed hard, regretting the string of lies that had come so swiftly to her lips during her insecure youth. By the time her path had crossed Mark Toddman's, she had felt like an ensnared rabbit—too paralyzed to escape the shelter of her own fiction.

Paige closed her eyes. How she wished she could turn back the calendar. Mark's boyish image sprang to her mind's eye like a series of clearly focused snapshots:

> Bent over the drafting table in the public relations department, diligently cutting and pasting Mark's photograph above an accompanying article, Paige nearly jumped out of her skin when the office door banged open against the inside wall. He had materialized before her, looking as if he stepped off the cover of *Esquire*. Mark's candid hazel eyes held hers for a breathless moment.
>
> "Sorry. Didn't mean to startle you," he said apologetically in a thick Boston accent, extending his hand as he introduced himself.

A few minutes later, Sonny kissed her on the forehead and headed out the door. The light in the room seemed to dim, and Paige felt the walls closing in on her.

Inwardly cringing, she thought back to the night of the Share charity extravaganza and how she had flirted with the incoming president of Wells Fargo. Had she been feeling insecure that night? Had her juvenile antics been aimed at getting Mark's attention? Ridiculous. She knew that Mark had neither the time nor the inclination for jealousy.

The following week, Dr. Gene—the portly, balding doctor who had been their friend as well as Paige's gynecologist since she and Mark had moved to the Los Angeles area—offered the logical explanation for her uncharacteristic behavior. "Paige, you're pregnant," he announced.

She had stared at him in total denial. Mark had had a vasectomy earlier that year so that she could go off the pill. "But I can't be pregnant!" she had protested, incredulous.

"I took the liberty of checking with Mark's urologist, and I'm afraid Mark never found the time for his follow-up exam to recheck his sperm count." The doctor paused. "Although the success rate of a vasectomy is high, it isn't 100 percent. It seems we do, indeed, have a little freeloader here."

Paige now worried about her uncharacteristic flirtatiousness with the Wells Fargo president, caused most likely by her raging hormones. She prayed it hadn't triggered a faulty assumption about her pregnancy. Mark was the only man she had ever loved.

CHAPTER

3

Viviana De Mornay awoke with a start, well before dawn.

Her pulse thundered in her ears. Slowly raising her head from the pillow, she peered into the darkness and waited for her eyes to focus. At the sound of Philip Sloane's rhythmic breathing, her tension began to ease.

Gazing at his sleeping face, she recalled their lovemaking and almost blushed at her immodesty. She'd given an Academy Award performance, concealing her sense of betrayal, her rage, and her fear. She felt certain that she had skyrocketed him to sexual peaks he had never climbed before.

She eased herself off the bed and picked up Philip's hastily discarded shirt. Pulling it on, she tiptoed out into the hallway. Moonlight filtered through the domed skylight, illuminating her path as she made her way to the dressing room in the guest suite.

She brushed her hair, deftly reapplied foundation, and added a light touch of blush to duplicate the youthful glow of nature. She downed a little red pill. Wide-awake, she felt ready to begin again.

Viviana crept back into the master suite and draped Philip's shirt across the settee before slipping, naked, between the sheets. She nuzzled possessively into the hollow of Philip's body. He moaned sleepily, pulled her close, and ran his hands over her pelvis and along her thighs.

When she reached out and stroked him gently, he groaned. Showing no sign of drowsiness, he rolled her over and kissed her greedily.

"Umm," she murmured, gently biting his earlobe. "Don't hold back, Philip," she whispered. "Don't be gentle. I want you. I want all of you. I want to be . . ."

"I know what you want."

That afternoon, in the garden-view office of his Greenwich country home, Philip Sloane's grip on the receiver tightened as Murray Levich, the so-called prince of mergers and acquisitions, spoke. Sloane felt the hairs on the back of his neck snap to attention. They'd had this same go-around over the Amalgamated deal.

"Damn it, Murray. Don't use that patronizing tone. If it were just a few shopping malls or department store divisions I was after, I wouldn't need you. We'll get financing for the whole deal. Not bits and pieces. Of course I'll need to spin off a few divisions, but I'll do the choosing."

Levich remained silent on the other end of the phone. He and First Commercial stood to make an astronomical $200 million in fees once Amalgamated's junk bonds and sixteen divisions were sold. The hungry bastard knew damn well Consolidated would be even more lucrative.

"The immediate priority is our preemptive bid," Sloane hurried on. "I don't care if it takes all night, get your top number crunchers to generate models to cover every contingency."

Philip set up an 8:00 a.m. breakfast meeting in his Manhattan suite, and then he went in search of Viviana. Unbelievably patient during his marathon of business calls, she had periodically poked her head through the open doorway of his study and blown him a kiss. With a loving smile, she would slip away to entertain herself.

"Viviana." He never used the diminutive. Viv didn't seem to suit her, if her body language were to be trusted. He found her sitting stiffly on the sofa, staring out the bay window. "Sorry, kitten, I had no idea I'd be tied up so long."

She turned to face him, her pale-blue eyes brimming with tears.

"What is it?" he asked. "Are you upset with me?"

She averted her eyes, but then she held out her arms to him. "How could I ever be upset with you, Philip?"

"Then tell me what's wrong." He felt her tremble as her arms went around him. He pulled back to look into her eyes. "Please, kitten. I can't help if you don't tell me."

She gazed at him, her eyes wide and wet. "Oh Philip . . ." She hesitated. "It's just so awful. I can hardly believe that someone I considered a friend could be so vicious."

"Vicious? Who? About what?"

"Darling . . ." Her voice wavered. "I haven't had time to think this through, but Lois, my so-called friend, called this morning . . ." Viviana broke off, appearing to struggle with her emotions. "Before I repeat what she told me, I want you to know I didn't believe a word she said. I know the kind of man you are. You could never do what she says you've done."

Sloane's patience began to unravel, and his voice turned harsh. "Stop talking in circles, Viviana."

She looked at him as if he had slapped her, and he instantly regretted his tone.

Viviana began again. "Lois told me you were using me to get insider information and that you had no intention of making me your wife."

"I'd say your so-called friend is out to stir up trouble," Philip quipped somewhat nervously. Gently wiping the tears from the corners of her eyes, he traced her cheek with his fingertip. "How about dinner at Le Paroquet?"

Ashleigh paused beneath the porte cochere of Bentleys Royale's flagship store on her way to her office. Conrad had officially resigned from the presidency of Bentley's, and she missed him more than she thought possible. Unconsciously, she gazed in the direction of downtown Los Angeles, visualizing Conrad's empty office at Bentley's headquarters. Her departure from Boston had been less than twenty-four hours earlier, but to Ashleigh it now seemed as distant as another planet.

Before meeting Conrad, Ashleigh viewed this elegant store as the epitome of all her hopes and dreams. Charles Stuart, the inspiration behind this legendary cathedral of merchandising, had been like a father to Ashleigh. Her own parents had died in a plane crash when she was only two, and although she had no *blood-ties* to Charles Stuart, he and her grandmother had been her parents—the only ones she remembered. They had instilled in her a love and respect for the Bentleys Royale and all it stood for. This elegant store had become Ashleigh's obsession, as well as her salvation, after her first love was killed in an auto accident the night before their wedding.

But today, as she walked past the familiar etched-glass doors, memories of her grandmother and of Charles Stuart eluded her.

Replacing those memories was the article in the *Los Angeles Times* that lent credibility to rumors of more takeover threats aimed at Consolidated. The reporter's interpretation of the division's structure, while technically correct, had seemed cold and clinical.

Among Consolidated's vast holdings is its distinguished division of stores situated on the West Coast, known as Bentley's. Bent-

ley's is a giant in the retail industry. Their organization chart shows a block of corporate offices at the top. This division is currently headed by Mark Toddman, CEO, and Conrad Taylor, President. Under them, the chart divides, showing two uniquely separate subdivisions; each manages and merchandises its goods autonomously. The larger of the two subdivisions is made up of twenty-six suburban stores, known as Bentley's Department Stores. *The smaller subdivision is made up of seven upscale specialty stores, known as* Bentleys Royale, *with its own president and headquarter store . . .*

Conrad's resignation had been withheld from the media, but the fact that he no longer sat in his office at the corporate headquarters tugged at Ashleigh's heart.

At the door to the associates' entrance, Ashleigh heard rapidly approaching footsteps that pulled her away from her introspection. She looked over her shoulder and spotted the fashion merchandising director, Viviana De Mornay.

The two women quickly exchanged greetings as Ashleigh held open the door. Viviana looked as though she had just stepped out of a designer ad. She wore a Sonia Rykiel three-piece deep-red wool suit. The long knit jacket over the short skirt created a lean look to perfection. Her accessories were a combination of Chanel and Ferragamo. Viviana had always dressed beyond her means, but since her liaison with Philip Sloane, she allowed nothing ordinary or second best to adorn her body.

In spite of the arrogant set of Viviana's chin, her facial expression spoke of chagrin. Having made no secret of her coast-to-coast romance with Sloane, she now encountered open hostility from peers and other fiercely loyal members of the Royale team. That hostility was bound to increase, Ashleigh realized, and Viviana would become a scapegoat in Sloane's quest to capture the Consolidated empire. Ashleigh felt genuine compassion for this woman whose pride and love for the stores nearly equaled her own.

Ashleigh's ability to look beyond the surface had been an important asset in her job as director of human resources. Whether it was a blessing or a curse, she didn't always know. Inevitably, she focused on what was not being said. In her personal life, this trait drove those close to her wild, but at Bentleys Royale, it served her well.

As they walked along the corridor together, Viviana said, "I understand Conrad Taylor has already jumped ship."

Caught unprepared, Ashleigh stopped and turned to face Viviana. How could she know of Conrad's resignation?

While Ashleigh considered her response, Viviana continued, "Don't worry; I won't say anything until it's been officially announced."

Ashleigh quickly changed to a neutral subject as they signed in at the check-in desk, then she took her usual shortcut down the back corridor to her office. Viviana headed for the double doors that led to the bank of elevators that would take her to the fashion offices on the fourth floor.

Ashleigh unlocked the door to her reception area, pausing before her secretary's cluttered desk. The small Lucite phone-message holder was stuffed to capacity. No surprise, after a week's absence and the threat of a hostile takeover. Job security was bound to be an issue—particularly at the executive level. Shifting her organizer to the crook of her arm, she picked up the pink memos and opened her office door. Pushing it shut with her foot, Ashleigh sidled between the étagère and the large circular table that dominated her office and slipped into her desk chair.

Usually, the moment she stepped inside these familiar blue walls, the outside world evaporated. Today, however, everything felt different. She looked up at the painting of the colorful clown Emmet Kelly, made on an aged copy of the *Wall Street Journal*, and thought how he was privy to all the secrets that came to light within this room. But on this day, even Emmet seemed oddly distant.

Ashleigh quickly rechecked her calendar and then twisted her chair around to the credenza. Ignoring her fistful of messages, she dialed Charles Stuart's number.

Charles answered on the second ring, his familiar baritone full of warmth and good humor. He asked about her trip to Boston and meeting Conrad's family.

"I'd like to tell you all about it tonight if you're free for dinner."

"That would be lovely."

"Any more developments on the lawsuit, by the way?" Ashleigh asked. Charles's daughter had inexplicably been released from the Rancho Mirage Mental Hospital three weeks before, and she had promptly initiated a lawsuit against him. Caroline's claim stated: "I am entitled to my dead mother's entire estate and a large portion of my father's. Mother told me to go after it before Ashleigh McDowell got her greedy paws on it."

"Caroline thinks I'm the one who had her committed."

But that isn't true, Ashleigh wanted to say, but Charles's next revelation shifted her focus.

"Her attorney gave me a list of assets she feels she should have. It includes my shares of Consolidated stock."

"Do you think she knew the company would be forced into play?" Ashleigh asked.

"As we suspected, Caroline's former husband signed for her release and immediately remarried her. She either doesn't know or has forgotten that he was the one who had spirited her off to that abominable state mental facility. Then he managed to keep her mother and me in the dark about it for several weeks while he transferred Caroline's assets to a Swiss bank account. After that, he quickly divorced her. Caroline would never have fallen for his remarriage scheme otherwise. But I'll fill you in at dinner."

Ashleigh felt chilled to the core as she set the receiver back in the cradle. She never would understand how his own daughter and son-in-law, whom Charles had trusted and appointed president of his beloved Bentleys Royale, could have plotted against him all those years ago. But that was exactly what they had done. The vast stockpile of Bentley's shares that they had secretly accumulated tipped the scales against Charles in 1965, and Bentley's had fallen to Consolidated Department Stores. The son-in-law collected his money and bailed out, leaving Charles to handle the transition.

Charles joined Consolidated's board of directors after his company fell into their hands. Times changed, but Charles had not been left behind. With the power he retained, he continued to make his contribution to the integrity of his former empire. Now, it seemed, his daughter and son-in-law might be plotting to take that role away from him as well.

Viviana De Mornay strode through Active Sportswear to the fashion offices without stopping to check her appearance in the floor-length mirror outside her office, her usual habit. She went directly to her desk, picked up the phone, and dialed David Jerome. His line rang and rang. The president's phone seldom went unanswered. For a fleeting moment, she experienced a sense of relief. But as soon as the receiver hit the cradle, the urgency to reach him returned.

She clicked on the speaker button and hit redial. As the phone rang, Viviana locked her handbag in the closet and checked her face closely in her well-lighted makeup mirror. The two weeks' rest had not worked the hoped-for magic, but fortunately, she didn't look as drained as she felt. Gingerly patting a generous portion of concealer under each eye, she allowed her mind to return to her early days at Bentleys Royale. Nostalgia tugged at her.

David Jerome had been her Professor Henry Higgins, and she had fallen blindly and hopelessly in love with him. He had taught her a true appreciation for quality by taking her to museums and encouraging her to enroll in art classes. Under David's tutelage, she had earned a master's degree in business at UCLA and had become a name in the fashion industry. She had loved those days and felt good about herself and her accomplishments.

When he ended their brief affair, she had wanted to die. Instead, she gathered up the remnants of her wounded pride and took advantage of what he had given her. She even legally changed her name to De Mornay, her mother's maiden name, for its ring of prestige, and she felt herself elevated above her humble upbringing. How different her life might have been if she'd gone through school as Viviana De Mornay rather than Vivian Brown. Her love of art and beauty was not middleclass. When she had heard the words "good enough" during her childhood, she had felt diminished. Now, as a leading fashion authority and looking every inch the part, she refused to settle for anything ordinary.

The passionate sexuality David Jerome had awakened in her also served Viviana well. She had loved him with all her heart and had given of herself completely. She vowed never to do so again with any man after David had severed their intimate relationship. Never again would she risk that kind of pain. She was not bitter, however, nor did she regret her affair with the president of Bentleys Royale. It had strengthened and armed her for the future.

Viviana was not in love with Philip Sloane, but she *was* infatuated with him, his wealth and power as potent as any aphrodisiac. She hungered for the luxuries his money could buy. When she walked into a room on his arm, all heads turned toward them. She liked that. And, unlike David, Philip would make her his wife.

A takeover was sure to be the end of David's own dreams. She could not bear the thought that he might think her a traitor.

"David Jerome." The deep voice above the background hum jolted Viviana from the past. Her hand trembled as she grabbed the phone and flipped off the speaker.

Viviana marched past the secretary's office, straight into the president's. David Jerome looked up briefly.

"Please, sit down." He nodded toward the chair in front of his massive desk and wordlessly continued to sift through a stack of phone messages.

Her antennae went up. She recognized that deadly, polite tone. Trying to gauge the exact moment to speak, she focused steadfastly on his face until he made eye contact.

David defied the passage of time. Now in his mid-sixties, he seemed more attractive than when she had first come to work at Bentleys Royale. Although his gray hair wasn't as thick as it had been, his face remained relatively unlined and his body trim. His energy level in business, as well as on the tennis court, surpassed that of men thirty years his junior.

When he looked up, Viviana began, "Before things get all blown out of proportion . . ."

David held up his hand and leaned forward. "Forget the platitudes. You're not responsible for Sloane's actions. However, you are responsible for your own. And I expect you to conduct yourself as the professional I know you to be."

She held her silence as he removed his glasses and began to polish the lenses with a white linen handkerchief. "Philip Sloane is an emotionally unstable and dangerous man. You must end your affair immediately."

Viviana felt paralyzed with disbelief. He had no right to make such a demand. Though she had prepared herself for his inevitable challenge, this was too much.

"Under the present circumstances, for you to continue to be seen in the company of Sloane or his cohorts," David continued, "is not only an embarrassment, it is an outright betrayal to this organization. A betrayal to me and to yourself as well. Despite your intelligence and considerable talent, your value to Bentleys Royale is nil without your total commitment."

Viviana rose on unsteady legs. "How can you question my loyalty or devotion, David?" She swallowed the lump in her throat, disbelief turning to self-righteous indignation. She rattled off her stellar record of outstanding contributions to the quality and high standards that epitomized Bentleys Royale.

A moment later, having been summarily dismissed from David Jerome's office, Viviana felt her face burning. How dare David talk down to her as if she were some expendable piece of shit?

Now, as she thought of their brief affair, the sweet nostalgia vanished. She had an image of the two of them entwined on the blue velvet couch in the corner of his office. She had spread her legs and opened her body to him. She had not felt like a whore then, but that is how he had made her feel today. He had absolutely no right. Oh, how she wished she could erase that holier-than-thou expression from his distinguished face. She should have asked him how undivided his commitment to his wife had been during their torrid affair. But she never would. After their affair ended, they never again spoke of it. But he knew, as well as she, that neither had given any less to Bentleys Royale during their days of passion. If anything, they had each given more—their quest for excellence a strong bond.

Ashleigh heard raised voices outside her office. Without warning, the door sprang open and banged against the wall. Viviana burst in, slamming the door behind her.

"I have no intention of resigning," the fashion director announced.

Ashleigh gestured for her to be seated and buzzed her secretary. "Betty, please hold my calls for the next fifteen minutes."

Viviana folded her arms in front of her. "Sure you can spare the time?"

Ashleigh, used to all the colors of Viviana's moods, took no offense. Nothing in Viviana's world was viewed in half measures. She saw black or white, entirely full or completely empty. Her demeanor, when it was not calm, cool, and collected, was hyper-agitated, as it appeared now.

Ashleigh met Viviana's gaze. "I have a meeting in twenty minutes," she said. "How can I help you?"

Viviana's pale skin turned a deep shade of raspberry in splotches. It was a blessing that she couldn't see herself. "I'm telling you—I have no intention of giving up my position. I've worked damned hard creating this store's quality image . . ."

Silently nodding her head at appropriate intervals, Ashleigh listened to Viviana's tirade. Finally, when the monologue seemed to be over, Ashleigh asked, "Has it been suggested that you resign?"

"Not in so many words," Viviana replied as she laced her slender fingers and began turning her thumbs in circles. Then, in an uncontrolled outburst, every word the president had uttered moments before gushed through Viviana's tight lips.

"You know better than to take his every word literally," Ashleigh chided. *God, what an understatement*! Inwardly, Ashleigh cringed. If only Mr. Jerome practiced his well-honed skills of diplomacy with his own management team. Unfortunately, he continued to say exactly what he felt, giving no thought to possible ramifications. And while Ashleigh did not disagree with his conclusion regarding Sloane, she was responsible for preventing brouhahas in the personnel arena. "As long as you continue to perform, no one can force you to resign."

"You're damned right!" Viviana rose, thrusting the now familiar, dog-eared issue of *Women's Wear Daily* across Ashleigh's desk. Below her picture, the article proclaimed Viviana as one of the nation's top fashion merchandising directors. "I won't be pushed around. I'll resign when, *and if*, it suits me."

Viviana sank back into the chair, her voice softening. "He knows how much I love Bentleys Royale. I've poured my heart and soul into it. And Philip won't sacrifice quality or try to run Bentleys Royale like a department store. Philip knows—"

"Hold it," Ashleigh interjected. "Let's not speculate."

With an exaggerated lifting of her brows, Viviana said, "Well, la-di-da. I bet you'd have sung a different tune if Mitchell Wainwright had been the one to put Consolidated in play when you two were hot and heavy."

Ashleigh felt her hands close into tight fists and sought the words to put Viviana in her place. But before she could form her first syllable, Viviana uttered a hasty, though transparently insincere, "Sorry. My relationship with Philip Sloane is no flash in the pan romance. When his divorce is final, we're getting married. He is an intelligent and powerful man. The media gives a distorted picture, but it's nothing more than sour grapes. Both Philip and Mitchell have had more than their share . . ."

When Ashleigh did not immediately respond, Viviana drummed her fingers on the tabletop and shifted focus. Staring unblinkingly into Ashleigh's eyes, she asked, "Isn't it illegal to dictate what I do on my own time?"

On Friday afternoon Philip Sloane climbed out of the subterranean pool of his Greenwich estate. Shaking purified water from his hair, he flung his goggles onto a nearby lounge chair and gingerly patted his head. Reassured the transplanted follicles were secure, he finished drying himself and wrapped the maxi beach towel around his trim nude body. Liposuction had been only the start of his new image. Health food and workouts were now a daily ritual and an effective stress reducer. But today, his fifty laps had done little to relieve the gnawing in his gut.

His wife's unannounced visit to New York the previous weekend had been more than a surprise; it had shocked him to the core. Although he had feigned delight and hastily revised his plans, it had not gone at all well. Predictably, through overheard comments and innuendos at the extravaganza at Carlingdon's, she'd learned of Viviana De Mornay's presence in his public and private life. He'd been a damned fool to take Helga there.

Thank God she hadn't made a scene. What she had done, instead, was disappear from Carlingdon's and New York. When he returned to his hotel suite, he'd found a scrawled note propped against the table lamp—blunt and to the point.

> *Returning to Melbourne to begin divorce proceedings. Your things will be shipped to you.*

What utter bullshit. He'd give her a week to cool down, then fly to Melbourne and set her straight. For now, thankfully, he had Viviana. She was loving, genuinely supportive, and believed what he told her. But, in spite of her smashing good looks, incredible intelligence, and uninhibited sexual appetite, a divorce from Helga was out of the question.

With an audible sigh, Philip turned his attention away from personal problems. Somehow he'd sort things out with Helga; Consolidated was another story. He could leave no stone unturned in his quest for control.

He quickly made his way up the spiral staircase and trod barefoot to the master suite. He donned a silk robe and sheepskin slippers and perched on the edge of the Georgian settee to contemplate his strategy. Then he dialed the Cincinnatian Hotel. After a bit of fast-talking, he was put through to Mark Toddman's suite.

Mark heard an insistent blare in a distant corner of his mind. He blinked his eyes and squinted at the illuminated dial of the digital clock beside his bed. The time, 3:24 a.m., slowly came into focus as he grabbed for the phone.

"Sloane here," came the familiar Aussie accent.

Philip Sloane was notorious for his late-night or early-morning calls, but Mark had no intention of conforming to his idiosyncrasies or whims. Sloane had been courting him hot and heavy since the tender offer. But if Consolidated fell to Sloane, divisions would be spun off and thousands of jobs would vanish. Mark's title of CEO would be meaningless.

Sloane was far from victory, however. If rumors were to be believed, his tender offer had been launched without the support of a bank—not even a commitment or a highly confident letter.

Mark, having been in bed less than a half-hour, struggled to rouse himself from his initial deep slumber. Running his fingers through his thick hair, he drove the grogginess from his tone. "This better be important."

After a slight hesitation, Sloane spoke. His voice lacked emotion. "I assume you're part of Learner's in-house management buyout team?"

The campaign that Ralph Learner, Consolidated's current CEO, attempted to mount had no more appeal to Mark than did Sloane's. The churlish Learner, who'd come up through the ranks, ran a combative administration. Under his leadership, Consolidated first began to lag behind. His ventures into diversification—aptly tagged "diworsification" on Wall Street—had spawned the depressed stock price and targeted them for a hostile raid.

giddy with excitement. Everything would be all right between them. After twenty-two years, how could she have doubted their bond?

For a moment they stared at each other. Then, without warning, Mark literally swept her off her feet.

"Tonight is totally ours," he said. "I told the world to go away, and I've ordered a fabulous dinner to be served right here in our suite. All of your favorites." He gently set her on the sofa and then kissed her, a thorough loving kiss.

"That's perfect," she said, feeling that she'd received the most marvelous gift. "I couldn't be happier."

"Good." Mark began to unbutton his shirt. "First, I'm going to take a bath," he announced with that youthful glimmer that made Paige's heart beat faster. "Did you remember to bring that green velvet jacket you bought me for Christmas?"

Paige nodded. "It's time you christened it."

Paige had already bathed and was wearing a beautifully fitted robe. Delighted that they would have dinner in their room, she slipped out of the robe and selected the hostess gown that was Mark's favorite from the closet. She pulled it over her head, ran a brush through her close-cropped hair, and returned to the sitting room.

She smiled when she saw Mark's Dewar's White Label on the wet bar. While his taste in food, clothing, and art had escalated with their income, he was still unpretentious. He'd never trained his palate for fine wines and drank Chivas Regal only when it would be rude to ask for his old standby.

When Paige walked into the steam-filled bathroom to hand Mark his drink, his eyes were closed. Her pulse quickened. "Are you asleep?" she asked.

"Just resting my eyes." He smiled and reached for his drink, his eyes now full of enthusiasm. "I've so much to tell you, Paige. Things that will change our lives in ways we've never imagined. Soon as I get dressed, I'll share my news, then you tell me yours."

"Over dinner," Paige suggested. She handed him a large white bath towel. Her confidence dwindled as she thought of her own life-altering announcement.

When Mark emerged in the green velvet jacket and beige trousers, Paige felt a tiny somersault in the pit of her stomach. Baby or nerves? She couldn't tell. All she knew was how much she loved this man and how much she feared the unknown.

Mark refreshed his drink and came to sit beside her on the sofa.

"It's a good thing I arrived when I did," he explained, leaning toward her, his eyes holding hers with unblinking intensity. "The chaos is unreal. Worse than we suspected. The organization has been poorly managed for years, so whoever takes control will have to do a lot of fancy footwork just to keep it afloat."

Paige was incredulous. While she knew Mark had a major philosophical difference with the current CEO, she also knew that Consolidated sold more merchandise than any other department store retailer in the country—more than May Company and Macy's. The only exceptions were Sears and Kmart, but they were in a different ballpark, with a distinctly different customer base.

"You've uncovered more problems than the ones we discussed the other night?"

He emphatically shook his head. "Same ones that led to our depressed stock prices and Wall Street's dissatisfactions. Ergo, a hostile takeover ploy."

"If only Philip Sloane had stayed in Australia!"

"We were ripe," Mark said. "If it wasn't Sloane, someone else would have stepped forward."

"So, what's the next move?" Paige asked, attempting to move on.

"That's what I want to talk to you about . . ." Mark fell silent at the sound of a double knock at their door. He opened it, and he and Paige watched while the waiter unfolded a small table, covered it with an alabaster-colored linen cloth, and arranged their food.

When the waiter disappeared, they clinked their glasses. Mark picked up where he'd left off. "Yesterday, I couldn't muster a single thread of hope," he confessed, shaking his head. Then, uncharacteristically, he rattled on about the CEO's shortcomings. "He pits one executive against another. Morale is at rock bottom. He's perpetually trying to save money,

Viviana De Mornay squinted at the illuminated dial on her bedside clock and fumbled for the phone beneath her extra pillows. At the sound of the muted tone, or perhaps the vibration, she struggled to surface from the deep slumber of her Halcyon-induced sleep. As much as she hated Philip's proverbial calls at odd hours, her fear of missing one was stronger. The stack of pillows dulled the harsh intrusion of the blaring phone and gave her time to plant a smile and a hint of seduction into her sleepy tone.

"Philip, darling," she purred, not waiting for him to speak. No one else would dare call at this ungodly hour. "I was hoping you'd call."

He apologized for the early hour.

"I'm thrilled to hear from you at any hour," she lied. Once she was Mrs. Philip Sloane, she'd put an end to his disturbing her beauty sleep. But until then, she'd give nothing but adoration and unconditional love.

As Philip talked about his world, she saw that it wasn't quite five o'clock. Closing her eyes, she concentrated on murmuring her approval at appropriate intervals.

When his monologue came to an end, Viviana said, "I'm terribly proud of you." Then, taking a steadying breath, she asked, "What time will you be here?"

"Afraid I can't make it, kitten. I'll be working round the clock all weekend with Levich and his number crunchers."

"Oh," she said, unable to keep the disappointment from her tone. Having no idea whether his wife had returned to Australia or not, Viviana had to keep her insecurity and rising bitchiness from reaching his ears. "I'll miss you, darling," she purred again. While business and his wife made their demands, she would be the one to provide him with a blissful haven.

For a few timeless seconds after Philip said good-bye, Viviana held the receiver in her hand as if it held the answers to her future.

"Either I've got an acute case of paranoia, or I've put too much stock in the rumors of Sloane's arsenal of professional stalkers and Mafia hit men," Mark joked.

"Not too professional, since you've spotted him," Conrad observed as they turned into Consolidated's headquarters.

"If Sloane had those so-called ties to the Mafia, though," Mark continued, "then Mitchell Wainwright would have been dead meat long ago. But Amalgamated would have fared a lot better if they'd fallen to Wainwright rather than Sloane. At least he knows when to leave the hands-on management to an experienced team." Mark hadn't intended to surface Wainwright's name before nailing down Conrad's commitment, but now he might as well deal with it. Wainwright was one of the pioneers in the wheeling and dealing of successful leveraged buyouts. Unfortunately, he was also Ashleigh McDowell's former fiancé. If Conrad could set his personal bias aside, Mark would enlist Wainwright's expertise and make use of his contacts in his bid for Consolidated.

The ground floor of the headquarters building, manned by a single security guard, seemed unusually quiet without the weekday hustle and bustle. Conrad noticed the ominous high-pitched hum of the florescent ceiling lights as he and Mark strode across the lobby.

After clearing security, they stepped into the center elevator. Mark said, "The board voted unanimously to turn down Sloane's bid and to put you on an extended leave of absence."

What was he talking about? "Leave of absence?" Conrad echoed.

The elevator opened on the third floor into a reception area, which was vacant. Mark nodded toward one of the small conference rooms on the outer perimeter. "Hear me out. If the numbers don't make sense to ward off a hostile takeover, at least you'll be in on the $28 million golden parachutes we've loaded into our poison pill."

Conrad turned the concept over in his head. "Thanks for the thought. But a leave of absence can't be open-ended."

Mark held up the palm of his right hand and proceeded to pull a bulging manila folder from his briefcase. "We've got that covered, while we're working on this White Knight proposal—"

"Hold it," Conrad broke in, "I'm intrigued and willing to listen, but—"

"Fair enough," Mark cut in. "Sloane's bound to raise his lowball bid, and with three or more bidders waiting in the wings, a bidding war is inevitable. If the price escalates too high, we pull out."

Conrad leaned back in the swivel chair as Mark separated his papers into three stacks. Mentally taking a step back, Conrad repeated skeptically, "The board voted to turn down Sloane's tender offer *without* taking it to the stockholders?"

"Our attorneys have poured over every detail." Mark pulled a paper off the top of his first stack and handed it to Conrad. "This is going out to the stockholders mid-week."

Conrad scanned the document.

> February 5, 1988
> Consolidated Stockholders,
> You have undoubtedly heard of the tender offer made by Philip Sloane. In your best interests, the Board of Directors has turned this offer down.
> Mr. Sloane will not be given an option on Consolidated for the following reasons:
> 1—Mr. Sloane has not produced satisfactory evidence of his ability to finance his offer.
> 2—Mr. Sloane has stated he needs four months to close a fully negotiated transaction.
> 3—If we were to give Mr. Sloane this long-term option, Consolidated could be in an extended state of turmoil. (There is already a degree of unrest among our employees, customers, and suppliers who are aware of Mr. Sloane's past record. After assuring Amalgamated stockholders that he would not sell their assets to pay for the takeover, he disposed of 16 out of their 24 divisions and terminated more than 4,000 employees.)
> 4—There is far too much uncertainty as to Philip Sloane's current financing.
> Sincerely,
> Ralph Learner
> CEO, Consolidated Department Stores

Hardly believing what he had just read, Conrad exploded. "Jesus! Sloane's bid is a joke. Or there's a lot I need to learn about these leveraged buyouts—what you call LBOs."

Conrad was acutely aware that in the market a deal was no longer defined as selling a company's stock or underwriting its bonds. Those old-school activities had become passé. To keep Taylor Commercial Investments afloat, an M&A division must be established as soon as possible. He'd intended to immerse himself in all facets of mergers and acquisitions. Mark's call had merely accelerated his research.

"Let's get all our cards on the table," Conrad said. "I'm interested, but wary." Distracted by Mark's restlessness, Conrad paused. "Look, ol' buddy, give me five minutes. I'll tell you why I'm interested . . . as an *investment banker*," he clarified. "Then you tell me why you want my firm, rather than a financial firm with an impressive track record, to spearhead your bid."

Mark gestured for Conrad to proceed and sat back in his chair.

"Being the new kid on Wall Street, I've immersed myself in the subtle nuances of leveraged buyouts. I've read or at least skimmed through tons of written materials from every reliable source I could lay my hands on, and I've done a fair amount of networking with experts in the field. Still, I've got a lot to learn."

Conrad rose and poured a cup of coffee from the pot Mark had turned on when they first entered the conference room. "To understand my position, you need a certain amount of background." He then launched into an abbreviated version of what he'd learned over the past few weeks. "The price-cutting and discounting, prevalent in the airlines, have taken their toll on Wall Street. Since deregulation, it's been impossible to earn a decent profit in the gentlemanly old-fashioned way. Profits were virtually wiped out of stock trades in 1975 when the SEC abolished fixed commissions."

To avoid covering unnecessary ground, Conrad asked, "Are you familiar with the infamous 415 rule?"

Mark nodded. "It more or less eliminated the profits for underwriting, didn't it?"

"Exactly. Even the so-called white-shoe firms like Morgan Stanley and First Boston began undercutting their competition. In desperation, rather than pure greed, they made plays for each other's formerly untouchable corporate clients. And with the demise of the 'Gentleman's Code,' a long list of unthinkable practices have become the norm.

"Dad's been slow to come to terms with today's predatory atmosphere—to grasp the fact that reputable Wall Street firms are now engaged in buying and selling corporations. A large proportion in hostile takeovers."

Conrad noticed Mark's fingers strumming a steady tattoo and cut his overview short. "In essence, Dad's reluctance to enter into M&A ventures could turn us into dinosaurs in the financial marketplace. A situation I intend to rectify ASAP. We've missed the astronomical fees enjoyed by our competitors. However, I'm also leery of hostile LBOs, comprised of astronomical amounts of borrowed money and their debt potential."

"I wholeheartedly agree," Mark confirmed.

"Taking the lead position in a bona fide acquisition could be the opening we need to move into the 1990s. Therefore, your White Knight proposal has tremendous appeal. My loyalty toward the organization is as strong as ever, and sharing your optimism toward the future of department stores, I'd like to be a part of derailing Sloane's power quest."

Mark's straightforward gaze locked with Conrad's. "On or off the management team, I know you will work in Consolidated's, as well as my own, best interest," Mark asserted. "My motivation is simple. Number one, I trust you. Number two, you know and understand the business and can interpret the numbers. And number three, while I know you intend to bring your firm out of the Dark Ages—your words, not mine—I'm confident you won't push for a deal that doesn't make good financial sense. Bottom line, you're the partner I need to determine the maximum bid."

"Okay," Conrad continued. "You know my strengths and my limitations. To proceed, I'd like to bring in an M&A expert."

Mark nodded. "I agree. I've given it a great deal of thought and have come up with a name."

"Mitchell Wainwright?" Conrad offered.

Again, Mark nodded. "I know you've had your differences—"

"Jesus, Mark," Conrad blurted, "this is business. I don't have to like the bastard. He's not my first choice as a working partner, but he's one of the LBO pioneers, so if he's the right man for the job, I can work with him." Then he smiled and added, "Should be interesting to see how Wainwright handles a White Knight campaign." As far as Conrad knew, the notorious corporate raider had spearheaded only hostile takeovers.

Mark smiled. "Should be a piece of cake. Now that Learner's stepped aside and the board's swung their support to me, we'll have access to actual sales, profit, and operating numbers. Something Wainwright's never had before. And his ongoing rivalry with Sloane should provide sufficient motivation."

Conrad thought of Sloane's unprecedented tactics, spearheaded by Murray Levich. The M&A mastermind's eleventh-hour ploy had snatched the predicted slam-dunk victory of the Amalgamated Department Stores from Wainwright and granted it to Sloane—as unexpected a victory as Harry S Truman's over Thomas E. Dewey.

16

Scores of partygoers poured out of limousines and high-priced automobiles at Casa Pacifica, Mitchell Wainwright's oceanfront estate. Many came to celebrate the charismatic corporate raider's forty-fifth birthday. Far more came to be seen and captured by the media, their photographs to be among the elite in the Long Beach *Press Telegram* society column.

Tuxedoed waiters passed hors d'oeuvres as Wainwright laughed and joked with guests, shaking hands and slapping backs. Throngs of beautiful people milled around the outdoor gardens sipping champagne, while others toured inside to view all the exquisite treasures acquired over the years by the Wainwright family.

Christine Wainwright, though no beauty by any stretch of the imagination, was an attractive and well-bred woman. Tall and stately in her tailored black and cream-toned Armani suit, she stood out in the sea of ladies dressed in short black cocktail dresses. As cool and efficient as she'd been in her role as Mitchell's personal assistant, Christine wove her way through the hordes of well-wishers to find her husband.

She spotted his thick mass of silver hair, head and shoulders above the others, in a small group at the far end of the garden patio and felt a surge of pride. "Mitchell," she called, when she drew near. "Sorry to interrupt, but you have a phone call."

Mitchell glanced up, his brow lifted. "Excuse me," he said to the group. Then, without a moment's hesitation, he followed Christine toward the house. He knew it must be important; otherwise, his wife would have taken a message.

"It's Mark Toddman," Christine said. "I didn't think it wise to make him wait."

Mitchell picked up his pace. Christine stopped at the entry to his study, gave him a knowing smile, and closed the door behind him.

Wainwright's team of accountants had been crunching Consolidated's numbers around the clock. Although he and Toddman did not travel in the same circles, Wainwright had enormous respect for the merchant. His goal from day one had been to entice Toddman into his camp. But before approaching the golden boy of retail, he was waiting for the dust to settle. He'd planned to flush out every detail of his strategy and then attempt to lure Toddman into his corner. With Toddman on board, the Consolidated takeover would be a slam-dunk.

After a perfunctory greeting, Mitchell found himself on the listening end of the conversation. He instantly began counting his blessings as Toddman outlined his strategy and Wainwright's role in it. Had the victory of Amalgamated Department Stores not fallen to Sloane, Mitchell wouldn't be having this conversation. Thank God he wasn't the one buried in *that* enormous sea of debt.

"More than a little interested," Wainwright admitted. He smiled, picturing Sloane's face when he found out that Toddman had come to him. Amalgamated was small potatoes compared to Consolidated. News of this partnership might even drive the feisty Australian into a third nervous breakdown.

"Saturday at eight," Mitchell confirmed. "I'll be there."

Mitchell sighed after bidding farewell to the last of the guests. He gave Christine a perfunctory kiss on the forehead as he commented, "A memorable affair, my dear."

"I hope so," she said, and then she asked—as he knew she would—about Toddman's call.

His smile broadened into a wide grin. "I'll be heading my first White Knight crusade."

Christine, who had been turning out lights as they made their way to the bedroom, stopped in the wide, Italian-tiled corridor. "It appears Toddman has topped even my gift of the original Norman Rockwell 'Four Freedoms' painting."

He studied Christine as she methodically removed her earrings. She was the perfect wife. As his personal assistant, she'd handled almost every detail of his business and personal life and had been his most reliable hostess. Yet, it had taken him nearly seventeen years to take stock of his life—to take a long hard look at where he was going and what was in his own best interests.

Finally, he'd looked beyond Christine's cool efficiency. She was no raving beauty, but she was an asset. Unlike his former wife or the string of glamorous women he'd unwisely pursued in his past, Christine was intelligent and had no mountains of her own to climb, as had Ashleigh McDowell, his former fiancée. While Christine lacked Ashleigh's youth and vitality, she understood his business. Most important, Mitchell was Christine's number-one priority. Even after the birth of their son, on whom his dreams of immortality now rested, Mitchell remained the focus of Christine's life.

"We've been invited to the Toddmans' this coming Sunday," he said. "The only fly in the ointment is that Toddman wants to involve Conrad Taylor's rinky-dink investment firm, but I'll soon put an end to that notion."

Christine's body stiffened, and a spark of emotion flashed in her hazel eyes. Anger or fear, he wasn't sure. "Isn't he engaged to Ashleigh?"

"Yes. He left Bentley's to head his family's investment firm. And Toddman has some wild hair about him being the lead investment . . ." Distracted by the uncharacteristic hard lines of his wife's expression, Mitchell broke off. "What is it?" he snapped.

"Will *she* be at the Toddmans'?"

"She . . . Ashleigh? Jesus Christ, Christine. What difference does that make?"

"That skinny bitch nearly got you killed," she shrieked.

Mitchell stared up at the ceiling, mentally counting to ten, and then he slowly lowered his eyes to meet hers, which were parallel with his own.

Her posture remained rigid.

Mitchell detested this kind of bullshit and made no attempt to conceal it. "I never imagined *you* would turn into one of those proverbial insecure, bitchy wives."

Elated with their progress, Mark left Conrad to sort out his personal business.

Mark planned to spend the rest of the day with Paige. In time she would come to her senses, but for now, they'd put this nonsense behind them. Maybe take in a movie.

Mark and Paige seldom missed a major film. Theater was as integral to keeping in touch with today's opportunities as the networking and deal making on the golf course were. Going to movies and theater with a keen sense of observation—taking in what was being worn and said—was key to predicting emerging trends. And Paige, with her shrewd eye, invariably pointed out something Mark might otherwise have missed.

Thankful that the man in the blue blazer was nowhere in sight, Mark walked around to the front of the Cincinnatian rather than ducking into the side entrance. He picked up a newspaper and headed for the elevator.

As Mark pushed open the door to their suite, he called out "Paige?"

She turned from the window, but instead of running to meet him with the childlike enthusiasm she'd showered on him the day before, she gave him a tentative smile. "How'd it go?" she asked.

"Better than expected." The joy he'd felt moments before vanished. He saw pain in her enormous green eyes, but he resisted the urge to reach out and comfort her, fearing she might misinterpret his affection. Instead, he filled her in on the day's developments—avoiding any mention of the man in the blue blazer.

She responded like some goddamned robot, asking only a few perfunctory questions.

"Christ, Paige. I may as well be talking to the wall."

"Sorry," she said, stepping closer and reaching out to touch him. "I can't stand having our lives so unsettled."

When he didn't respond, she went on, "I'm not talking about business, I'm—"

"I know what you're talking about," Mark exploded. "You know how I feel. I can't force you to have an abortion. I just hope you'll come to your senses. In the meantime, there's nothing to discuss."

"Mark, please. Nothing can be solved if we don't talk it out."

"Not now. Give it time." He would never change his views about a child. It would wreak havoc on their lives.

"How much time?" Paige asked, the set of her chin unyielding, her eyes locked on his.

"Let's just say we'll discuss it when one of us has a change of heart."

"That's not good enough, Mark . . ." She broke off and then said with no uncertainty, "We'll talk when you come home."

"Fine," he agreed hastily. Opening to the entertainment section of the newspaper, he offered, "In the meantime, how about transporting ourselves to eighteenth-century France?"

"What?" she asked. Then her mind apparently clicked into focus. "*Dangerous Liaisons*?" They'd planned to attend the film's premiere in Westwood the day Sloane's hostile bid was announced.

At 8:00 a.m., on the upper floor of the First Commercial building, a loud cacophony of voices boomed through the partially opened door of Lawrence Drew's corner office.

Louise, Drew's secretary, lifted the phone and began to punch in the numbers of the NYPD. The noise broke off, however, and an unsettling silence filled the room. She aborted the call, rose, and headed toward the CEO's office. From halfway across the room, she saw the door swing open, and Stephen, a recently hired arbitrageur, emerged.

Beyond the open doorway, Louise could see her boss extend his hand to Murray Levich. As the two men stood shaking hands, she noticed that the lanky CEO's precisely knotted tie had been loosened and the sleeves of his oxford-cloth dress shirt had been rolled up to the elbows. Ironically, Levich—who generally was unabashedly rumpled, with his shirttail hanging out—looked as if his suit and pink dress shirt had come straight from the cleaners. Even his wiry hair was combed in place.

Drew did not take his eyes off of Levich and Stephen until they disappeared into one of the elevators. He chewed nervously on his bottom lip. His worst nightmare had turned into reality. When word of Levich's exit got out, First Commercial's competence, its prestige, and even its masculinity could be questioned.

Walking back into his office, he pinched his eyes closed and tried to shut out visions of resignations en masse shadowing the superstar's departure. The lure of not having to share their profits with an "antiquated trading department," as Levich labeled it, and working with the king of mergers and acquisitions could be an irresistible temptation—and tough to overcome. No doubt, Levich's departure could cripple or, at the very least, seriously erode the momentum of the bank's M&A department.

As Drew mulled this over, the intercom buzzed.

"Philip Sloane is on line one. When I told him Levich wasn't in, he demanded I get you on the line immediately."

"See if we have a signed contract with Sloane for the Consolidated deal," Drew instructed his secretary. His heart pounded hard against his rib cage as he thought of the expected fee—close to $250 million. No matter how much he'd resented Levich's smart-ass attitude, he and his M&A department made 90 percent of the firm's profits. It would take a goddamned miracle to find a replacement with a fraction of Levich's deal-making know-how and creativity.

He sighed, remembering how Levich had pulled off one of the most sensational and unlikely triumphs of the corporate age. Only Perelman's Revlon and Peltz's National Can Company rivaled the Amalgamated deal, and Perelman and Peltz had each had Drexel's Michael Milken in their corners.

Louise walked in with the fourteen-page contract opened to the last page. The unsigned document blurred before Drew's eyes. He swallowed hard and pressed line one. "Sorry to keep you waiting, Phil."

He didn't have a chance to say much. He just listened, holding the receiver away from his ear as a torrent of loud expletives assaulted his ears.

Philip Sloane slammed the phone down with such force that it was a wonder the receiver hadn't broken in two. *Those bloody bankers aren't about to maneuver me into taking any second-rate negotiator. Levich is the best, and that's who I'll have.*

Sloane mentally counted to seven, his lucky number, then picked up the phone and pounded in the number for his attorney. He had kept Howard Greenfield on retainer, not only for his superior knowledge of mergers and acquisitions but also because Sloane didn't want his competitors to be privy to Greenfield's expertise.

Greenfield answered on the second ring.

"You were right. Levich bailed out of First Commercial," Sloane said. "Turned in his resignation this morning. Effective immediately."

"I knew it," Greenfield confirmed, "but I'm surprised Drew didn't try to keep it under wraps for a while."

"Didn't give him a chance." Sloane spat out the words. He was fed up with the world of greedy fee-snatching bankers. "Whatever it takes, Levich is to be our principal negotiator. Work out the details. And don't let First Commercial pull any shenanigans."

"No problem. We're in the driver's seat," Greenfield responded. "With Levich gone, they're vulnerable. And they stand to lose a lot more than megabucks in fees if they're locked out of the Consolidated deal"

"Right you are," Sloane broke in. "Negotiate with Levich. He's too damn smart to have burned bridges at First Commercial. Have him push for commitment letters, then let the bloody bankers worry about pedaling the paper."

"Sure. I take it we're not to expect you here for the ten o'clock meeting?"

"Right. I'm going to Bermuda." With no further explanation, Sloane added, "If you run into trouble, you know how to reach me."

He strode across the room and peered into the large mirror above the sofa. He looked tired and was losing his tan. What he needed was complete relaxation. His course of action was clear. He again picked up the phone.

"I'm sorry, Ms. De Mornay is in a meeting."

"Tell her Philip Sloane's on the line," he insisted. "It's important I speak to her now."

Viviana De Mornay's face flushed at the unrelenting buzz of the intercom. "Ignore it," she said to the four buyers who sat at her round table. "As I was saying, the key colors for the season will be navy and scarlet and this muted burgundy." She held up color swatches and then she frowned as the intercom buzzed a second time. Shoving her chair back from the table, she trod across the room and pushed the speaker button. "I said no interruptions."

She was about to disengage the intercom, when her secretary said, "It's Mr. Sloane. He says it's important."

Viviana turned to the buyers, "Would you mind stepping out for a moment?"

As they filed out, Viviana pressed the blinking light on her phone. "So sorry to keep you waiting, darling. Lisa should have put you straight through."

"Good news," he said, ignoring her apology. "I'm leaving all the piddling details behind, and we're going to Bermuda."

"When?" she asked. Her mind raced, fear quaking through her as his enthusiasm echoed in her ear.

"I'll dispatch the Amalgamated jet to LA. You have close to six hours to get to the airport. Don't worry about packing a lot of clothes. I plan to take you on a shopping spree."

"Phi . . . Philip," she stammered. "I want to be with you, of course, but I'm a working girl." If only she could take off at a moment's notice. She'd been afraid this might happen. Before she had discovered he had not yet put his divorce in motion, she had been confident. Not always being available would make him desire her all the more. But now she was unsure. What if he turned back to Helga? In the uncomfortable silence, she prayed that he'd once again assure her that he'd always take care of her.

"I need to get away before the onslaught of all-nighters with the bloody bankers, lawyers, and accountants begins. But since your agenda's full . . ." His voice was cold and dismissive.

Goose bumps sprang to her arms, and the roof of her mouth felt dry. "I'll resign," Viviana said hastily, the words rolling off her tongue before she had thought it through.

"No, kitten," he said, his tone softening. "I know how much your career means to you. We'll make it another time."

Even if she gave up her job, it would be nearly impossible to take off this afternoon. But damn it, she was entitled to pursue her own dreams. She would not jeopardize her future. She must continue to convince Philip he was her number-one priority. "I want to be with you. Nothing means more to me than you, Philip. Not Bentleys Royale, not anything!"

Ashleigh sat with her arms wrapped around her legs, her back to the crackling fire in the living room of Charles Stuart's two-story home in the Naples community in Long Beach. On this unusually chilly Southern California evening, the warmth of the fire felt comforting.

Enjoying a glass of the older man's favorite sherry, she marveled at the dashing figure in the armchair just inches from her. No one would guess that Charles would soon be eighty-eight. Heads still turned when the silver-haired octogenarian strode into a room, his posture erect, his suits precisely tailored. And his mind was still as sharp as when he'd been the inspired creator of Bentleys Royale.

This man had given Ashleigh so much, and now it seemed she brought him nothing but pain. If it weren't for her, his own daughter might not have turned on him. "There must be something I can do, Charles."

As he shook his head, she noticed the deep lines and shadows beneath his eyes. "No, love. Caroline is a very sick young woman and very much under the influence of her husband."

"Obviously, he signed her release from the hospital and remarried her to gain access to your holdings. He's a bona fide sociopath."

"It's time we stopped dwelling on things we have no power to change. Caroline's mother claimed my single-minded devotion to Bentleys Royale robbed our daughter of a normal childhood, and there's some truth to that. Caroline's my daughter, and I love her. But let's move on to more pleasant horizons. What I want to know is, when can I expect to give the bride away?"

Ashleigh smiled, her thoughts returning to her future with Conrad. She reached up to take hold of Charles's hand. "I love you both," she said.

Charles scowled. "You don't have to choose between us."

"I know. I know," she hurried to explain. "It's just that there's a lot I have to do here before I can think of uprooting myself and moving to Boston."

She edged closer. "I just don't feel I can bail out on Bentleys Royale."

Her deeper concern, of course, was Charles. She simply could not abandon him.

She squeezed his hand. "Let me explain. Conrad is far more important to me than Bentleys Royale, a career, or living in Southern California, but I wouldn't feel right about leaving while there is such uncertainty within the organization. Conrad left because he had no choice, but I . . ." Then, before he had a chance to say what she knew he would, she continued, "I know I'm not indispensable, but with such unrest, I feel that it would be wrong to abandon my position. When I returned from Boston, I was flooded with calls from executives in need of reassurance."

"And could you provide that?"

"You know I couldn't. But often a sounding board is what's most needed."

"That seems to be your forte." Charles gave her a knowing smile. "I guess that's why they call you the 'company shrink.'"

"Guilty. But apparently, there's just as much turmoil among the sales associates. My personnel managers are spending much of their time reassuring the associates of their unique value and telling them that, no matter what happens, their jobs are secure." Ashleigh hesitated. "For now, this is where I'm most needed. Besides, Conrad needs time to settle into an entirely new business."

"And how does Conrad feel about your decision?"

"He never would have left Bentley's if he hadn't been forced to. And he has no idea how long he'll be in Boston. I'm sure he'll understand." When she again sensed that Charles was about to speak, Ashleigh quickly added, "And no matter what you say, I want to stay until Caroline's lawsuit is behind us."

In Cincinnati, a team of Consolidated attorneys washed down the remains of Chinese takeout with a steady stream of caffeine while they worked through the night drafting emergency legislation on the state's anti-takeover law with the assistance of Marvin Marshall, chairman of the Ohio Senate financial committee, a friend and neighbor of Ralph Learner's. A bill that applied directly to hostile acquisitions by foreigners was being sent to the Ohio House through Senator Marshall.

While Mark Toddman attempted to make contact with the chairman of the Ohio Senate's finance committee, Sloane got wind of the proposed legal maneuvers.

A phone never far from his ear, Sloane cursed the rotten timing and barked orders to his squadron of attorneys. "Counteract any legislation that might impede our progress. Can't wait to see whether the courts declare the measures unconstitutional. Make sure nothing is left to chance . . ."

He slammed down the phone moments before the jet touched down on his private landing strip just outside of Melbourne. He was paying the bloody attorneys a fortune; they damn well could handle the legal shenanigans. Viviana's hesitation over his spur-of-the-moment trip to Bermuda had prompted him to switch his destination to Australia.

Sloane planned to persuade Helga to accompany him to Bermuda, where he would set his domestic life in order. He must avert the risk of plunging into more courtroom drama. Their agenda would be nothing like the one he'd planned with Viviana, but maybe he and Helga could recapture what they'd had so many years earlier in the humble one-bedroom house he'd built with his own hands. He remembered the laughter and good fun of those early days. They had been the happiest years of his life.

The plane rolled to a smooth stop on the airstrip. The glorious Australian summer day brightened his spirits as he watched the workmen wheel the stairs into place. Withdrawing sunglasses from his shirt pocket, he saw his Land Rover at the edge of the runway, the motor running and his chauffeur beside the open door.

The Rover pulled into his circular drive about ten minutes later and stopped at his front door. Sloane sprang from the back seat of the air-conditioned vehicle, pulled a long velvet box from his inside breast pocket, and mounted the stairs.

Opening the magnificently carved door, he felt a blast of hot air. The house was hot as hell. If only Helga would take advantage of the air-conditioning he had had installed. It had cost a bloody fortune . . . This was no time to get himself in a lather, though. As he passed the thermostat in the wide corridor, he flipped the switch to 70 degrees.

"Helga?" he called out as he made his way to the back terrace. "Helga, where are you? I've brought you a surprise."

"In here." Her icy response came from the direction of the kitchen.

He stopped short in the doorway. Helga was on her hands and knees, scrubbing the floor, her forehead dripping with sweat and a babushka covering her damp hair. As she heaved herself to her feet, she reached up with one of her bony washerwoman hands to wipe the perspiration from her brow. His visions of recapturing a spark of romance disappeared. "Helga, for God's sake, what are you doing?"

"What does it look like I'm doing?" She planted her hands firmly on her hips, bunching up the fabric of a faded, loose-fitting housedress. There was a hard edge to her voice.

No matter how many times Sloane had pleaded with her to get help for the heavy work, Helga insisted that she didn't need anyone cleaning up after them or cooking their meals. At his station in life, it was downright embarrassing. She answered the door herself no matter how dirty and sweaty her attire or how unkempt her hair.

His sons had chided him about how hard their mother worked. And the looks they gave him when he said she *liked* doing all the housework herself and refused to have help. If his own sons didn't believe him, what must outsiders think?

"You don't need to be doing this," he shouted, throwing his plans for reconciliation out the window. "I'm getting sick and tired of having you play the proverbial martyr."

"Would you like me to be all tarted up like your fancy American whore?" She spat out the words, but her face crumpled, and she fled from the kitchen.

Sloane walked slowly out the back door. As he stood by the edge of the Olympic-sized pool looking at his reflection, he thought about his life with Helga. She had been an attractive woman, could even be a stunner when she fixed herself up, but those times had become less and less frequent.

The more money he amassed, the more resistant Helga was to change. She'd always been a strong-willed woman, and this was not the first time she'd threatened him with divorce. When she'd found out about another woman in his life when the boys were still young, she'd told him in no uncertain terms, "I won't put up with your carrying on. And I'll see to it that the boys know you for what you are." He had quelled that storm, but theirs had been a rocky, uneasy peace.

Lately, Sloane had talked to her about her appearance and how she might spend her time, but Helga was steadfast and inflexible. "I won't put on airs or become some sort of window dressing. If you want to pretend to be someone you're not, I can't stop you, but I want none of it. Cosmetic surgery and all that other folderol won't make you a single day younger. You'll never be the man you once were," she had said, glaring at him.

Sadly, Sloane realized that while Helga was the mother of his children, and he had no desire to hurt her, she would never be a woman that he'd be proud to have pictured by his side on the cover of *Time* magazine—or any other publication. A discrete divorce might well be his only option.

21

Mitchell Wainwright's capacious office, ensconced in the most desirable high-rise building in downtown Long Beach, had a magnificent view of the harbor, Catalina Island, and the Pacific Ocean. In recent years, it had become the deal-making mecca of the West Coast.

At the familiar beep of the fax signal, Wainwright pushed his desk chair back from the six-foot Mediterranean-style table at the far end of his office. He turned to see the current CEO letter to Consolidated's stockholders that Toddman had promised to send him rolling out of the fax machine. Wainwright had his fingers on the paper before it even finished printing. Here it was, in his hands at the same time it hit the wire service.

Wainwright knew all the ins and outs of LBOs, but Sloane continued to astound him. His low-ball bid in the initial stages of a hostile bid was unusual, but hardly earth shattering. What was staggering was his flimsy financing, with no visible equity.

Wainwright buzzed his secretary on the intercom. In seconds, she appeared in the doorway.

"Make a couple of copies," he said, handing her the fax. "And get Dick Landes on the phone."

As Wainwright strode back to the table, he tried to predict Sloane's next move. With all the suits and countersuits, his legal clocks had been ticking at a merry pace of $150-plus per hour for weeks. It wasn't a question of whether Sloane would bump up his bid—it was a question of how much? Wainwright scanned the figures in front of him. A White Knight bid for a deal of this magnitude was almost too good to be true. He would have access to the actual figures, while Sloane and other rivals would have only those in the public domain, and their best guesstimates.

He knew damn well Consolidated was more than a bunch of numbers. It was a huge operation, averaging $10.5 billion in annual sales compared to Amalgamated's $4 billion.

Wainwright closed his eyes and sank back against the soft, Italian-leather headrest of his desk chair, thinking about how he'd outmaneuver his chief rival. That damn foreigner had been engraving his mark on Wall Street while he, Mitchell, had been losing ground. And this deal required no less strategic planning than a ploy to take over the U.S. Navy.

"Mr. Wainwright." His secretary's voice floated in from the open doorway. "Mr. Landes is not in, but a Mr. Ross Pocino said he'd take the call. He's on line one."

With no preliminaries, Wainwright asked, "What did you find out?"

"Toddman's been a busy boy. One damn meeting after another. I don't think he ever goes to bed. He hasn't once returned to his hotel before three or four in the morning, and he's out again by seven. He was dead-on about having a tail, but it sure wasn't one of Sloane's. The jerk who's been shadowing Toddman is a novice; the thugs on Sloane's payroll are pros. We've spotted them, but Toddman doesn't have a clue."

22

Ashleigh passed through the lobby of the Portofino. She paused in front of the elevators and, balancing a bag of groceries and a large bunch of tulips in her arms, fumbled for the small elevator key that would allow access to Conrad's penthouse.

Her fingers touched the tiny key as she stepped inside the elevator. Setting the groceries on the floor, she inserted the key at the top of the panel, vowing to make the most of their two short days together.

She knew her way around Conrad's spacious kitchen and worked quickly. Although they had talked every night since she'd left Boston, it seemed much longer than a week and a half since she'd felt his arms around her.

Keeping an eye on the clock, she searched in the high cupboards for a vase. At the sound of footsteps just outside the front door, she froze. A visitor might have gained access to the lobby by entering with another resident, but not to this level.

As she was reaching for the phone to dial 9-1-1, she heard Conrad's voice calling her name. Abandoning the flowers, she flew out of the kitchen and tore through the living room.

They met in the marbled entry and stood staring at each other. He looked marvelously unrumpled in the familiar gray Oxxford suit and a blue dress shirt, the same shade as his deep-set eyes.

He tossed his garment bag to the floor and held out his arms to her.

"Your plane wasn't due for another hour and a half."

"I got on an earlier flight," he said as he drew her into his arms.

She looked up at him, her eyes fixed on his face. "But, I could have met you if—"

"I'd have missed the earlier flight if I'd taken the time to call. And once I touched down in LA, I was too impatient to wait for you to come after me. Besides, if I'm not mistaken, you had your time planned down to the last second."

She smiled, encircling her arms around his neck. "You know me all too well. I'm just happy you're here."

They stood holding each other without speaking. Eventually they pulled apart, and Conrad took her hand and led her through the hallway to his bedroom.

They had so much to talk about, so much to settle, but for now, Ashleigh wanted him as much as he wanted her.

They stood for a long time beside the bed, just kissing and holding each other. They pulled apart briefly to gaze at each other, and Conrad moved his mouth down to the hollow of her throat and began to unbutton her blouse. Within moments, all her clothing had fallen to the floor.

Ashleigh began unbuttoning Conrad's shirt as he struggled out of his shoes and slacks.

They came together, holding each other tightly. Conrad ran his hands through her hair and down her back as they sank onto the bed. He pushed her gently against the pillows, kissing her eyelids, her cheeks, and her lips.

His mouth was soft, yet insistent, as he followed the curve of her neck. Ashleigh sighed, the pain of their separation fading as their kisses grew hot and more passionate.

When they paused to take a breath, Conrad said, "Being without you is unbearable."

"For me too," she said, reaching up to touch his face with her fingertips. Ashleigh felt heat surging throughout her body as she ran a finger around his mouth. Then she drew his face to hers. Desire flooded her as their mouths locked and their tongues entwined. She was blind to everything but him.

"I love you," they both said together, their voices sounding as one.

His eyes were vividly blue, so blue. She felt mesmerized. Suddenly she was enveloped in wave after wave of ecstasy. Her eyes closed. She rose higher and higher as he moved deeper and deeper inside her, saying her name over and over.

"Ashleigh . . . Ashleigh, I've never known this kind of love. Never realized it was possible to love so deeply."

"I love you too," she murmured, "forever."

She nuzzled his chest, marveling at her own unabashed sexuality. With Conrad, she'd discovered pleasures she had never dreamed of.

The crimson radiance of sunset filtered through the master bedroom windows. And as the magic of twilight settled around them, they lay content in each other's arms.

Throughout a leisurely dinner, Conrad watched Ashleigh with delight as she told one animated tale after another. She filled him in on the flourishing rumors about the eminent takeover and tried to explain, with humor, how the uncertainty was playing itself out at Bentleys Royale. Their nightly calls had touched only lightly on anything other than their love and longing for each other. He'd come with a full agenda of things he needed to discuss, but for now, he was content just looking at her glistening blond hair brushing her shoulders as she spoke. It was so wonderful to be beside her, to hear her voice, to share her concerns.

Finally, they cleared the dishes and took cups of steaming coffee into the living room. Sitting in front of the flickering flames of the circular fireplace, Ashleigh said, "We've talked about almost everything, but you haven't told me whether you've decided to back Toddman."

"I was saving it till the end."

"Does that mean you have decided?" She set her cup on the end table.

"I think so, but I'd like to bounce some ideas off of you first."

Her smile was quizzical. "What I don't know about LBOs could fill an entire library."

"From what I've learned so far, your observations about LBOs weren't far off target," he countered.

"You mean when I said that it seemed like a person needed more money in the bank to get a mortgage for a house than to buy a corporation worth billions?" Ashleigh joked.

He nodded. "Slightly over the top, but not much. It seems that Sloane has put Consolidated in play without putting one red cent on the table. Nobody knows where he plans to get the money; he hasn't come forward with any specifics. Yet, he wants the company to take his word that he'll come up with it.

"But don't get me started on that tangent. In the past weeks I've learned enough about this topsy-turvy era of investment banking to know I've got to initiate big changes. Taylor Commercial Investments has not kept in step with the times."

"Does your dad agree?" Ashleigh asked.

Conrad nodded. "Yes. But he's opposed to LBOs, particularly hostile ones."

A quizzical frown crinkled Ashleigh's brow. She'd been privy to his father's tirades on what he'd labeled the unconscionable shenanigans of Wall Street.

"And you're in favor of them?" Though her expression was one of puzzlement, it was uncritical.

"Not unilaterally. However, I'm seriously considering backing Toddman's White Knight bid."

"And your dad wouldn't veto it?"

"As long as I'm at the helm, the decisions are ultimately mine. Those were the ground rules. I can't operate as a lame duck, and Dad trusts I won't jeopardize the company.

"LBOs aren't my first choice, but we can't stay locked in the past. Deals worth about $200 billion are now being done on Wall Street every year. If we don't climb into that arena, we'll end up a dinosaur in the industry."

"When you say Wall Street, are you talking about the bankers and lawyers?"

He nodded. "Along with a sea of accountants. Astronomical fees are charged for each step of a deal. They've caused debts that have bankrupted scores of first-rate companies.

"If it weren't for Toddman and my department store expertise, I wouldn't be thinking about backing this kind of venture before getting myself well centered in the investment world. But Toddman is by far the most intelligent and respected merchant in the country. While he does have a healthy ego, he won't enter a bidding war if it could jeopardize the corporation or its backers. If the bids get too steep, we'll bail out."

Reaching for her hand, Conrad said, "Sorry, sweetheart. I don't want to waste our time on a diatribe about the woes of investment bankers, when all you—"

"Conrad," she interrupted, "learning about your world is not a waste of time. I don't want to be an outsider. If you're going into LBOs, I want to know all the gory details."

"Okay," he agreed, "but I'll make it brief. I can think of a lot better use of our time," he teased, kissing her fingertips.

Ashleigh showed no sign of impatience as she listened to his condensed report. When he had finished, she adjusted her position on the sofa, tucking her long legs beneath her. She looked at him intently.

"Now that you know some of the details," Conrad said, "you can imagine how foolhardy it would be for me to take this kind of plunge on my own. I haven't developed the contacts to form the necessary bank syndicates." He hesitated for a nanosecond. "I need an expert. Someone who knows the maneuvers and the players. Someone like—"

"Mitchell Wainwright?" she filled in.

"If his involvement would make you uncomfortable, I'll . . ."

She smiled, and leaned over to smooth his brow. "Not at all. Mitchell and I were wrong for each other. But he was into LBOs before most people even knew what the letters stood for."

Conrad pulled Ashleigh into his arms. "As much as I hated to abandon Bentley's to take over my dad's firm, it's a piece of cake compared to being away from you."

"I missed you, even before my plane left the ground in Boston," she said. But as she wrapped her arms around his neck and kissed him lightly on the lips, Conrad felt a strange sense of distancing between them.

Ashleigh was silent for what seemed a very long time. Then she took a deep breath. "Charles told me you had talked to him the other night. Did he tell you the latest news about his daughter's lawsuit?" she asked.

Early Thursday afternoon, Paige strolled aimlessly though her sleek, contemporary home, running her hand along the smooth surface of several of the lovingly selected art pieces.

She'd always known that she wasn't destined to live here in Hollywood Hills forever. New York is where she and Mark longed to be. But she'd never before considered a life without him.

During their brief time together in Cincinnati, they had said stupid, hurtful things to each other. She had apologized for her spiteful words. He hadn't. "Goddamn it!" she said aloud, her hands balling into fists. *I won't be a victim. I can take care of myself. If Mark won't stand by me now, he's not the man I love. He's someone else.*

She rubbed her hand across her middle. *Well, kid. It may be just the two of us. It's not what I want, but we'll manage.*

Paige strode purposefully into the library, sat down at her crescent-shaped desk, and pulled out a pad of paper. No point in getting carried away. She must be calm.

Naturally Mark was upset. She'd been unreasonable to think he might take her news in stride. With his entire world crashing in on him, he needed time to adjust. Though she still hadn't completely adjusted, adjust she would. Even now she was coming to terms with the rapid changes fate had dealt them. Hopefully, Mark would as well. She wouldn't give up. She would be fair and give this her best shot.

Nearly an hour later, she was still pouring her heart out on paper. At the sound of heels clicking across the tiled floor, Paige jumped up and accidentally kicked over the wastepaper basket, now overflowing with crumpled paper.

Anna, her personal secretary, rushed forward to pick it up, but Paige waved her off. Paige hadn't intended the communication for anyone but herself. And sorting out her thoughts on paper had done the trick. She felt a good deal better now that her mind was focused.

She took the next few minutes to recheck the details for Sunday. "All taken care of," Anna assured her. Then, consulting a square four-by-four-inch memo scrawled on the chef's familiar sand-colored memo paper, she continued, "There will be pitchers of water, pots of coffee, and soft drinks available in the conference room. Dinner will be at eight. Wes asked you to tell him as soon as possible if the meeting is expected to run late."

Paige nodded. "Tell him I'll do my best, but sometimes my crystal ball fogs over." She paused. "On second thought, ask Wes to change the dinner arrangements to a barbecue, an informal one like we did for the governor's victory party. That same menu would be perfect for Sunday."

Anna jotted down some reminders. "I'll tell him. I assume you'll want to use a half dozen of the outdoor heaters?"

"Yes. Thank you, Anna."

Then, as an afterthought, Anna added, "You were right about Mrs. Wainwright being a vegetarian. Wes said he had it handled."

Anna scurried out of the room. Paige let out an audible sigh. *Everything was set.* Mark had taken an early flight and should be home any minute. They were free until the weekend. And, damn it, Mark wasn't going to push this pregnancy off as her personal problem alone. No matter how lousy the timing, they had to deal with it together.

Moments later, Anna reappeared. "It's Mr. Toddman," she said, handing Paige the portable phone.

Alarmed, Paige asked, "Is everything all right, Mark?"

"Sorry, Paige, but I didn't get a chance to call before I left Cincinnati."

What new trauma, Paige wondered, steeling herself for the inevitable news that they wouldn't have the evening to themselves.

"Martha called just before I left for the airport. Walter is going downhill fast. She doesn't know how much longer he has. I told her I'd come right away. Got to run. I have a connecting flight to Palm Springs in less than ten minutes."

Tears pricked at the corners of Paige's eyes as she set the phone down. Life was so unfair. On his deathbed, Walter Winslow was faced with the hostile takeover of Consolidated—his father's legacy.

Paige scrunched her eyes shut to quell the tears rolling down her cheeks. From the very day she had met Martha and Walter Winslow, they had all felt a deep and lasting bond. No one knew of the longing in Paige's heart for the mother who'd abandoned her and the father she'd never known. The Winslows had made Paige feel as if she, as well as Mark, were a part of their family. Why, then, hadn't they asked her to come too?

As Conrad slipped behind the wheel of Charles's vintage Rolls Royce, Ashleigh felt thankful the two men, whom she loved with all her heart, genuinely liked and respected each other.

When they arrived at the Toddmans' princely estate, Ashleigh's eyes widened. The imposing sculptured iron gates spanned an area greater than her entire condo.

Conrad rolled down the window in front of the heptagonal kiosk and recited their names. The uniformed attendant scanned the top page of his clipboard, and the gates swung open. "Follow the drive to your right, please, and park in front."

They drove up the graceful winding road to the multilevel Mediterranean-style house. Ashleigh spotted Mitchell Wainwright's Cadillac and steeled herself. Mitchell was not the problem; it was his wife's open hostility she dreaded.

Ashleigh twisted around to Charles, who had insisted on sitting in the back. "It's hard to imagine this as a gambling den for Bugsy Siegel and his gang." Ever since she'd read the *Architectural Digest* article about the Toddmans and seen the pictures of their three-and-a-half-acre estate, she had been curious to see the results of the extensive renovation.

Sunlight danced off the dazzling white walls, and Ashleigh found it impossible to imagine the sinister clandestine meetings of the 1930s that allegedly had taken place on this very spot.

Tall and stately, the butler who greeted them looked as if he'd been chosen by central casting. "Mrs. Toddman is expecting you," he said, taking Ashleigh's coat.

Paige greeted them midway down the corridor, and the butler quickly disappeared. Paige gave Conrad an affectionate kiss on the cheek. "It's wonderful to have you on our team." Then taking a graceful step back, she made eye contact with the rest of their small party. Conrad introduced Charles Stuart. Paige extended her hand, saying, "I'm delighted to finally have the opportunity to meet you."

Ashleigh had seen Paige Toddman at several promotional events and a few black-tie dinners, but always from a distance. Up close, Ashleigh was surprised to see that Paige was not nearly as tall as she had appeared—perhaps only five-four. Her beauty was more gamine than classic, with her large expressive eyes, sculptured cheekbones, and lips quick to smile.

Paige displayed a friendly, unpretentious manner as she chatted with Charles.

At last, when there was a slight lull, Ashleigh introduced herself.

"I'm sorry!" Conrad exclaimed. "I didn't realize you two hadn't met."

Paige's smile was warm as she took Ashleigh's hand. "We certainly should have. I've heard so much about you from Mark."

They moved along the corridor and stopped outside a closed door. "Excuse me," Paige said to Ashleigh, and turned to Conrad. "Mark is in here, in the conference room, with Mitchell Wainwright and a couple of his staff. They're expecting you."

With a tap on the conference room door, Paige turned the knob and pushed it open. Conrad and Charles disappeared inside.

Paige turned back toward Ashleigh. "I may need your assistance to blast them out for dinner." Then, with a shrug of her slim shoulders, she led Ashleigh into the game room.

Stepping over the raised threshold, Ashleigh felt as if she'd been transported to another world—a gambling paradise of the future rather than a 1930s gambling den. Nothing dark or foreboding. The room appeared to be part of an ultra-classy Las Vegas casino, with everything custom made to blend with the dramatic white interior.

"I'll introduce you to the other ladies, then get you something to drink," Paige said, then gave an impish lift to her brow.

Ashleigh nodded. It would be difficult to find a more dissimilar group of women than the three sitting around the roulette table at the far end of the room. Mitchell's wife, clad in a business-like Anne Klein blazer, in navy, gray gabardine slacks, and a tailored blouse, towered above the others. Next to her was a leggy blond in a nondescript black mini-dress. Beside her sat a heavyset woman with limp mousy-brown hair, who wore a pair of polyester pants with a matching overblouse.

As they approached, Paige said, "I'd like you to meet Ashleigh McDowell. She's director of human resources for Bentleys Royale."

Before Paige had a chance to introduce the others, Christine Wainwright said, "We've met." Her greeting was as cold as Paige's had been warm. Ashleigh took this in stride, as did Paige, who went on to introduce the sexy blond, who'd come with Wainwright's M&A attorney, and plump Mary, the wife of Wainwright's lead accountant.

Turning to Ashleigh, Paige said, "Now, let's get you something to drink." Taking hold of her elbow, Paige propelled her toward the bar at the opposite side of the room.

Ashleigh felt an instant rapport with her hostess and was glad to have a few minutes to regroup before engaging in the expected idle chatter. She would never master Paige's ready smile and ease, but she was determined to do her best.

With a quick glance over her shoulder in Christine Wainwright's direction, Paige said, "I'd watch my back if I were you."

CHAPTER

25

A sudden and unnatural silence swept through the smoke-filled conference room when Charles Stuart and Conrad Taylor crossed the threshold.

Dressed casually in a vivid green polo shirt and gray slacks, Mark Toddman stopped pacing mid-stride. "Good timing!" he exclaimed, extending his hand first to Charles, then to Conrad.

A quick glance at the host's ruffled hair told Charles things hadn't been running smoothly.

Mitchell Wainwright stood and extended his hand, "Nice of you to join us, Charles," he said with an air of familiarity.

Then, turning to Conrad with thinly masked indifference, he stepped forward and shook his hand.

Toddman introduced Charles and Conrad to Larry Brighton, an attorney who worked with Wainwright on mergers and acquisitions. A stocky man with a well-groomed mustache, he appeared to be in his mid-thirties. His thick, dark hair was combed forward as if to cover a receding hairline.

Next, Toddman introduced the man with the curly brown hair that fell to his narrow shoulders. It was a style that would not have been tolerated in Charles's day, but in the past couple of decades, he had learned to look beyond first impressions. Steve Wilcox, a top-notch accountant who also worked for Wainwright, stepped forward and extended his hand as Mark explained, "Steve is one of the new breed of number jockeys known for crunching numbers round the clock when a deal's on the table." After shaking hands, Wilcox resumed tapping numbers into a book-sized calculator.

"The last thing in the world I want is for us to be apart," she said, her doubts miraculously melting away.

He looked at her as if waiting for the second shoe to drop, but there was none.

"Maybe I did have a case of cold feet, but I don't now. I want to be with you. I want to start our family, and I promise to stop hiding behind my inevitable wall of responsibilities."

"Hiding?"

"I'm afraid that's exactly what I've been doing," she admitted. "Although, until this minute, I didn't realize it. The responsibilities are real, but not as insurmountable as I thought."

The look of relief and love that swept over Conrad's face made her want to slip into the arms he held open for her, but there was more she wanted to say. "I'll need to fly back to California from time to time, but Charles is eager to give the bride away. As much as I regret leaving Bentleys Royale, my place is beside you."

Conrad smiled. "I guess I should count my blessings, but what made you change your mind?"

"You," she replied. "Time is precious, and it's time I put my fears and doubts behind me."

Conrad's forehead creased with a network of uneven lines. "Fears and doubts?" he repeated.

"Not about you, love. About me. I've never lived anywhere but Long Beach, and I don't know what I'll do in Boston." Then, before he could comment, she made a melodramatic sweep of the back of her hand across her forehead. In her best imitation of Scarlet O'Hara, Ashleigh sighed, "But never mind. I'll think about that tomorrow." Laughing, she quickly added, "Would three or four weeks be too soon for a small wedding?"

CHAPTER
28

Roused from bed at 7:00 a.m. by a burly bodyguard who introduced himself as Ross Pocino, Paige was now operating on automatic pilot. "How do you drink your coffee?" she asked as she poured beans into the grinder.

Pocino had plunked his ample form on a high stool at the breakfast bar. "Black. But don't go to any bother on my account," he said, glancing around the pristine kitchen.

Apparently noticing the tremor in her hand as she poured the ground coffee into the basket, spilling nearly as much on the counter, Pocino said, "Mrs. Toddman, your husband is in no real danger. We're keeping an eye on him to keep Sloane's goons from discovering his sources during the negotiations."

After handing Pocino a mug of black coffee, Paige excused herself and went into the library to call her trainer.

Sonny picked up on the first ring with his familiar, "Top of the mornin'."

After a brief greeting, Paige said, "Glad I caught you."

"Well, colleen, another two minutes and I'd have been winging my way to your doorstep. But perhaps you're thinkin' of clipping my wings?"

"Sorry, Sonny. This has been a Monday morning straight from purgatory. I promise not to let myself go to seed, but I'd like to postpone our workouts till next week."

"After I've spent the whole weekend studying all the yeas and nays about exercises for mamas-to-be?" he asked, an unmistakable lilt of laughter in his tone.

"Afraid so, my friend, but just till next week."

"Sounds like you've got a lot on your mind. How about us gettin' together for another wee chat?"

"Thanks, Sonny, but I've no time. Mark won't talk about the baby, and now that he has two bodyguards around the clock, the wee bit of privacy we had is shattered. I feel as if Big Brother is watching," she confessed, her laugh forced.

CHAPTER
29

Viviana's high heels clicked in a timid cadence on the hardwood floor leading to the president's office. She hesitated in the doorway and gulped in a deep breath. *God give me strength*, she silently prayed.

David Jerome sat at his desk, his custom-made shoes resting on top of the open drawer, a phone at his ear. When he looked up, she saw the unmistakable aura of impatience as he motioned her in. Hopefully, it had nothing to do with her.

She left the door open, took a seat in one of the familiar armchairs in front of his desk, and waited for him to turn his attention to her.

Finally, he terminated his call and indiscreetly checked his watch. "What was it you needed to see me about?" His brows pulled together as he glanced over her shoulder at the open door.

Viviana's initial nostalgic vein and nervous timidity shifted in an instant to self-righteous indignation. She wished she had just left her letter of resignation in his mail tray.

Holding her chin high, she simply handed an envelope to him. Then, casting her well-rehearsed speech aside, she said, "As much as I love Bentleys Royale, I'm unable to work in this perverse atmosphere."

She pushed back her chair, fastening her eyes on him as he stared at her in disbelief. "I hope you're satisfied," she added. Even as she spoke, she wished she could take back her hasty words and start over. Yet, somehow, she couldn't stop herself. Hurt by his dismissive manner, she wanted to hurt him.

David leaned forward and pushed a button inside his desk drawer. His office door shut.

A glance at his watch warned that time was running out. He had to be at the airport within the hour, and he no patience for this kind of bullshit.

He quickly opened Paige's bedside table and pulled out one of the hotel notepads she always collected. He scrawled:

> Paige,
> If you have something to say, join me in Boston and say it. Don't write notes!

He placed the note on her pillow, with the torn bits of her note on top of it. He turned to go.

Then, thinking better of it, he turned back, folded his note in half, and wrote her name on the outside. He threw the scraps of her note in the wicker trash basket and left.

CHAPTER
34

Morris Sandler was in a hurry to flee his home in Greenwich that night. It wasn't only because his wife vacillated over his pursuing the CEO slot at Consolidated. Depending on her mood swings, it was "Pull out all the stops and full-speed-ahead!" to "Who needs it?" Well, he did, and more than she would ever know. More than he could let her know. He was in too deep to take a breath without looking over his shoulder.

Gambling, which had at first been a lark and a thrill, had become his obsession. An obsession he kept from his colleagues and from his wife. Unfortunately, his good luck had soured, and he was so deep in debt that there was only one way out—he had to be named CEO of Consolidated. His creditors' patience had run out, and his life was in danger. He could no longer keep them at bay.

After discovering that his position as CEO of Amalgamated gave him no real power, and that his retail expertise was blatantly ignored, he'd stopped giving his all to the company. Instead, he began dipping into the till, but opportunity was limited. To keep his job, he couldn't dip too deeply.

Sandler was CEO in name only. And there was no security in working for the mercurial Sloane. No matter how much he accomplished today, he could expect no loyalty from the man tomorrow.

In the Amalgamated acquisition, for instance, Sloane had announced to the media: "I'm a tenderfoot; I know nothing about the day-to-day running of a retail giant. I'm leaving the management to the pros." He then explained that Sandler's old retail buddy, Samuel Golddapper, would be continuing as CEO and, thus, the man in charge.

Two weeks later, however, following a squabble over the use of the corporate jet, Golddapper was gone, and Sloane appointed Sandler to take over Golddapper's position as the one who managed the corporation.

Golddapper's exit was the beginning of a mass exodus. On the 25,000-foot executive floor there remained only Sloane, in Golddapper's old office, his two top lieutenants from the Sloane Corporation—Jules Ramsey, CFO, and Bob Talbert, his key adviser—and Sandler. In theory, Sloane's leveraged buyout of Amalgamated was seen as virtuously healthy and beneficial. Leaner and meaner after dumping do-nothing bureaucrats, the company was predicted to soar under the leadership of the flamboyant Australian risk-taker.

But Sloane had given Sandler's flowcharts—which identified areas to reduce expense and proactive measures to keep the business prosperous—no more than lip service. Now, Amalgamated faced selling off many formerly profitable divisions.

The ink on the sales document had barely dried before Sloane announced a party aimed at making the nation's corporate leaders stand up, take notice, and applaud his great victory. However, when Sloane launched into an extemporaneous lecture on the state of the world currency market, his audience, comprised of lenders and lawyers whose attendance was mandatory, tuned out.

Two weeks later, Sandler received the bills and targeted more heads to roll. But it would take more than expense cutting to turn the tide and encourage creditors to invest in Sloane's takeover of Consolidated.

At the sound of his wife's voice from upstairs, Sandler pulled himself from his mental analysis. Quickly running a comb through his toupee, he slipped back into his sports jacket and tiptoed from the downstairs bathroom into the kitchen.

He ran straight into the shapely blond nurse he had hired to care for his wife. "Oh, Nikki," he said, keeping his voice low. "Take Mrs. Sandler a cup of hot chocolate and tell her not to wait up."

At the provocative raise of her brow, Sandler said, "I'm afraid it will be another all-nighter." He ran his thumb along the curve of her breast and leaned in to kiss her when he felt her push her pelvis forward, her hand sliding toward the zipper of his trousers.

"Morris. Where are you?" His wife's voice rose to a frantic pitch.

Reluctantly, Morris grabbed Nikki's wrist and pulled her hand away. But it was too late. He already felt his rising desire.

"Later," he promised, giving her a conspiratorial glance. He pressed a finger to his lips and slipped out the door to the garage—and temporary freedom.

president. No matter what he said, the title he gave her did not hold the prestige she merited.

Well, that was behind her now. Once Philip acquired Consolidated, she'd be vice president of fashion for the entire corporation—not just one division. Viviana hadn't yet discussed this with Philip, but she would when the timing was right.

She glanced over her shoulder to the back of the plane where Philip was deeply engrossed in conversation with his two lieutenants. She thanked her lucky stars that they'd be dropped off at Kennedy Airport in New York. She hadn't had a minute alone with Philip since they'd left Los Angeles, but this evening she would have him all to herself.

Viviana busied herself checking each and every nail. Satisfied, she recapped the bottle, picked up all her nail paraphernalia, and strode back toward the bedroom.

As she approached the conference table, she overheard Talbert say, "Please, Phil, no more impromptu interviews." She knew Philip was passionately involved in his press campaign, issuing broadsides that invariably made people angry. As regular as the tick of the clock, he would fire B. J., his communications consultant, for not following his instructions. And just as regularly, Philip's staff would rehire him.

Viviana touched Philip's shoulder lightly as she passed his chair. She was rewarded with his boyish smile as he glanced up at her just before the bedroom door clicked shut.

Once inside the bedroom, she felt as giddy as a child. She kicked off her shoes and bounced on the side of the bed. It was hard to believe that all this luxury was within her grasp.

She wasn't kidding herself; there would be tough times ahead. But for now, she was going to sit back and enjoy the heady exaltation and powerful aura of Philip Sloane. Taking off for Bermuda in the midst of negotiations was a gutsy and powerful stance. She loved it.

She could hardly wait for her former management team to see the *Los Angeles Magazine* when it hit the stands. They'd be singing a different tune when they saw her on the arm of the man who was soon to be their boss. She'd show all those doubting Thomases, particularly her former boss, former lover, and former friend, David Jerome.

Philip had told her that he couldn't go forward with his divorce until the Consolidated takeover was a *fait accompli*. Now, as she looked at her reflection in the mirror beside the bed, she realized how badly she wanted to believe him.

Paige stared at the telephone, which had not rung since she had checked in. *No point in brooding over circumstances I have no power to change.* She tossed her belongings into her Gucci weekender and checked out of the Beverly Wilshire.

Paige felt driven to pursue her earlier dream, which had been short-circuited when she'd fallen in love with Mark. Life with him had been exciting and rewarding as he climbed the career ladder. By the time she had earned her degree in social work and finished her internship, Mark had been promoted to CEO of Mitchners, a Consolidated division head-quartered in Atlanta. This position required considerable networking, and Mark depended on her skills as hostess and informed companion, roles she loved and fell into easily. Yet she still yearned to do more than fund-raising to help the underprivileged. Now she could pursue her dream of one-on-one counseling, but her heart ached for what she must leave behind.

Her first stop was the E. F. Hutton building to meet with her broker. Gary didn't question the sizable withdrawal from her joint account with Mark, only the amount of cash she required. But after settling on the denominations, he said, "This shouldn't take more than five minutes."

Alone in Gary's office, Paige felt the weight of all she had to do. She closed her eyes and Mark's face dominated her vision. He'd been generous with her, even when they had had little money. And for the past few years, he had encouraged her to indulge in the very best. It gave him pleasure to see her reaping the rewards of his achievements. She focused on quality rather than quantity in her purchases, even though Mark encouraged her to have both. "What is money *for* if not to enjoy?" he'd quip.

Money and what that money could buy were Mark's measuring stick. He never challenged her purchases, but he turned a jaundiced eye to giving money to those he labeled too lazy to work for it. For him it was a matter of principle. "It's all wrong," he'd say. "Giving out cash doesn't solve problems. To feel good about yourself, you need to be in charge of your *own* destiny. Handouts send a wrong message." But Paige never handed cash out indiscriminately. She gave money only to help someone ready to get his or her life back on track. By limiting her extravagances, she could follow her heart without pushing Mark's hot buttons. She understood his point but was unable to convince him that a helping hand was often all that was needed to turn someone's life around. Had Mark known the child she'd once been, he might have understood.

Just then Gary popped his head back in the office and asked, "Would you like this cash in a manila envelope or—"

"A manila envelope would be fine," Paige replied. Though she doubted Mark would limit her access to money or credit, she had withdrawn enough to see her through the pregnancy.

Next on her agenda was to volunteer her services full time in working with the homeless. Having headed a number of fund-raising programs for the homeless and abused women and children, Paige already knew many department heads in Social Services. She had also recently volunteered at the Los Angeles Mission through the Celebrity Action Council to assist homeless women.

After an exhausting day and no real progress, Paige checked into the Sheraton Townhouses on Wilshire Boulevard. For the next three days she visited Social Services every day, talking with the director, Lee Preston. He and his staff acknowledged her credentials, which she hadn't allowed to lapse, but they assumed her drive would wane and that she would quickly tire of the daily grind and retreat to her life of wealth and privilege. Finally, however, Preston conceded and allowed Paige to join the orientation and training classes for volunteer counselors, most of whom were practicing professionals offering their services pro bono.

Conrad doubted that, but it was futile to argue once Mark made up his mind.

A few minutes later Mark returned, looking considerably improved but not exactly up to par.

Conrad gestured Mark into an armchair. As usual, Mark remained standing, claiming that his mind was most active while he was on his feet. To keep from having to look up, Conrad leaned against his desk and got straight to the point. "Now that Sloane's exceeded our drop-dead price, are you prepared to pull out?"

"Jesus, Conrad. I never thought the stakes would skyrocket to this level. At $61, the price is too rich."

Conrad gave a noncommittal nod.

"We can't ignore the balance sheets." Mark paused, then challenged, "Can you rationalize topping Sloane's bid?"

"Not without some drastic reorganization. If things remain status quo, it would be financial suicide."

Mark paced to the window and back twice before adding, "Okay. We know the risks. And the cost has exceeded our expectations by a long shot. So why aren't you pushing me to pull out? And why, in God's name, aren't I insisting on it?"

They both knew why. Had Conrad remained on the retail side of the table, he would have voiced his opinion in no uncertain terms. He'd have fought tooth and nail to prevent Sloane's takeover and the ultimate collapse of Consolidated. But his sphere had shifted. As Mark's investment banker, rather than his partner, he had no power to make structural changes in the organization. The decision to pull out or hang tough must be Mark's.

Mark stopped pacing and gave Conrad a penetrating look that demanded he verbalize his opinion.

"The decision isn't as clear-cut as we anticipated," Conrad stated. "We can always pull out. But, to compete at this inflated level without plunging the corporation into unconscionable debt, a drastic reorganization must be considered."

Always a quick study, Mark instantly read between the lines. "By reorganization, you mean spinning off divisions." It wasn't a question. They were both privy to the balance sheets. There was no other alternative.

Conrad nodded. There was no need to spell out which divisions; it would be the grocery store division and the two discount chains. Mark would not touch the department store divisions. Conrad was in accord.

"Cutting 'diworsification' to the core is not an unattractive alternative," Mark threw out, "but is it enough?"

Conrad lowered himself into one of the armchairs. "We'll have to rework the numbers."

"How long will it take to get a realistic handle on it?"

"Better part of a week. Wainwright will push for less time, but that's a minimum. In the—"

"Agreed," Mark said.

"In the meantime," Conrad continued, "I've got a hold of Dad's 'dirtball' list."

"Dirtball?" Mark repeated.

"At least I've got your attention," Conrad chuckled. He had had the distinct impression that he hadn't had Mark's undivided attention, but now he continued as if he did. "A dirtball list is more or less a Who's Who of financial daredevils. At this point, I figure we should have one or two deep pockets to count on."

Before Mark could voice the questions clearly registered in his expression, Conrad added, "If and when we present a bid to the board, we must produce solid guarantees. No matter how enchanted the board might be with your expertise, they can't afford to take a flyer on the financing."

Conrad had scanned the current list and made a few phone calls. He'd bypassed top real estate developers like Donald Trump of New York and Mel Simon of Texas. He'd also eliminated financiers like Ivan Boesky, who was knee-deep in problems of his own. In the final analysis, he'd decided on the billionaire Evonovich brothers of Canada, who though no risk-takers were certainly deep pockets.

He brought Mark up to speed and then said, "The Evonovich brothers are flying in tomorrow morning. They're known as family men, so it's important to include Paige and Ashleigh in the social portion of the evening. They're sure to be impressed. Your wife and my fiancée are head-and-shoulders above their 'little woman' image."

Mark rubbed his eyes and shook his head. "Not this weekend, I'm afraid."

"What do you mean, 'not this weekend'?" Conrad parroted. "This is no leisurely golf game. We get our ducks in order, or we fold up our tents and get out of the game."

Mark raised his hands in a gesture of truce. "I'm committed and available, but Paige isn't free."

Conrad didn't immediately respond. Maybe there *was* trouble in the Toddman marriage. After all, they were only human, and both were under tremendous pressure.

In the silence that followed, Conrad stepped out of his professional persona and asked, "Are you and Paige at odds over this takeover?"

"Hell, no." Mark's voice held an angry note of incredulity. But before Conrad could apologize, Mark continued, "Sorry, Conrad," and lowered himself into an armchair. "Shit. I'm not accustomed to distraction from the home front."

"This takeover is taking its toll," Conrad began.

"It's not that," Mark interrupted. Combing his fingers through his hair, he went on, "I have no idea where she is!"

"Paige?" Conrad asked, thinking he'd misunderstood.

"God, I feel like I've wound up in the starring roll of a B-movie." Mark rose and grabbed a handful of almonds from the open bowl on the side table. "This is strictly between us," he added, needlessly.

"Paige is missing?" Conrad asked in disbelief.

"Not exactly. What I am telling you is, I don't know where she is."

Conrad left the silence unfilled, waiting for Mark to clarify.

"God, I hate this. I've no experience—never thought I'd need it. But I could use a sounding board. So hear me out."

CHAPTER
39

Mark paced in front of the large office windows. Discussing personal problems was foreign to him. He took his time, wondering how far to go. He and Conrad had openly shared their trials and tribulations over business matters for the past five years as tandem heads of Bentley's, but this was different. He trusted Conrad without reservation, but he felt professional business executives should handle personal problems on their own. And yet, he could no longer deny that Paige's disappearing act was having a profound impact on his ability to think rationally. If he didn't get himself pulled together posthaste, it could jeopardize his entire future.

He confided that he and Paige had had a major disagreement, totally unrelated to the takeover. He bypassed the true cause of their disagreement. "Paige hates the round-the-clock protection and the fact that we haven't had any time to ourselves. With this round of meetings in Boston, I thought that we might be able to grab some time to get things back on track."

Fat chance, Conrad thought.

"When I got home Monday night, her car was gone, and I found a note artfully propped up against my bottle of scotch." He paused, quelling his rising anger. "To make a long story short, I was so irritated, I didn't do much more than skim it before dumping it in the trash."

Conrad leaned forward. "Just how serious was your disagreement?"

"Serious, but not catastrophic," Mark replied, willing it to be true.

"You said you didn't read the note carefully. Could she have mentioned where she was and when she planned to return?"

Mark shrugged, ignoring the question. "You know Paige. She never beats around the bush. She understands the demands of business. This disappearance is totally out of character." His voice rose with indignation.

"So where is she?"

"I told you, I don't know."

"And you're not concerned?" Conrad's voice rang with his own irritation and incredulity.

"Sure I am, but when I found out that she'd given her secretary the week off and her trainer hasn't shown up for the past week, I realized she must have planned this disappearance. But it's so out of character, I'm not sure what to think."

"Has she ever done anything like this before?"

"Never. Paige is no game player. I don't know what's gotten into her, but she couldn't have picked a worse time."

"How long did you say it's been?"

"Five days," Mark shot back. He'd mentally counted and recounted the days.

Conrad sprang from his chair, his eyes drilling into Mark's. "Five days! How can you be so damn passive?"

"I've traveled an entire gamut of emotions. First irritation, then anger, then concern. Very concerned, but that was before I discovered Sonny, Paige's trainer, must have also been given time off."

"Have you talked to the trainer?"

"Called several times, but all I get is the goddamned answering machine."

Mark picked up the phone on Conrad's desk and tried again. "Still only the message in his lilting Irish brogue."

"You're playing with fire, Mark. In your own words, a disappearance act is not Paige's style. Let's get Landes on this right away."

"Hold it. I've already called another agency in Los Angeles."

"Why not Landes? He's the best."

"The last thing I want is for this to get out."

"Jesus, Mark, forget the macho crap. If something happens to Paige, you'd never forgive yourself."

Mark slumped back in the chair. He couldn't fight Conrad's logic. He nodded. "Right. But I'm going through another agency. I can't imagine telling Pocino or any of Landes's so-called executive protectors that my wife is missing and I need help finding her." He had known Ross Pocino when he had worked for Bentley's. He was smart and an undisputed expert in security, but unfortunately, he had the finesse of a toddler.

"Talk directly to Dick Landes. He's the one I worked with on the computer fiasco at Bentleys Royale. I don't know about the other agency you contacted, but you couldn't get a more experienced or discreet investigator than Landes."

"Don't get me wrong. I know he runs a top-notch operation. The problem is, he's on retainer with Wainwright."

"Not a problem," Conrad said. "Landes's integrity can't be bought or compromised. I know what I'm talking about. The man lives by a high code of ethics. And believe me, nothing stands in the way of his principles. They've cost him a career in the police force and nearly cost him his lucrative retainer with Wainwright a few years back."

Mark was about to challenge Conrad's blind faith, but Conrad had sparked a dim memory. "I remember," Mark said. Although he hadn't been personally involved in all the details of the computer crime at Bentleys Royale, Conrad had filled him in on the major components. Landes had been called in to protect Ashleigh McDowell after she discovered she was being followed and a time bomb had been planted in her car. She'd been engaged to Mitchell Wainwright at the time, and he'd been the one to hire Landes. When Landes discovered that Wainwright was keeping him in the dark regarding his suspicions that his estranged son might be the mastermind behind the crimes, his actions putting Ashleigh's life at risk, Landes took himself off Wainwright's payroll but continued to provide Ashleigh with round-the-clock protection.

"Let's see if we can get hold of Landes now."

The phone rang and Conrad picked it up.

"It's for you."

The second the Irish brogue registered, Mark felt a brief sense of relief.

"Sorry I missed your calls," Sonny said, "but I've been away for a few days."

"Have you spoken to Paige?" Mark asked cautiously.

There was a slight hesitation before Sonny replied, "Not since the first of the week. I was just about to ring her when I spotted the message light. Is anything wrong?"

"No. It's just that I lost the phone number where she can be reached and thought you might have it," Mark lied.

"I thought she was with you," Sonny said. Then he quickly added, "Guess I wasn't listenin'."

Mark froze. "Did she say when she'd be ready to resume her regular workout schedule?"

"Monday mornin' at seven. Is everythin' okay?" Sonny asked, his Irish brogue barely evident as his concern spilled across the line.

"Just ask her to call me if you hear from her before I do, Sonny." Mark thanked him and said good-bye before the trainer could surface more questions.

Clicking off the line, Mark's professional shield of detachment crumbled. "Goddamn it!" he exploded.

CHAPTER
40

Mark reached Conrad's office around nine o'clock Monday morning.

"Any further word from the Evonovich brothers?" Mark asked, closing the door behind him.

"Any word from Paige?" Conrad asked.

"Not a peep."

"I still think you should get Landes involved."

"Back off, Conrad. I've got the other agency on it. She wasn't abducted; she left a goddamned note." A pause. "Sorry. I've got to handle this my way." He strode across the office to the window and looked north toward the John F. Kennedy building. He asked again if Conrad had spoken to the billionaire brothers.

"Briefly. They were impressed with your presentation this weekend. Enough so that their misgivings about Wainwright were overcome. Harry said they'd run through the numbers with their CFO, and if he found no new wrinkles, they'll put up the $400 million within the parameters we laid out yesterday. It should be a *done deal* by this evening."

Mark still wasn't convinced that the deal was doable, but he was willing to explore all the possibilities. The weekend meetings had gone well in spite of the rough beginning.

At dinner Friday evening Harry Evonovich had questioned Mark about Paige's absence. "A man needs the little woman's full support," he'd said. If his words raised the hackles on Ashleigh's neck, she'd given no sign. Instead, Ashleigh had jumped in—to Mark's great relief—lauding Paige's work with the underprivileged and expressing her own admiration.

"Have you touched base with Wainwright?" Mark asked.

Conrad nodded.

A shadow fell across Viviana's legs. She looked up, shading her eyes from the sun. Philip Sloane stood beside her, his lean body, with its firm taut stomach muscles, handsomely tanned.

She pulled in her own stomach and adjusted the strapless top of her maillot swimsuit as he squatted down beside her and handed her a glass of mineral water.

His eyes gleamed with amusement as he gazed down at the copy of *Cosmopolitan* on her lap. It was open to an article titled "Why Men Don't Get Enough Sex and Women Don't Get Enough Love." She quickly snapped it shut.

"Is that so?" Philip teased. A smile warmed his face and caused his eyes to crinkle in the corners as he leaned to kiss her.

"Not for us, Philip," Viviana replied.

"You sure?"

"That's almost insulting."

He looked at her, his eyes steady and unblinking. Ignoring her comment, he asked, "You're not getting bored, are you, kitten?"

"No," Viviana lied. "It's a beautiful day, and you've given me a whole new world." The truth was, the last few days had held little of the idyllic life she'd dreamed of. When not on the phone, Philip exercised. He seemed more focused on his own body than hers, and their lovemaking had dwindled to no more than once a day. Philip's tremendous energy was unquestionably not directed toward her.

Viviana no longer crawled out of bed at three in the morning to join him in a glass of fresh-squeezed orange juice. Nor did she paddle around the pool while he worked out. She hated exercise and had given up the pretense of being invigorated by an early morning swim. She needed her beauty sleep. Besides, what was the point? The minute Philip emerged from the pool, he was back on the phone.

"It is truly beautiful here," he agreed. His tone held a note of pride as his gaze took in the width and breadth of his estate. From where they sat on the terrace, trellised with vines, he could see a path leading to a small tangled garden that spilled down to the swimming pool—the clear water glinting turquoise in the afternoon sun. Set high on a cliff, Philip's house commanded an uninterrupted view of the sea. Viviana gazed wistfully seaward. A stairway zigzagged down the steep cliff to a boat dock where Philip's seventy-five-foot yacht was moored.

She turned back to Philip, who was gnawing on his bottom lip. A queasy feeling stirred in her stomach. "What's wrong, darling?" she asked, quelling the anxiety in her voice.

"I've got to fly back to New York."

"But, I thought—"

"Kitten, it can't be helped. But there's no need for you to come. It's strictly business, and I'll most likely be in round-the-clock meetings." Then he gave her a wink and said, "Just sit tight, and I'll bring you one of those marvelous trinkets from Tiffany's."

Oh, God, he's beginning to treat me like a brainless bimbo. Viviana couldn't stand it. She wouldn't let him. She took a deep calming breath and patted the spot next to her on her lounge chair. She'd come too far to blow it now. "Please don't keep me on the outside, Philip," she pleaded. Not trusting herself to say more, she let a silence settle between them.

Taking her hands in his, Philip raised them to his mouth and kissed one, then the other. "You've hardly been kept on the outside. You're my number one asset, as well as being my most valuable retail barometer."

"I know," she quickly agreed. "I just don't want to be dropped from your need-to-know list." She formed her lips into a pout, the mood light and nonconfrontational.

"Never, my love."

Viviana knew Sloane's team of lawyers was simultaneously making court appearances in Delaware, Florida, South Carolina, and Nebraska. She prayed they would be successful in striking down the antitrust issue and could acquire a restraining order blocking Consolidated's poison pill. But those battles were in competent hands.

"So, tell me then, what's propelling you back to the big city?"

"Number one, Levich has set up meetings to discuss selling a division or two."

"Consolidated divisions?" Viviana asked.

He nodded. "The longer we fight amongst ourselves, the higher the ante."

Viviana frowned, trying to take it all in. How could Philip negotiate on divisions he didn't yet own? He must know what he was doing, but it was difficult to grasp.

"The price is too rich to hold on to every division," Philip went on. "Would-be buyers have been preselling the best divisions to other would-be buyers any number of times. Like a national convention of baseball cards enthusiasts—'You take this one, and I'll take that one'—and so it goes.

"Between the main game and these side games, there's a tremendous shifting of alliances among potential bidders. Debacus has signed on with Jordon's, for instance."

"That wealthy Texan who agreed to put up $600 million in loans for you?" She knew that was the tycoon Phillip meant, but Viviana wanted him to know she had kept track of the players and the figures.

He nodded. "All part of the game. First Commercial's shenanigans may be worse. Rumor has it they're in on a portion of the financing with all six possible buyers. There are so many Chinese walls inside their New York headquarters, insiders have dubbed the building 'Peking.'" He shook his head. "There's no end of activity between the principle negotiators and . . ."

Viviana wanted to ask what divisions he had in mind, but she decided to wait. "It's all so exciting," she broke in. A surge of energy swept through her, strengthening her resolve not to be left behind.

CHAPTER
43

Conrad snapped the lock on his suitcase and hit redial. At the click of the answering machine, he hung up. He'd already left messages on both Ashleigh's and Charles Stuart's machines. It was eight-ten on the West Coast. Since he knew they had planned to watch the *Hard Copy* segment on hostile takeovers at seven, he'd expected no problem in reaching them.

He dialed a third number in LA. Ross Pocino answered before the first full ring.

"You on duty tonight?" Conrad projected his voice above the blare of Pocino's TV.

"Nope. What's on your mind?"

"I need a favor." Conrad began. "I'm on my way to New York with Toddman, and I can't get hold of Ashleigh." He explained his concern.

"Gotcha. I'll get on it ASAP."

Same old Pocino, Conrad thought. "Thanks. There's probably some logical explanation, but I'd appreciate you looking into it. I'll pick up the tab for your time, of course."

"Don't give me that crap."

"Sorry," Conrad said, "I just thought—"

"Forget it. Maybe they set the VCR to record the program and went out to dinner. But if there's any chance Ashleigh's in danger, I'm your man."

"Don't go off the deep-end. Ashleigh's not on the firing line like she was before."

"We didn't figure she was before."

"Just make sure there's been no accident."

Drifting through darkness, Ashleigh felt as though her eyelids were weighted. *Too heavy to lift.* A high-pitched wail vibrated in her head, and her prone body floated back and forth. Along with the sensation of motion, she heard the pinging of small objects on metal.

A gentle hand pressed against her arm. Ashleigh instinctively shrank away. Where was she? Unable to voice the question, she slowly began to piece together a disconnected stream of vague memories.

She felt as if she were running in slow motion against an unseen wind. Her head ached, no less than if she'd crashed into a brick wall. She struggled to lift a hand to her head, but her body refused to respond to the simplest command.

"Try to relax." The voice sounded like it came from the bottom of a barrel. The vehicle rounded a corner, and she realized she must be in an ambulance. It jerked to a stop. Eyes wide-open, Ashleigh's mind snapped into focus, and she tried to push herself up on her elbows.

"Please, try not to move." The voice came from a young woman clad in a mint-green tunic top over slim-legged trousers. It looked nothing like the traditional white uniform Gran had worn as a nurse. Maybe this woman was a paramedic, not a nurse. Did it even matter?

Ashleigh didn't speak for a moment, determined that the first words out of her mouth weren't going to be, "Where am I?"

A picture of Mary's prone body on the kitchen floor flashed in her mind as she touched the lump on the side of her head. "Where is Charles Stuart? Is he all right?" she blurted in rapid succession.

The woman responded with a blank stare. "I'm sorry. Was he inside the house?"

"I think so," Ashleigh said, shifting her legs to the side of the bed in an attempt to sit up. The woman restrained her as the rear doors of the ambulance swung open and two clean-cut young men climbed partway inside.

Ashleigh eased herself back down, and the two men lifted her gently out of the ambulance. She noticed a few specks of dried blood on her fingertips and realized that Mary's grandson must have hit Mary a lot harder than he had her. But why?

Now in the emergency ward, with a white curtain pulled halfway around her bed, she heard other voices. A woman in a yellow smock pulled back the curtain to ask Ashleigh, "May I see your insurance card?"

"My insurance card?" she repeated.

"Do you have it?"

Was the woman blind? "I don't have my handbag."

After posing a few more questions, the woman left, and Ashleigh glanced around the cubicle for a telephone. No phone on the bedside table. She spotted one at the nurses station, and seeing that no one was near, she released the bed rail, eased herself to a sitting position, and swung her legs over the side of the bed. She sat there for a few seconds waiting for the room to settle down. She grasped the bed frame and slid her feet to the floor.

A police officer suddenly materialized. He grabbed hold of her forearms as she swayed precariously on rubbery legs. "Ashleigh McDowell?" he asked, helping her back onto the bed.

She nodded. Her head reeled. *Not a good move*, she thought, as a wave of nausea hit her. "Charles Stuart," she said. "I have to find out what happened to him."

"He's all right," the officer said.

"Thank God. I was so afraid that Mary's grandson had hurt him—"

"Ms. McDowell," the officer interrupted, "Mr. Stuart was shot, but he's okay."

"Shot," she parroted and then rattled on incoherently. "Shot where? How? Are you sure he's okay? Where is he now? I've got to go to him." She tried again to get up. She couldn't lose Charles. Not like this.

"Please," the officer said as he restrained her. "He's not here yet."

"Where was he shot?" she insisted. The blood thundered through her temples.

"It was an off-center gunshot wound to his head."

"To his head?" She felt her eyes glaze over and she involuntarily drifted back toward the pillow. "Why? He doesn't have an enemy in the world . . ." Her voice faded as she lost consciousness.

CHAPTER

46

Pocino left the crime scene a little after nine and pointed his Mustang in the direction of Community Hospital. He'd call Conrad Taylor again after he had more information. First, he'd talk to Ashleigh about the housekeeper's grandson, whom she'd mentioned to the debriefing officer. He'd said he hadn't gotten much out of her because she drifted off, but he'd stick around until she could talk.

Pocino planned to be on the scene when she came out of her stupor.

In the emergency ward, he was told that Ashleigh had been assigned a room and was en route. Arriving ahead of her gurney, Pocino stepped aside while she was wheeled inside. He paced outside her room waiting for her to be settled. When he was finally able to enter, he saw that, unlike Charles Stuart, she had only an IV in her arm. There were no other tubes or equipment attached to her pale form. And there were no bandages wrapped around her head, just a trace of dried blood in her matted hair.

He saw that her breathing was steady and unlabored. Pocino slumped down in a bedside chair moments before the police officer appeared. The officer was merely there to get the facts, not for Ashleigh's protection. The assailant had already bought his ticket to hell.

The officer stuck out his hand. "Duke," he said by way of introduction. "Just got off the horn with Telford. They've done a thorough sweep of the house and grounds. No sign of stolen property or drugs, other than prescription. The old man's wallet was on top of his dresser with $125 in cash still in it."

"Easily explained," Pocino said. "The shit hit the fan, and the perp hightailed it out of there."

Conrad nodded. "Maybe I'm a victim of too many all-nighters and late-night movies, but a weird plot began weaving its way through my head."

"Yes?" Mark prompted.

"What if the present scenarios don't check out? What if this is some-how connected to this takeover? Paige's disappearance might even be connected."

"Christ. You're really stretching it. Paige was ticked off, and she left a goddamned note. Besides, how can Ashleigh be connected?"

"Not Ashleigh," Conrad said. "I buy the fact that she just arrived at the wrong moment. But Charles Stuart is a stockholder with a sizable number of shares, as well as being a respected member of the board."

"So, what's to be gained by knocking him off?" Not waiting for a response, Mark continued, "If Sloane or any of the contenders wanted to eliminate anyone, it would be me." He pointed his head in the direction of the second bedroom where his bodyguard was ensconced.

"I think it's pretty clear after last night's phone call that Sloane hasn't given up the idea that he might lure you to his side." Conrad braced his chin between a thumb and forefinger. "Forget it. I see now that the web I was spinning doesn't hold together."

Then, abruptly changing the subject, Conrad added, "Ashleigh's pretty unnerved. Not about what's happened to her, but to Charles."

"Understandable," Mark commented. "He's in his eighties, isn't he?"

"Eighty-eight next month. He's in excellent shape for his age, but a head injury, if not fatal, is bound to be disabling." His fervent hope was that Charles had not suffered any brain damage.

Mark nodded. "So what are your immediate plans?"

After a long moment, Conrad responded, "To take care of business. At this point, there won't be any wedding bells interfering with the Con-solidated negotiations. Although Ashleigh didn't mention it, we'll have to postpone—at least until Charles is out of the woods."

CHAPTER

48

Paige loosened the laces of her tennis shoes and pushed them off. This break hadn't come a moment too soon. She wiggled her cramped toes and leaned back in the swivel chair, again taking in the austere surroundings. The stark white walls and serviceable round table and chairs in the counseling room, though immaculately clean, lacked the slightest hint of warmth.

Paige's designer jeans had given way to Levis with elastic waistbands. She wore one of her new cable-knit sweaters—brightly colored and tunic length. The pastor had given her permission to add splashes of color to the walls, but with so many people to counsel and convince that their lives had value, she hadn't yet found the time.

If only there were more hours in the day. And yet, having no spare time kept her from dwelling on the life she'd left behind, and on her uncertain future. Here, she felt needed. The problems of others helped push away thoughts of Mark and how he had so callously discarded her and their unborn child.

She stretched out her legs, resting them on the rungs of the straight-back chair, and picked up the business section of the *LA Times*.

Each night, after her twelve- to fourteen-hour days, she would pick up a paper at the corner newsstand and immerse herself in the blow-by-blow accounts of the ongoing negotiations for Consolidated. She had read of the suits and countersuits being filed by lawyers across the country, the so-called final bids, and the inevitable sweetening of those bids. One-by-one, bidders emerged from their walls of secrecy to rival Sloane. Just last week, she'd read that Sloane had bumped his bid to $61 per share. Why hadn't she read that Mark had thrown in the towel? No doubt, after losing the last big deal to Sloane, Wainwright would maneuver to stay in the game, but Mark was not one to be swayed. From what she knew of Conrad, neither was he. The possibility of Mark emerging as an eleventh-hour White Knight was widely rumored, but no news had been issued from his camp. Powerless to predict the outcome, Paige thought, simply, *Whatever will be, will be.*

She had drifted off when she was only halfway through the Dow Jones report the night before. She already felt like an outsider in the world of high finance. Now the world she'd occupied for the past twenty years seemed unreal. At this point, only her new world, void of fancy clothes and pretension—a world filled with hunger, lack of shelter, and mental retardation—was real. For many, it was a world with little hope.

Paige did not deceive herself. Hurling herself into this world was no act of nobility. It was one of necessity—for her own survival. She would not be a victim. She would regain control of her destiny. But first, she must step away from the world Mark had carved out for them. Only then could she get a fresh perspective and make concrete plans for the future.

And yet, not able to completely let go, she found herself following the ups and downs in the market—her one remaining tie to the past—and now, her only tie to the world she had shared with Mark.

A knock on the door brought her reflections to an abrupt halt.

"Please come in," she called out, raising her voice above the hum and clank of the old radiators. She refolded her newspaper and set it on the floor beside her handbag.

A pretty young woman who Paige doubted was even twenty stood in the doorway, holding the hand of a little girl. Paige guessed the child to be four or five. She wore a bulky jacket, with patches on the elbows, over a faded cotton dress. The dress, more than a size too large, hung to the child's ankles. But when the girl looked up, Paige was taken aback by the natural beauty that seemed to radiate from within her. Paige forced her attention from the girl to the woman, who was dressed in a thin cardigan sweater over a low-cut blouse and black miniskirt. Despite the nip in the air, she wore no coat.

Paige slipped back into her shoes and crossed the threadbare carpet to meet them. She greeted them warmly before introducing herself.

The child clung to her mother's skirt. Her enormous brown eyes were soft as velvet and held traces of sadness and fear. The mother had the same large dark eyes, but they lacked even a hint of inner light.

Gesturing for them to be seated, Paige asked, "How can I help you?"

"My name's Patti, and this is April," the young woman said, her eyes rapidly scanning the bleak surroundings. "I need to find a good home for April."

"No, Mommy. Please, no. I promise I'll be good."

Paige felt her heart being squeezed as she watched the mother stroke the child's head. "There's no one to look after her, and I must work."

Paige should have referred them to Social Services, but she found she couldn't turn them away.

"Tell me about your work," Paige said. "Maybe we can sort something out."

The woman's face colored. Her eyes fell away from Paige's, and she stared down at the faded carpet pattern. She shook her head. "There's nothing you can do. I want more for April than the kind of life I can give her."

What twist of fate had brought this young woman to such desperation? It tore Paige apart to see the small body of the sobbing child and the love in the woman's eyes as she tried to comfort her. A tear slid down the woman's cheek, and she balled her hands into tight fists.

Paige swallowed hard, watching the little girl fling herself across her mother's lap. She held on to her with all her might, pleading, as if her heart would break. "I won't be any trouble. I promise I won't. Please, Mommy, please." The child repeated the words over and over like a mantra.

Paige felt herself go soft inside, and an eerie feeling of déjà vu washed over her.

"Bentleys Royale. We've got a round-the-clock watch on Charles Stuart at the hospital, but I'm keeping an eye on Ms. McDowell," Pocino said. "Landes is out of range, so I'm calling you for the go-ahead."

"You've got the approval for Stuart, but Ashleigh's no part of this deal." Without so much as an "Adios," Wainwright ended the conversation, the phone thudding in Pocino's ear.

51

Murray Levich lit up. He took a long drag from his Salem and gazed around his domain. The fee-generating hum within his own office complex gave him a thrill.

In spite of Sloane's past blunders, Levich felt optimistic about interesting CEO Robert Denton of Dudley's department stores in Arkansas in a particular Consolidated division currently on Sloane's presale auction block.

At the sound of Denton's voice, he ground out the Salem in the overflowing cloisonné ashtray and said, "I understand you and your collaborators have pulled out of the Consolidated deal."

"You got that right. Bailed out late last night. Where I come from, to get a fee you've got to earn one. The M&A gang we've been working with pressed for huge up-front fees. We eventually got their fee down to $8 million and told them we'd pay when we had something to show for it. They were still clamoring for fees long after midnight. Unbelievable," he said with a ring of incredulity.

Levich felt like pointing out that if the experts worked their tails off on a buyout without collecting fees up front, there was little chance of collecting them after. Instead, he asked, "How about a smaller piece of the deal?"

Denton shot back in less than a heartbeat, "Not one of Sloane's on-again, off-again deals. Burned once, shame on Sloane; burned twice, shame on me."

Levich removed his coke-bottle-thick glasses and rubbed the bridge of his nose. Denton's reluctance came as no surprise. Six months before, Sloane had approached Denton on the sale of an Amalgamated division.

cal, but then he cautioned, "No matter how dirt poor or down on their luck, some folks could be offended by handouts."

"Don't I know it," Paige reminded him. "And Patti, that's April's mother, wouldn't have taken a cent if I hadn't convinced her it was a routine loan from Social Services, and she was expected to pay it back when she got on her feet." She paused. "Just a little white lie. Patti's so young. She never had a chance, and she loves her little girl. Even before I found out for sure, I suspected she had turned to prostitution to take care of her daughter."

Sonny lifted his brows. "Maybe the child would be better off—"

"Let me finish. I've been meeting with them for the past couple of weeks in the evening when Patti gets off work. I found another young girl at the shelter who needed to make a little money. She looks after April so Patti can work during the day at a local coffee shop. Patti never wanted to give up her daughter. She was just afraid. She wanted April to be safe and have a chance to go to school."

She paused, trying to organize her thoughts. "I told Patti what it was like growing up in foster homes. I think I'm getting more out of my counseling than anyone else. Things that happened to me when I was April's age are seeping through the wall that you said I've built around me. Nothing is coming in lightning flashes, but I'm starting to fit things together bit by bit. And maybe my mother wasn't the monster I made her out to be."

The Irishman grinned. "And she probably loved you just as this mother loves her little lassie."

Paige shrugged dismissively and continued. "Patti was only fifteen when she found herself pregnant. The baby's father left her with no money and nowhere to live. She had no education or job skills, but she desperately wanted to keep her baby."

Paige's breath caught in her throat as she told Sonny that Patti had come upon one of her johns slipping his hand up April's skirt. "It stirred something deep inside me, Sonny. I had a memory of my mother throwing dishes, one after another, at a tall ruddy-faced man who wore nothing but a pair of jockey shorts. She was screaming at him to keep his dirty hands off her little girl, and to get out. She was very small next to the big man," Paige said, her voice choked with emotion as the trauma unfolded once again before her.

Sonny set down his glass. "Did the man molest you?" he asked, his voice etched in concern for the innocent little girl she had been.

Paige nodded. Sonny had uprooted her last remaining secret. "His hands were enormous. Or maybe they just seemed enormous because I was only four or five." In her mind she saw him lift her nightie and push her down. And now, as if still held by the rough ropes, she began rubbing her wrists. The memory was so vivid she couldn't push any sound past her dry throat. Instead, she stretched her arms, palms up, toward Sonny so he could see the thin, almost invisible, red scars on the inside of each wrist, where the skin had been broken.

"He tied you up?"

He didn't ask her to fill in the gaps, which somehow freed the block in her throat. She nodded. "I think my mother must have walked in while I was still tied to . . ." Paige frowned as the next picture flashed before her. It was different from the one in her nightmares. She was going to say "tied to the bedposts," but she'd been on the floor, and her hands were tied to the drainpipe beneath a sink in this fleeting vision. "I remember him raising his fist as if he was going to hit my mother. Maybe he did hit her. Then another man bolted into the room. He caught hold of the ruddy-faced man's fist, twisted him around, and knocked him to the floor. That's all I remember. I don't know what happened next." Chilled, Paige rubbed her hands up and down her folded forearms.

Finally, shaking her head as if to clear away the vision, she said, "When I set my problems in perspective, right now my life is a piece of cake." The truth was, however, that her life had gone to hell, and merely thinking of a worst-case scenario didn't help one iota.

When Paige tumbled into bed that evening, she slept fitfully. Her nightmares had not been put to rest, and now there was a new dimension. She woke up in a cold sweat. Not once, not twice, but three times. In these nightmares she was a child again, and like the child at the shelter, she clung to her mother's shabby dress. But Paige's faceless mother kept drifting farther and farther away from her clutching hands. This time, before the silhouette drifted out of sight, Paige clearly saw the mother figure lift the back of her hand and wipe a tear from her cheek.

CHAPTER

53

Ross Pocino had followed Ashleigh's Thunderbird to Community Hospital, and he had stood in the corridor outside Stuart's room exchanging information with the agent who stood guard.

Now, he entered the dark room as quietly as his crepe-soled shoes would permit. At the sound of his muffled footfalls, Ashleigh looked up. He heard her voice, soft and low, a split second before she came clearly into focus. She sat at the old man's bedside holding his hand. Had Stuart come out of the coma?

After a perfunctory greeting, Pocino pulled up a chair and plunked himself down beside her. A stiff and unnatural silence permeated the room.

Finally, Ashleigh turned and said, "I'm flying to New York tomorrow to see Charles's daughter who now lives in Greenwich. I need her to sign a medical power of attorney so that I can get Charles moved to his own home."

Like hell you are, Pocino thought. Instead, he simply commented, "Stuart can't be released from the hospital until he's well out of the coma—power of attorney or no power of attorney."

She shook her head. "I won't have him wake up to these sterile hospital walls. I want him home." She paused. "I've already arranged for a hospital bed and round-the-clock nursing care in his own home. But since I'm not officially next of kin, I have no medical say-so without a power of attorney."

She'd taken the wind out of his initial objection, but the idea of her hotfooting it to New York before they got a bead on the assailant at Stuart's home rattled him.

"Can't you just call?"

Ashleigh pushed a wispy strand of blond from her cheek. "I tried, but Caroline won't talk to me."

"Why not?"

Ashleigh sighed. "It's a long story. But bottom line is, she thinks I'm after her father's fortune. I'm sure that's why she filed the lawsuit."

Pocino shook his head. "Ever met this charming daughter?"

"No, but I intend to." She didn't tell him Caroline had had her share of mental problems. Nor did she share that Charles felt she was strongly influenced by an overzealous husband. "She's his daughter, so I can't get a medical power of attorney without her consent."

"Most likely, you'll get the door slammed in your face."

"I don't think so. A fax will precede my arrival, and I don't believe she'll be able to pass up the offer I intend to make."

CHAPTER
54

A hush fell over the room as Conrad Taylor silently read the printout hot off the wire services.

Wainwright sensed the unspoken tension before he glanced up to see Taylor's weary, last-straw expression. Without a doubt, the deal had come unhinged.

Wainwright then turned his gaze to Toddman, who was looking over Taylor's shoulder at the ominous piece of paper. Undoubtedly, the stakes had again jumped. Toddman had been close to the end of his rope with the previous bid. Now, it appeared, the ball game was over.

For two-and-a-half days the team had worked nonstop. Buyers had been approved for the sale of the Silver Triangle and Budget Plus discount divisions. Around 2:00 a.m., an agreement with the management team of John's Markets had been reached. To avoid being offered for spin-off, the management of the grocery store division had obtained the necessary financing for an in-house buyout. They had firm commitment letters from credible banking institutions—more proof of concrete financial backing than Sloane had produced to date.

"Sloane leapt to $67," Taylor announced, not bothering to embellish.

Ironically, Toddman seemed relieved. Making direct eye contact with Wainwright, he said, "That's it."

Wainwright mentally counted to ten, cursing himself for wasting time with the retail king and his rookie investment banker. Neither knew the first thing about playing to win in the LBO game. He'd never take a backseat for another White Knight fiasco—actual sales figures hadn't turned out to be the advantage they were cracked up to be. But to win at this late date, he needed a leg up with the board. To pull out without Toddman's blessing would be a distinct disadvantage. It took all his well-honed negotiating skills to keep from blasting Toddman and his conservative cohorts. Swallowing past the lump of contempt wedged firmly in his throat, he said, "We've got a few new models for you to take a look at, Mark."

"Forget it." Toddman was adamant. "I wasn't convinced that it was doable with the previous jump. Even at our original drop-dead price of $60, after cutting a minimum of $3 million in expenses, we'd have had to increase sales by 5 percent each year, with no new locations . . ."

Wainwright held his tongue. The CEO's position was clear and unalterable, and he no longer wanted him in the deal. Wainwright was about to take charge. He'd let Toddman have his say, and then get on with his own agenda.

Toddman made eye contact around the room before concluding, "I'd like to thank all of you for your time and diligence. You will receive the fees we agreed on up front. And now, unless anyone has something to add, it's time to clear out and go get a good night's sleep."

"Before, we call it a day, I'd like to run something by you," Wainwright said. "I understand you have no interest in a deal that includes spinning off department store divisions. Under those parameters, I can't argue with your conclusion. The price is too rich for any single buyer." He paused, glancing in Taylor's direction before making eye contact with Toddman. "However, spin-offs are inevitable. Whether it's Sloane or someone else, it's going to happen. KKR and Denton dropped out in the low $60s, and to date, the rumored bid from Jordon's has not materialized. If I pull out, that might leave Sloane without a rival.

"In my judgment," Wainwright continued, "with proper reorganization, which must include selling off the lower-producing department store divisions, Consolidated is still a viable acquisition." He raised his hand, sensing a rebuttal from Toddman or Taylor, and met Toddman's gaze head on. "I understand that you've run the course. Therefore, I'd like to pick up the gauntlet. You can rest assured that I will seek a top-notch CEO." His gaze now included Taylor as well as Toddman. "I seek your support in stopping Philip Sloane."

Toddman nodded. "My priority is to get the top dollar for our stock-holders. And I'm acutely aware of the downside of a Sloane victory. I'll give you the names of three top-drawer CEO candidates. You can count on my support . . ."

Wainwright rose and was about to offer his hand when the codicil to Toddman's statement stopped him cold.

". . . provided Jordon's doesn't enter the game with a formal offer. If so, I'll have to shift my support to a team with a proven track record in department store management."

Paige flipped on the radio and listened to the news as she dressed for work.

> *Philip Sloane, a relative newcomer to Wall Street, having announced his equity lineup early this morning, appears to have Consolidated in the bag.*
>
> *CEO Ralph Learner confirmed that Consolidated's legal maneuvers have failed, and the company has not come up with defensive restructuring to compete with Sloane's $67 per share offer. Opposing bidders have dropped out, and there is no longer the potential of a White Knight on the horizon. This leaves only an untested poison pill to protect the company's management. Though not stated directly, the signal is clear. Consolidated is on the verge of surrendering to the Australian raider.*

No White Knight? No White Knight? The words echoed in her head. Paige reached for the phone, wanting Mark to know how deeply she shared his sorrow. But her hand froze on the receiver. Mark no longer wanted or needed her comfort. Her love for him had not altered or diminished, but she now had another life for which she alone was responsible. With that reality had come an inescapable shift in her priorities. She would give Mark time to accept the takeover, and then she would arrange a convenient time for them to get together to settle their affairs. She prayed they would not end their lives together on a bitter note.

The very idea of parenthood brought to mind the Winslows, the closest she had ever come to having parents of her own. The collapse of Walter's family legacy was bound to take its toll on the cancer-ridden retail icon. Suddenly, her plans for the weekend changed. On Saturday, Paige would spruce herself up and head for Walter and Martha's desert home.

In New York, at the small writing desk of their spacious bedroom, Viviana turned out sketch after sketch of exciting new couture designs while Philip immersed himself in a marathon of negotiations in the next room.

Taking a deep breath, she stopped to admire her creations. She fingered through two days' worth of work, confident the drawings were superb. She no longer held a single doubt as to her talent. With Philip's money and power, becoming a top designer was nearly within her reach. Why be satisfied with predicting fashion when she could create it? Why even settle for vice president of fashion merchandising for the Consolidated Stores when she could open her own shop on Fifth Avenue and hire a high-caliber sales force to equal that of Bentleys Royale Carlingdon's, Bergdorf Goodman's, I. Magnin's, Neiman Marcus, and Saks? Viviana grinned thinking of the endless possibilities. And all the top fashion houses would vie for her exclusives.

Absorbed in her dream of fame and fortune, Viviana didn't hear Philip come into the bedroom. She started, but quickly pulled herself together. Patting her hair into place, she reached for him, an adoring smile planted on her face.

He bent and kissed her on the forehead. "Pack your bags, kitten. It's time we got away. I've worked solidly for days. It's time we took a vacation."

She smiled, her heart swelling with pride. "It's a done deal?" she asked.

"Ninety-nine percent fait accompli." Then, affectionately patting her derriere, he teased, "Now get that sexy bottom in gear. We're off to the Alps."

CHAPTER
57

Conrad tipped the bellman who had come for the luggage to be loaded into the Consolidated limo. "I'll be right down," Conway promised. Realizing it was nearly seven o'clock on the West Coast, he decided to try one more time.

There had been no answer in Charles Stuart's room, so he'd called Ashleigh at home. Hearing another series of unanswered rings, his mind filled with possibilities. She could have gone for a cup of coffee; she could be on her way home; she could be any number of places. But since the break-in, anytime she couldn't be reached was unsettling. Conrad quickly punched in Pocino's number.

"Pocino."

"Hate to bother you, Ross, but I'm clearing out of the Waldorf Towers and on my way back to Boston. Ashleigh's not answering her phone. Do you know where she is by any chance?"

"Didn't she call you?" Pocino replied.

Conrad glanced down and saw the steady red glow of the message button on his room phone.

Without waiting for a response, Pocino said, "I told her taking off for New York on her own was crazy. But you know Ashleigh."

"New York?" Conrad's voice exploded.

"Damn. She promised she'd call. I thought you might be able to talk some sense into her."

"Why is she coming to New York?" Conrad repeated.

"Said she had to talk to Stuart's daughter about a medical power of attorney."

Conrad sat down on the arm of the sofa, his heart thudding against his rib cage. This was no time to panic; Ashleigh's life might depend on his ability to stay coolheaded. "My God! Stuart's daughter is not only schizophrenic but is also married to Morris Sandler. I never put it together before, but Sandler has more to gain by Stuart's death than anyone."

"Sandler?" Pocino echoed. "Name's familiar."

"He's CEO of Amalgamated. He has his sights set on Consolidated as well," Conrad explained. "Did Ashleigh leave the address in New York?"

"No. It's not New York City. She mentioned a suburb."

"Greenwich?"

"That's it."

"Get hold of Landes. Update him, and tell him I need one of his New York agents. Have him call me on my cell phone."

Conrad had nothing but adrenaline to keep him going. The instant he and Pocino terminated their call, a vision flicked through his mind. A long shot, but he wasted no time calculating the odds. When he and Toddman had cleared out of their temporary New York office suite, he'd noticed a Greenwich Homeowners Association directory left beside a house phone and had taken it to the front desk.

With no time to spare, he went straight to the lobby. The woman at the desk opened a large drawer and pulled out the book, no questions asked. He looked up Morris Sandler, was rewarded with the address information he was after, and strode purposefully toward the outside doors.

Conrad didn't know Sandler's whereabouts, but he prayed that he was still in Manhattan, not at his Greenwich address.

CHAPTER

58

By Friday afternoon, Murray Levich found himself hopping from one conference room to the next at First Commercial's headquarters on lower Wall Street. The surface of every desk and tabletop was still littered with papers and Styrofoam cups of stale coffee.

Once the decision had been reached to retain only the department store divisions east of the Mississippi, the negotiations had been nonstop.

Side games did not fall within his bailiwick, but with the shortage of equity, Levich intended to keep tabs on every avenue of revenue. "Such a fuss was made over the shortage in Amalgamated," Sloane had said, "I'll raise more equity than we need for Consolidated." Not out of his pocket, of course—he flatly refused to sell his properties in Australia. Instead, he got a couple of dirtballs to put up equity loans, securing them with property rather than selling it outright.

Levich collected Howard Greenfield, Bob Talbert, Jules Ramsey, and Morris Sandler from various conference rooms. The latter had no place in the financial negotiations, but he hung in as a self-appointed observer.

When Sandler started to follow the others to Lawrence Drew's smaller conference room, Levich turned to him and said, "We need the complete rundown of expense cuts for a $68 bid."

Sandler stared at him for a few awkward seconds, then he replied, "I'll need a quiet corner somewhere." He picked up his pile of black notebooks from a nearby chair and headed down an adjacent corridor.

Ashleigh slammed the trunk of the rental car and slipped behind the wheel, taking a few minutes to review the directions on the Hertz map. A red pencil line marked the route to Greenwich. Her priority was to avoid the inevitable Friday commuter traffic beating a path out of New York.

Eager to get to Caroline's before dark, Ashleigh had arranged a late check-in at the Warwick Hotel in Manhattan and left word for Conrad Taylor to be given a key if he arrived before her. If only she could have talked to him before confronting Charles's mentally deranged daughter. She longed for his calm, unemotional logic. Far too close to the situation, she could no longer count on her own.

Ashleigh negotiated her way onto the expressway, her hands damp and unsteady on the wheel. Caroline Stuart Sandler was an enigma. A name Ashleigh had known since childhood, ironically, the two had never met. Years prior, Ashleigh had seen a picture of Caroline as a beautiful young girl. Ashleigh had no idea what she looked like today, but for now, that was the least of her problems.

Whether Caroline was truly evil, a victim of mental problems beyond her control, or merely a pawn in the hands of an ambitious and amoral husband, Ashleigh didn't know. What she did know was how much pain she had caused Charles.

Finally able to turn off the expressway, Ashleigh drove through a panorama of rolling pastures, horse ranches, and winter foliage. On the lonely roadway, bordered by a heavily wooded area, the final landmark she was looking for came into view as she bumped over the metal bridge spanning a gurgling steam.

Even by Greenwich standards, the Sandler property was well off the beaten path. Ashleigh braked beside a small kiosk. It was empty, and the gates to the property stood open. Odd, she thought, but after a slight hesitation, she shrugged off her misgivings and proceeded down the pebbled drive.

The house resembled Tara in *Gone with the Wind*, but not in its days of glory. Ashleigh parked the rented Mustang in the circular drive. Her heart hammering, she made her way past the pillars to the massive double doors and rang the bell.

Loud chimes echoed from inside as she shifted her weight from one foot to the other, trying to keep warm.

A sexy blonde in a tight-fitting, miniskirted uniform swung open the door, and Ashleigh stepped into the spacious entry. The blonde introduced herself as Nikki, Mrs. Sandler's nurse.

"I'll take your coat," Nikki offered, stretching out her thin arms.

"No, thank you. I'll keep it on." Ashleigh hoped she didn't offend, but the outside temperature was 30 degrees, and to her, it seemed nearly as cold inside.

"Suit yourself," Nikki said as she led Ashleigh into a large, dimly lit room. "Please wait here in the drawing room." She gestured toward one of the leather sofas. "I'll tell Madam she has a guest." She turned and flounced out of the room.

As the door clicked shut, Ashleigh wondered what she'd walked into. At first her attention had been on Nikki, who dressed more like a hooker than a nurse, and whose verbiage was as strange as her appearance. "Drawing room" and "Madam" sounded like something straight out of a Victorian novel. In addition to the affectations, her speech hinted of a lack of education—not at all typical of a registered nurse.

The so-called nurse faded from Ashleigh's thoughts as she took in the ominous room, with its dark burgundy and brown furnishings and the dozen or so candles scattered about the room—on the mantle, on the low coffee table, on each end table, and on the grand piano. Each one was aglow and gave off a pungent aroma, transforming the ambiance from foreboding to downright macabre. Had Caroline been expecting company, or was this setting indicative of her madness?

Ashleigh's thoughts turned to what she would say. She'd rehearsed her lines all the way from Los Angeles, but now, as she heard the click of heels on the hardwood floors outside the double doors, her brain turned to mush.

The door flew open dramatically, and a tall angular woman in her mid-fifties stood poised in the doorway, a wine glass held between her fingers at a precarious tilt. She wore a black velvet hostess gown, her face was heavily made up, and her obviously dyed auburn hair was swept up and held with tortoiseshell combs in a tousled arrangement.

Ashleigh stood and introduced herself.

"I know who you are. Mother's scrapbooks are filled with photos of father's bastard child."

Ashleigh, taken aback, fell speechless. To deny the ridiculous allegation was more than it deserved. But how on earth had Caroline's mother gotten hold of pictures of her (if, indeed, she had)? And why?

Her thoughts were cut short as Caroline swept into the room. "Well, don't just stand there with your mouth hanging open. That nonsense was Mother's hang-up. I don't believe that garbage, and I don't believe she really did either. She loved to torment Father by making him think she really believed you were his daughter. Thank God, you're not. The private eye Mother hired to trail your whore of a grandmother demolished that theory. Thank God," she repeated, "I have no half-sister. I am Charles E. Stuart's only child and rightful heir."

To be called a bastard child, though untrue, did not rattle her—she wished Charles were her father. But to call her saintly grandmother a whore was more that Ashleigh could take. "Mrs. Sandler," she began coldly, "what I came here to discuss—"

"Doesn't our weather suit you?" Caroline eyed Ashleigh's fitted cashmere coat, then sauntered across the room to the wet bar, downed her glass of wine, and poured another. "Did you mean what you said in this?" She fished a letter-sized sheet of paper out of her pocket and waved it in the air.

"Yes. I'm not interested in your father's money."

"How terribly noble." Caroline swayed back across the room and gingerly lowered herself onto one of the leather sofas. She pointed with a long red fingernail to the other. "Sit down. I can't stand people towering over me."

Ashleigh felt every nerve in her body contract. Her first impulse was to remain standing, but she wasn't here to win a moment's satisfaction. She forced herself to do as Caroline had requested or, more aptly, had ordered.

"You've been estranged from your father for a very long time. It hurts him deeply," she began.

"Would you like me to bring out the violins?" Caroline said, a snarl curling her upper lip. "It's all well and good that you say you're not interested in wheedling money out of my father's estate, but how can I be sure that you won't go after it when he's dead?"

Even if Caroline had had all of her mental faculties, Ashleigh was powerless to change the perceptions so deeply imbedded by Caroline's vindictive mother. Nodding her head in the direction of the paper Caroline waved at her, Ashleigh said, "As I stated, if you will back out of lawsuits against your father during his lifetime, I will sign over my rights to his estate upon his death. I've had papers drawn up to that effect and will sign them before a notary tomorrow, if you will sign this one." Ashleigh pulled out several sheets of paper from her Fendi handbag and unfolded them. "This details the provisions of my relinquishing my rights—"

"Rights," Caroline spat out. "You have no rights."

Ignoring the outburst, Ashleigh handed her the papers. "This states that you will refrain from legal maneuvers to gain control of your father's Consolidated stock. It further states that you will make no further financial *demands* while he is alive."

Caroline's expression was unreadable for a brief moment, and then she gave a sardonic smile. "I understand your fiancé is trying to get in on the act."

"You're mistaken," Ashleigh said. On the way to Greenwich she had heard the news that Philip Sloane was the only remaining bidder for Consolidated. Quickly shifting her thoughts, she continued, "This last document is a power of attorney . . ."

Again, Caroline cut her off mid-sentence. "You must think I'm an imbecile."

This time Ashleigh wasn't surprised. The woman was mentally unbalanced, but not stupid. She couldn't blame her for being leery of the power of attorney, and yet Ashleigh must have it. At first she thought a medical power of attorney was all she needed, but Charles's attorney informed her she must have a full power of attorney. Besides, in Caroline's or her husband's hands, such a document could be lethal.

"You have no reason to trust me, nor any reason not to. However, until your father can again manage his own affairs, I need to provide for his care. An executor can be assigned to monitor all expenditures."

Caroline glared at her and headed back to the bar. She poured herself another glass of wine, halfheartedly offered one to Ashleigh, then picked up the bottle and swayed back across the room to the sofa.

Ashleigh waited silently as Caroline shuffled through the papers. Although the older woman's skin was deeply lined and marred by broken capillaries around the nose and chin, she still bore traces of the beauty she had once possessed.

Finally, Caroline spoke. "You've no right to ask me to sign anything. But it would be convenient to have your signature on *this* document," she said, pointing to the faxed letter.

Ashleigh rose. "This is a package deal. If you refuse to sign the papers I need to protect your father, I see no need to hand over what you obviously don't deserve." As the words passed her lips, she realized she'd made a horrible mistake. Antagonizing someone who'd been diagnosed as schizophrenic was just plain stupid.

Caroline staggered to her feet, casting a malevolent glare. Ashleigh took a step backwards an instant before Caroline swung the bottle in a wide arch, barely missing one of the candles.

"Morris will sort things out when he gets home."

In a flash of illumination, Ashleigh's blood ran cold. If the perpetrator at Charles's home had been hired for the assault, there was no more likely suspect than Caroline's husband.

"I can't stay," Ashleigh said. "I have someone waiting for me in Manhattan. I'll call tomorrow after you've had a chance to talk with your husband."

"No. I want you to stay." The woman's voice was that of a petulant child.

"I'll call tomorrow," Ashleigh promised, picking up her handbag from the sofa.

Just then she heard a heavy thud and a sound she couldn't identify. Turning her head to look over her shoulder, she straightened upright.

Caroline was beside her, a broken wine bottle in her hand. She was waving the jagged edge dangerously near Ashleigh's face.

Ashleigh stood frozen in place. How did you reason with someone in Caroline's mental state? She didn't have long to ponder.

The older woman sprinted to the double doors with amazing agility and turned to face Ashleigh, the jagged bottle waving haphazardly in Ashleigh's direction. "You will stay until Morris gets home," she repeated. Then she slipped out of the room, slamming the doors behind her.

Through the echoing vibrations, Ashleigh heard a key turn in the lock.

Conrad made a dash for the Consolidated limo, removed his luggage from the open trunk, then said to Mark, who sat in the backseat, "Go on without me. I'll catch a later flight." Taking no time for further explanation, he turned and dashed off to meet the Avis driver who had delivered the Lincoln sedan.

The driver handed him the keys and a map to the Greenwich address. Conrad hurriedly signed the contract.

The Friday traffic was predictably heavy, and it seemed that he'd never get out of Manhattan. Even the expressway was bumper to bumper.

Conrad flipped open his briefcase and took out the cell phone. For now, he left the nine-millimeter semiautomatic handgun Landes had given him on top of some folders. "It carries eighteen bullets in the clip and doesn't have to be reloaded," Landes had informed him. "That's why it's become so popular." Popular or not, Conrad hoped he wouldn't have to use it.

He kept his eye on the road and thumbed through his address book. The phone rang before he located the number.

"This is Dustin, with Dick Landes's agency," a deep voice announced.

"Was just about to check in with your agency," Conrad said.

"I've run down Sandler; he's tied up in meetings at First Commercial. Hasn't been home for the past two nights. The agent tailing him is to report back the minute it looks like the meetings are about to break up."

Conrad pressed the accelerator to the floor.

CHAPTER
61

The sound of a key turning in the lock brought back a memory Ashleigh had long repressed. The terror of being locked upstairs in Wainwright's luxurious mountain retreat a few years earlier. She had been bound to a straight-back chair, and Mitchell had been tied spread-eagle on the bed. Then the horror of watching Anthony Wainwright fire a revolver at his father and seeing the blood slowly seeping from Mitchell's body. The episode came back to her with such startling clarity that Ashleigh could almost feel the bite of the sheets bound tightly around her wrists and ankles.

Ashleigh felt her throat constrict. She stared at the double doors, and all thoughts of the past disappeared. She'd been a fool to attempt to reason with Caroline. And yet, Ashleigh thought she had detected a flash of terror in Caroline's eyes just before she'd slammed shut the doors.

Ashleigh tried not to think about the dark splashes of red wine flowing down the side of the mantle, nor the jagged pieces of glass scattered on the hardwood floor. Instead, she turned her mind to discovering a way out.

She wanted to be far from the Sandler property when Caroline's husband returned. She had no idea what role Caroline's nurse might play but knew she had no one to count on but herself.

Tiptoeing across the floor to the windows, she pulled the cord on the first panel of drapes. It revealed a solid wall—no windows. The second panel revealed the same.

Her heart quickened as she opened the final panel. There were three windows, each with large square panes.

At the bottom of each window was a rectangular brass plate with a round grooved top where a handle should have been. None of the handles was attached.

Ashleigh considered breaking the panes of glass, but even if she managed not to be heard, the squares were barely large enough for her to squeeze through; she would be cut to ribbons on jagged edges of glass. Panicked, she searched desk drawers and shelves in vain for a window handle.

Abruptly, she stopped her frantic search. She stood perfectly still and let her mind take over. A moment later an idea clicked into place. She pulled one of the chairs from the game table to the window and climbed on top of the seat. She felt along the top of the molding, and just above the middle window her fingers came across something cold and hard. It was one of the handles.

Stepping soundlessly to the floor, she tried the handle in the brass plate of the corner window. A perfect fit.

She had cranked the handle only a couple of turns when she heard the spray of gravel under fast-moving tires, saw the glare of headlights, and instinctively jumped back from the window.

Morris Sandler? If so, she hadn't a minute to spare. She dashed around the room on tiptoe, blowing out the many candles. Soundlessly, she returned to the window and looked out. Nothing but darkness.

She cranked the window fully open. Then she hooked her handbag over her shoulder and, peering into the darkness, quickly raised herself to the windowsill. She swung her legs to the outside and looked down.

It was more than two yards to the ground, but this was no time for caution. She slipped off her shoes, jamming one in each coat pocket, then pushed off the window ledge, aiming for a soft landing on the other side of the thick hedge.

As she landed on her hands and knees, she heard light footfalls and the rustling of the hedge just inches from her.

"Ashleigh!" She heard a muffled shout as a hand gripped her arm firmly.

She tugged against the firm hold and turned to look at her attacker. It was Conrad. She literally fell into his arms. She didn't care about the hows or whys of his sudden appearance, only that he was there.

62

On the West Coast, Mitchell Wainwright's priorities shifted unexpectedly.

He had catnapped on the plane from New York, planning to go home and shower before taking up residence in his office suite for as long as it took to pull the Consolidated deal together. But when he pulled up to his waterfront property, he found it veiled in darkness. Only the outdoor lights glowed. Christine's car was parked in the opened garage, but there was no sign of life from within Casa Pacifica.

Letting himself in the door from the back garden, Wainwright let his eyes adjust to the dark, and then he found the nearest light switch. In the flood of light he saw the note by the telephone written in his wife's precise, perfectly legible handwriting.

> Mitchell,
> Come straight to the emergency room at Memorial Hospital. Your plane was already in the air when Jeanette reached me. I came straight home. Mitch is very sick. I have gone with him in the ambulance.
> Christine

Sick? Ambulance? What did that mean? And when did she write the damn note? *Some time in the last six hours*, he answered himself as the words "your plane was already in the air" echoed in his head. If anything happened to his son, Christine would pay for her negligence. If he hadn't wanted another son, he never would have remarried. Mitch was his chance to do things right—to prove that he could father a son to be proud of. And, ironically, this tiny child had aroused within him the first authentic stirrings of love and caring for another human soul. Christine had no right to leave Mitch in the hands of a nanny.

Less than half an hour later, Wainwright marched through the emergency entrance of Long Beach Memorial Hospital.

A line of people was waiting in front of the receptionist, all candidates for emergency services. But Mitchell hardly registered their presence. He barged to the front of the line.

"My name is Mitchell Wainwright. Where is my son?"

The uniformed woman's head shot up, and it looked like she was about to ask him to wait his turn. Instead, she consulted a clipboard and said, "14 B. Go through that door," she said, pointing down the hall, "turn to your right, and then make an immediate left."

Just inside the door to Room 14 B, Christine sat in the chair beside Mitch's bed. A large oxygen mask covered his tiny face. His small chest rose and fell in spasmodic, labored breathing.

"What's wrong?" Mitchell asked upon entering the room, his tone accusatory and louder than he had intended.

Christine turned, and her dead-looking eyes met his briefly then slipped away. Her prim unruffled appearance, with every hair precisely in place, grated on his nerves. "He has pneumonia," she said in a voice barely above a whisper. "But the doctor suspects he might have leukemia."

"Leukemia," he repeated. His hands drew into tightly clenched fists as he stared helplessly at the tiny form on the sterile white sheets. "That's irresponsible. How can a doctor make that kind of diagnosis? Test results must take more than a few hours."

"I didn't say he had diagnosed leukemia, but it is a possibility. The doctor has ordered a bone marrow biopsy, but we won't have the results for a few days."

Her gaze was unsteady. It fell to her hands. She was wringing them like some nervous old lady.

"Mitch hasn't felt very well for the past few weeks. At first, the doctor thought he might be anemic. He ran a number of tests a couple of weeks ago."

"A couple of weeks ago? Why didn't you tell me?"

"You were busy," she said, "and I didn't think it was anything serious. But today, when his temperature shot up to 106 degrees . . ."

Wainwright wasn't listening. He had to get out of the claustrophobic room before he strangled her.

He had to find the doctor.

Morris Sandler shook with rage. Being excluded from negotiating sessions at First Commercial left him feeling impotent. It was goddamned demeaning. That prick, Levich, really pissed him off. But he had had to take it. His entire future rested on Levich's ability to eliminate the competition. Sandler shoved papers back into his briefcase with a vengeance. If Sloane didn't emerge the victor, Sandler might as well put a bullet in his own brain—it was better than the alternative. He had to find a way to pay his gambling debts, pronto. Otherwise, he was dead meat.

At 2:00 a.m., when Sandler left Manhattan, he had the road to himself. His mind began to wander. After a nice hot shower, he planned to screw his brains out with Nikki. She was no mental giant, but intelligence in a woman didn't turn him on. He'd had enough of that in Caroline before she'd gone round-the-bend.

Caroline Stuart had been an ultra-classy beauty. She'd also been an ice queen. Making love to her was like screwing a statue. But since he'd sprung her from the loony bin, he'd had her adoration, and he'd continue to play it for all it was worth. Having Caroline released into his custody was far from problem free, though. He'd remarried her, knowing she was spoiled, willful, and demanding. But it was doable as long as he didn't set her off, kept the liquor and tranquilizers flowing, and had Nikki on hand to satisfy his libido. Nikki was willing to bide her time too. Sandler had told her he'd divorce Caroline and send her back to the funny farm after she inherited her old man's money. He was the one who'd control all of her millions. What Nikki didn't know was that at that point, she'd be history.

He smiled thinking of Nikki's voluptuous body and sexual know-how. No class, but boy did she know how to please a man. She was a fantastic fuck, and banging her gave Sandler an enormous sense of power. As he neared the house, he saw the outdoor lights all ablaze. "Goddamn it," he swore under his breath, "I might as well flush my money straight down the damn toilet!"

Nikki rushed toward him from the far side of the house as he parked his car by the front steps.

Thrusting open the door, he wondered what was going on.

"Mrs. Sandler's missing. I can't find her," Nikki cried out. Her face was flushed, her blonde hair untidy.

"Missing?" He swallowed a lump of contempt. "My God, she didn't get hold of the car key again, did she?"

Nikki shook her head. "Car's in the garage."

He felt the muscles in his neck and shoulders begin to relax. "Well then, she has to be nearby."

Nikki was still shaking her head. "I'm not so sure."

"What do you mean?"

"Come inside to the drawing room," Nikki said, gripping his hand firmly and leading him into the house.

When Nikki switched on the overhead light, the first thing he noticed was the drapes. They were all open, even those covering the plastered walls. The corner window stood open—the handle attached to the brass plate.

Simultaneously, his eyes glimpsed the deep-red stains on the carpet.

"This afternoon, this skinny blonde comes to see Mrs. Sandler."

"Who?"

"Don't remember her name. Says she's from California—Long Beach, I think."

It had to be Ashleigh McDowell, but what could she be after? Sandler's heart thudded in his throat. "You didn't let Caroline leave with her, did you?"

"No. Well, maybe. Don't know for sure."

"What do you mean, you don't know? Why do you think I brought you here?" His hard-on for Nikki went limp. He felt like killing the flashy bimbo.

Nikki's brows shot up, but she answered calmly, "Let me tell you; it's real confusing."

Better to let her talk. "Go ahead," Sandler said through clenched teeth as he leaned down to examine the red stain on the carpet. He also saw a thin red line running down the front of the mantle. Instinctively, he wet his index finger and ran it through the carpet stain, confirming that it was wine rather than blood, as he'd first suspected.

"After I let the blonde in and get Mrs. Sandler, I go upstairs to my room," Nikki said in her perpetual present tense. "Mrs. Sandler and the blonde are in the drawing room. Later I hear Mrs. Sandler come upstairs. She's drunker than a skunk, and she goes to sleep, or passes out on top of the bedspread. I put a blanket over her.

"I thought the blonde was gone, but when I look outside, I see her red Mustang. It's still there. I start to go downstairs to see what she's up to when I hear another car coming up the road real fast. So I go down the hall to the window and look out. Thought it might be you. But it's a big black car. Some tall guy jumps out and, instead of coming to the door, he runs to the side of the house." Nikki hesitated, then took a big gulp of air and began again. "I'm afraid to go outside, but I tiptoe down the stairs to lock the front door. That's when I see that the doors to the drawing room have been locked from the outside."

"Are you telling me that Caroline left with some guy in a black car?"

"Don't think so; she's still upstairs. But there's more. While I'm locking the front door, I hear another car. I look through the peephole and see a Ford Escort skidding up in front of the house right behind the other cars. Now I'm really scared out of my skull, so I call the cops."

"The police?" shouted Sandler. *God, that's all I need.*

Nikki nodded. "All three of the cars are gone by the time they get here, though." She gave a frustrated wave of her hands. "But before that, I wake Mrs. Sandler up. She's real upset and runs downstairs and unlocks the door to the drawing room. Then she starts screaming at me. She accuses me of letting her out."

"Who?" Sandler asked. "The blonde?"

Nikki nodded. "Guess so. Madam's really in a state by now. She runs outside in her stocking feet, without no—any—coat."

"Were the cars still there when she ran out?" Sandler asked, wiping the sweat from his forehead with the back of his hand.

"Don't think so, but can't say for sure 'cause that's when I call the cops."

"You called the police *after* you woke Mrs. Sandler, *after* she ran outside?"

Again, Nikki nodded, as though leaving a madwoman to her own devices was rational. "I'm too scared to go out before I call the cops."

Sandler's nails dug into the palms of his hands. He could hardly believe Nikki's stupidity. Bad enough that she had called the police. The last thing he wanted was to have them poking into his business. But letting Caroline out on her own was unforgivable.

Morris Sandler fixed his eyes on Nikki. "Did you tell the police Mrs. Sandler was missing?"

She shook her head. "I figured I'd find her. After the cops leave I go out and start looking, then I hear your car and remember all the commotion with the other cars and think maybe she climbed in one."

Sandler, breathing like a runner who'd just finished a marathon, inhaled deeply and said, "Let's keep the police out of this." Then, with as little show of emotion as he could muster, he suggested they get into his car and . . .

He cut off mid-sentence as he heard the creak of the front door.

Caroline limped across the threshold, her bare feet cut and bleeding, her pupils dilated. She looked like an inmate from *One Flew Over the Cuckoo's Nest*.

Sandler ran to his wife's side. "Thank God, you're safe," he said and wrapped his arm around her slender waist to keep her from losing her tenuous balance. The flush of relief was instantly transplanted by a need to get answers to a long list of questions—answers she most likely would be unable to give.

"She took all the papers." Caroline said as Sandler led her to the foot of the stairs.

"Papers. What papers?" Then, looking at his wife's disheveled appearance, he realized it was futile to begin asking random questions. He needed to start at the beginning. "Angel," he said, "I want to hear all about it, but you've hurt yourself." He gestured to her bleeding feet. "Nikki must take care of these cuts and get you into some warm clothes. I'll make some coffee." He wanted her as wide-awake and alert as possible.

In less than twenty minutes Sandler had filled and arranged the coffee service on a silver tray. He was nudging the bedroom door open with the toe of his shoe when Nikki stepped into the hallway.

"She's in the bath," Nikki said, twisting her head in the general direction of the master bathroom. And without as much as touching his hand, she took the tray from him and headed back into the bedroom. Her miniskirt swung rhythmically from side to side as she crossed the room, and when she bent over to put the tray on the bedside table, it was obvious that she wore nothing underneath.

In the few minutes since she had left him downstairs, she had repaired the damage to her makeup and her hair. The transformation was amazing. She was an entirely different woman. His anger faded to a vague memory. Sandler felt the familiar stirring in his groin.

With one eye on the bathroom door, he pulled Nikki to him and ran his fingers up her thighs and between her legs. She moaned softly. At the sound of a loud gurgle from the bathtub and water rushing down the drainpipes, he dropped his hands to his side, and Nikki straightened her skirt.

Moments later Caroline hobbled from the bathroom wearing a terry-cloth robe.

Unable to conceal the signs of his recent desire, Sandler maneuvered himself behind the chaise longue. "Stretch out here, angel," he said, patting the chair.

"If only you'd come earlier," Caroline lamented, pulling her robe above her ankles. She looked accusingly at the young woman who knelt beside her dabbing her feet with hydrogen peroxide. "*You* let her out."

Sandler handed his wife a steaming cup of coffee as Nikki began to wrap gauze around each foot. With a quizzical raise of her brow, Nikki paused. "You mean the blonde?"

"You know damn well that's who I mean."

Nikki shook her head. "Didn't even know she was still in the house. The doors were locked from the outside. She must've climbed out the window."

"Liar. The windows are all locked," Caroline protested.

Nikki shot up from her kneeling position, her shoulders thrown back and her sweater taut across her ample bosom. "Not all of them. One of them's wide open." Her eyes bore into Caroline's. "And I'm no liar. I don't lock people up. And I didn't turn that blonde loose."

"Enough," Sandler broke in. Then, turning to Nikki, who seemed to be looking to him for support, he said, "That will be all for tonight." But with his head turned away from Caroline, he was able to give Nikki a provocative raise of the brow, an unspoken message.

Without another word, Nikki sashayed out, and as the door clicked shut behind her, Caroline raised her coffee cup. "How about a little brandy?"

He poured more hot coffee in the fine china cup. "As soon as you get this down, I'll get the brandy."

She wrinkled her nose but began to drink the black liquid. "Nikki unlocked the door, then covered up by unlocking a window."

"Hold it, angel, I'm lost. Please start at the beginning."

Caroline again asked for a drink, but Sandler managed to keep her talking without one. Apart from a non sequitur or two, Caroline's account of Ashleigh McDowell's visit was fairly easy to follow. "She actually said she'd turn your father's entire estate over to you upon his death if you dropped the lawsuit?" he asked.

"Don't keep asking me the same questions, Morris. According to her, I get everything he's got, even if his will says it's hers."

"But she took the papers?"

"Yes. I told you she did."

Sandler saw the blood drain from her interlaced fingers as she squeezed them together. It was time for him to back off.

"You did the right thing," he said. "Giving that young woman power of attorney could cause no end of problems."

"That's what I thought you'd say." Caroline's bony fingers relaxed. "I tried to keep her here till you came home."

He covered the hand that rested on the cushion of the chaise longue with his own and began rubbing the icy cold fingers. "It doesn't matter," he lied as he poured an ample portion of brandy into her cup.

Sandler kept the conversation going and continued to pour brandy until he saw she was feeling no pain. "Angel," he said, "I think it's time we paid your father a visit."

"Why?" Caroline asked, her eyes widening. Sandler felt her hand begin to tremble. "I don't want to see him. He doesn't care about me. Ashleigh lied. Besides, she said he isn't even conscious."

"Does she expect him to pull through?" Sandler asked.

"She says she does, but that might be a trick to get me to give her power of attorney."

Caroline's account of Ashleigh McDowell's ridiculously generous offer had launched him in the direction of a new and more lucrative plan. Why settle for a percentage of Stuart's estate when, after a day or two on the West Coast and a little luck, he could have it all?

CHAPTER

64

The instant the clock struck seven on Saturday morning, Paige dialed the Winslows' number in Palm Springs. She closed her eyes, hoping they were still early risers.

Martha's cheerful greeting was all the reassurance she needed. But before Paige had a chance to ask about Walter or to tell her that she'd like to come to see them, Martha said, "We were so sorry you hadn't been able to join Mark last week."

So it was Mark, not Martha, who had chosen to exclude her.

"I've been trying to get hold of you ever since Mark left."

Paige's heart plummeted to her toes. "Is Walter—"

"Walter's holding his own. It's you we're worried about."

"Me?" Her antennae went up. Mark was far too closemouthed to speak of their personal problems. What on earth had he said to make Martha suspicious?

"Please don't shut me out, Paige. Mark is as tight-lipped as ever, and he insists everything is all right, but I know better."

"Nothing too serious," Paige lied, and then she rushed on to ask about Walter's health and how he'd taken the news of Sloane's imminent takeover of the corporation his father had founded.

Martha answered each question politely, but her tone, though maternal, held an unmistakable note of determination.

There was no point in Paige pretending all was well. Martha knew, or at least suspected, that it wasn't. Paige wondered how much she dared confide. She would not cover up or lie in response to any direct question. But before she could formulate a single coherent sentence, Martha said, "It's clear something is very wrong. And before you try to tell me that

I'm imagining things, I want you to know how much your happiness means to us. I pray that you haven't fallen out over the takeover."

Paige broke in before Martha said any more. "You have enough to contend with without me dumping our problems on you."

"Nonsense. You and Mark have been a godsend in what might have been quite a barren life for Walter and me."

As Martha spoke, Paige wondered why she had ever doubted their deep and mutual kinship.

Paige said, "And you've been a godsend to us." Knowing Martha couldn't possibly understand Mark's views, she hesitated, looking for the right words to relieve Martha of worry and yet not lie. "I can't deny the takeover threat has created a lot of pressure, nor that Mark and I have had a serious misunderstanding, but it has nothing to do with Consolidated. Please don't worry." She wished she could reassure Martha by saying that she and Mark would work things out, but of that she was not sure.

CHAPTER

65

In the waiting room of Dr. Chang's office, Christine Wainwright's posture was ramrod straight as she sat watching her husband's relentless pacing.

Neither had had any sleep the night before. She was at the breaking point. "Mitchell, please talk to me. It's not fair to accuse me of not loving our son."

"Words. I don't need words or platitudes. Mitch is your responsibility. Not a goddamned nanny's."

"I was gone less than two hours. You can't possibly think that little Mitch contracted pneumonia, much less leukemia, in that little time."

"You could have made the arrangements from home."

"I did," she said, "but I had to go to your office for the SEC manuals. Larry Brighton told me you'd need a couple of copies of several of the regulations before your first session."

If only she hadn't been so quick to revert to her past role. She couldn't stand it when Mitchell disapproved of her behavior. She'd been so careful not to let little Mitch take her focus from her husband. That's what had happened in his first marriage. She would not lose Mitchell in favor of caring for any sticky-fingered little creature. Maybe that was why she'd never bonded with the boy as *her son*. She thought of Mitch as a gift she had produced for Mitchell. In her mind, although she was always careful to call him *our son*, Mitch was no more than an extension of Mitchell. Her lack of maternal feelings occasionally troubled her, but not much.

"Christine." Mitchell's voice roused her from her introspection. "Did you hear what I said?"

Marshaling her wandering mind, she replied, "Sorry, I'm afraid I didn't. I was just thinking about our son."

Ignoring her last remark, Mitchell said, "I'm washing my hands of the Consolidated deal. Too bad it's taken something like this to bring me to my senses. Sloane's lost his perspective. To top his inflated bid would be financial suicide. Besides, compared to the battle we'll be up against if Mitch has leukemia, victory over that cocky Australian is damned unimportant."

The receptionist called their names, and Christine struggled to stand on legs that had turned to jello. It was shockingly clear. While she had tried, in vain, to win Mitchell's love, a four-year-old child had effortlessly succeeded. Her husband, who claimed to be incapable of deep emotion, could have given no greater proof than setting his ego aside and allowing Consolidated to fall to his archrival.

CHAPTER
66

As Conrad walked Ashleigh to the departure gate at Kennedy Airport, he wished he were going with her. But there were too many loose ends at Taylor Commercial Investments to resolve.

Reluctant to let her go, Conrad held Ashleigh tight as the boarding call boomed over the loudspeaker. "Give Charles my best when he comes around," he said. "And promise you won't . . ."

She covered his lips with hers in a deep penetrating kiss, then tilted her head back and met his eyes. "I promise. My Nancy Drew days have come to an end. But if I hadn't made this last foray, no telling how long it would have taken to connect Morris Sandler to the break-in."

Although they had no proof, Conrad was every bit as convinced of Sandler's involvement as Ashleigh was. "And, there's no telling what might have happened if Sandler had arrived before your precarious leap to freedom." She'd given Conrad credit for rescuing her, but she had, in fact, freed herself. He didn't want her taking any more chances.

"Stop worrying. I know I'm out of my depth. I'll leave the rest of the investigation to Landes. I just hope you're right about the power of attorney. I've got to get Charles out of the hospital and into familiar surroundings."

"Let me know if you run into any problems, but stay clear of the Sandlers."

Conrad had retained Landes Investigations and arranged for Ross Pocino to meet Ashleigh at LAX. She'd have twenty-four-hour protection until Sandler was either arrested for the crime at Charles Stuart's home or found innocent "beyond a reasonable doubt."

Paige drifted in and out of sleep in ten-to-fifteen-minute intervals. It was the worst night she'd had since making her painful decision.

Yesterday, when Martha had described Mark's recent visit, Paige's anger and resolve had begun to dissipate. She had even found herself empathizing with Mark. If only she'd handled things differently. If only he'd called.

A moment later, her resentment again began to fester. If only he had tried to understand. She didn't love this unborn child more than she loved him. He was too much a part of her. The simple fact was that Mark could take care of himself; their baby could not.

Clearly, Paige thought as she finally drifted off to sleep, she had no choice. She couldn't hold on to both worlds.

A surreal sensation washed over Mark as he pulled up to the address that he had coaxed from Paige's Irish trainer.

He'd heard a woman's stability could be altered by pregnancy, but this was bizarre. No woman in her right mind would live in a neighborhood like this if given a choice. So why hadn't Paige ended this stupid charade and returned home? It was irrational.

As he slid from behind the wheel, he saw that Paige's car was nowhere in sight. The only car in front of the apartment building was a beat-up blue Ford Taurus with a faded bumper sticker that read Rent-a-Dent. Well, if she wasn't home, he'd wait till she returned. They were going to have it out today.

He didn't think of himself as a snob, but as he'd driven past the line outside one of the soup kitchens and past the shelter in this neighborhood, he had felt the need for a good hot shower. It's a wonder Paige hadn't been attacked or raped. Although her apartment building was in a reasonably safe area, Paige certainly didn't belong here.

As he stormed up the front steps of the apartment house, he abandoned all thoughts of diplomacy. Paige had no right to play this juvenile game. She damn well better start acting her age. What he needed was the wife and partner he'd come to rely on—not this ongoing melodrama.

He marched down the freshly painted corridor, then stopped in front of the door marked six. Seeing no doorbell, he knocked on the door and waited. He heard no response and banged harder, then listened. He heard footsteps approaching the door and a tentative, "Who is it?"

At least she hadn't completely taken leave of her senses and flung open the door to anyone who might appear. "It's me. Open up."

The door opened slowly, then nearly closed again as Paige removed the safety chain.

"Come in, Mark," she said, showing no sign of surprise.

Sonny must have told her about my call, Mark thought to himself.

She was clad in the bright-red velvet robe Mark had given her for Christmas. Stifling a yawn, she gestured him toward the sofa—one that obviously hadn't come with the apartment. "Make yourself comfortable while I put some coffee on and wash my face," she said as she glanced at a clock on one of the end tables. "I was planning to call you first thing this morning. Afraid I overslept."

As he watched her disappear into the small kitchen, he was taken aback by her nonabrasive manner. It took a bit of steam out of his rage.

He looked around the room and recognized that the furniture, while not expensive, was well made, and that the interior of the small apartment was a product of Paige's unique creativity. His left eyelid began to twitch. How long did she intend to remain in this godforsaken neighborhood?

Paige hurried into the small bathroom after putting on the coffee. She splashed cold water on her face and ran a brush through her hair, wishing she'd taken the time to have it cut.

In her bedroom she stared into her three-foot-wide closet, then merely straightened the collar of her loose-fitting robe. Her hand shook as she applied lipstick and a touch of blush.

Although she hadn't planned for Mark to see this apartment, she was relieved they weren't meeting in the home they'd once shared. As she reentered the kitchen, the song lyric "say a prayer for me tonight" ran though her head. It had been etched in her brain since she'd first spoken with Martha.

She felt a pair of eyes on her and looked up to see Mark casually leaning against the doorjamb. He looked amazingly well rested and carefree, not at all as Paige expected. Paige poured the coffee and popped a couple of slices of bread into the toaster. "Be just a minute," she said, as if speaking to a relative stranger.

Moments later, when Paige set the enameled tray on the coffee table, Mark glanced meaningfully around the small living area. "Mind telling me what this is all about?"

Unprepared for such a beginning, she ignored it. "How did Walter take your decision to leave Consolidated?"

Mark's gaze revealed that he hadn't forgotten there were more pressing issues to discuss, but he briefly summarized his conversation with Walter.

"He's one of a kind. When I told him how sorry I was that I couldn't hold on to Consolidated, *he* tried to cheer *me* up. He hasn't lost his keen sense of humor, but he's got to be in a lot more pain than he admits to. Martha said he takes only a fraction of the morphine the doctor prescribed. He told me, 'Till the day they stick me in the ground, I'll not allow my brain to be turned to mush.'" Mark's voice faltered. "I don't see how he can hold on much longer."

A drawn-out silence followed, neither of them daring to speak. Mark felt his eyelid pulsate again and instinctively raised his finger to the corner of his eye. There was a great deal he had to say to Paige about her selfish and irrational behavior, but what he said was, "I hope you had the good sense not to burden Martha with our problems."

"Martha asked me to confide in her, but I didn't spell them out." There was now a cold, determined look in Paige's eye.

"Was it really necessary for you to even hint about our differences?"

"How would you have handled it?" Paige challenged, her green eyes flashing. "After your visit, the one *you* excluded *me* from," she couldn't help from adding, "Martha sensed that all was not well between us."

"If you'd behaved like an adult, rather than pulling a melodramatic disappearing act . . ." He broke off as Paige sprang to her feet, the fabric of the robe pressed against her body revealing a small dome-like protrusion below her waist.

"When I left the note, it seemed like a good idea. If the two of us could get away from the constant interruptions for a short time, we might be able to talk things out."

"Like I could just drop everything and trot off to a hotel."

She nodded as she settled herself in the rocking chair directly across from him. "In retrospect, I wish I'd confronted you at home."

"That would have been the grown-up way to handle it, rather than this blatant attention-getting ploy."

Mark had risen and was pacing the floor in front of the small windows.

She felt heat rise to her cheeks. "Maybe I didn't think things through, but things wouldn't have gone this far if you'd had the decency to call rather than leaving me tied to the phone, waiting for a call you had no intention of making."

"In case you didn't realize it, I was working round the clock on our future while you were doing your Agatha Christie number."

"You son of a bitch." Paige's voice cracked. "You knew exactly where I was. But you're more into control than—"

"I'm no clairvoyant," Mark broke in.

"You didn't have to be clairvoyant. I told you in my note. I even stayed at the Beverly Wilshire Hotel an extra two days."

"You told me nothing. You just left a note filled with the same damn platitudes I'd already heard. I had neither the time nor the energy to wade through the whole diatribe. If you had something to say, you should have said it to my face."

"I tried. You wouldn't listen."

"The fact that I didn't agree doesn't mean I didn't listen," Mark countered, his jaw rigid enough to crack teeth.

"Mark, please. Let's not quarrel."

"Great idea. Now, why don't you pack your bags, and we'll go home and talk."

"You just don't get it, do you?" Paige said in exasperation. "I had no intention of getting pregnant. But I am. And I want this baby. I'm not having an abortion."

"Obviously. If you were deeply religious or anti-abortion, I might understand. But you're just damn stubborn." He raised his palm, warding off response. "But this appears to be a battle you're determined to win, so I've just got to accept it."

"What does that mean?" Paige asked.

"It means that in spite of *my* feelings, you're taking on another responsibility for both of us. So be it," he said with a sigh of resignation. Then leaving no space for Paige to comment, he said, "I realize this is a losing battle. You win. We'll hire a competent nanny—"

"My child isn't going to be brought up by a nanny!" she exploded.

"Jesus, Paige. What do you want? Do you plan to become a house Frau and let some goddamned kid turn our world upside down at this stage of our lives?"

The battle went round and round until Paige threw up her hands and said, "Mark, this isn't getting us anywhere. It's clear that there is no room in your life for our daughter. Which means there's no place for me. I'm truly sorry, but you leave me no choice. I love you, but I must make a life for our child and myself. I'm in no hurry, and hopefully we can avoid the normal bitterness of divorce."

"You're in no hurry? How magnanimous." Then, with a gesture encompassing the tiny apartment, he said sarcastically, "And what a magnificent beginning."

CHAPTER
68

Now that it appeared that all the competitors for Consolidated had dropped out, Sloane's staff, along with Murray Levich and a team of accountants, lawyers, and bankers, held nonstop meetings at First Commercial to settle the takeover deal.

James Kelsey, one of First Commercial's managing directors, shook his head and turned to Levich. "Next I suppose you'll want a highly confidential letter from us," he said jokingly.

"Naturally," Levich said. The firm had too much riding on this deal to back out.

Jules Ramsey, who'd been stretched out on the couch in the corner of the conference room, hadn't missed a beat. Sloane's CFO rose and approached the table. He cleared his throat loudly. "We've been at this for three days. It's time you stopped questioning the boss's credibility." He looked pointedly at First Commercial's entourage. "You told Sloane he'd get no more than $450 million for the Babcock division. He negotiated the deal at $750 million."

Levich jumped in. "Not only did his lordship pay the sucker's inflated price tag, Sloane also sold him an option to run the food concessions in all his stores."

"That was no con job," Ramsey said defensively. "Sloane knows Babcock's is worth every penny, which is the key to his negotiating edge."

Amazing how Sloane's crew jumped to his defense when he was on the other side of the Atlantic, Levich mused. And, free of their mercurial boss's interference, not nearly as many snags developed in the negotiations. They were smart to avoid Sloane's harangues by not answering the phones—or leaving them off the hook.

Levich finally wangled the "Prepared to Commit" statement out of First Commercial for another billion-dollar bridge loan—to be repaid with the proceeds from yet another junk-bond sale. This allowed the use of First Commercial's name without having to pay for it up front.

After ironing out the major kinks, Lawrence Drew spoke up. "One stipulation is that we're directly involved in all pertinent negotiations in obtaining commercial banks."

"Done," Ramsey said. "But I have another issue to discuss." He paused, gave Levich a meaningful nod, and turned his attention to Drew. "Another $5 million fee to First Commercial for simply writing a letter expressing confidence in Sloane's already proven ability to find willing lenders is excessive. Every time we turn around, we're stuck with another outrageous bill." By the end of the hour, First Commercial dutifully reduced the earlier agreed-upon fee to $1.85 million.

CHAPTER
69

David Jerome glared at the empty chair. With one exception, the entire Bentleys Royale management team had filed in on time and had taken their customary seats around the large table in his office.

He strode to the table, his thumbs hitched in the waistband of his trousers. "Has anyone seen Ashleigh?" he asked, his agitation apparent. As president of this sinking ship, his role became more difficult by the day. It had become impossible to walk through the store without being bombarded with questions. Naturally, the associates were concerned, but he had more important things to do than smoothe ruffled feathers. That was Ashleigh's role, but lately, she was absent when he needed her most. Morale was at rock bottom, and he needed her here, not just counseling executives but also walking the sales floors. The sales associates trusted her, and it would relieve him of having to give reassurances that he knew, in his heart, could be false.

Jerome respected Charles Stuart—it would be a shame to lose that brilliant mind—but he had a business to run. And there wasn't a damn thing Ashleigh could do for Stuart while he remained in a coma. But there was plenty for her to do here.

About fifteen minutes into the meeting, Ashleigh slipped into her seat. She was cradling two thick black binders in her arm. As she set them on the floor beside her, he remembered that she had told him she would have to attend a meeting at the corporate office. She represented Bentleys Royale on a task force with Bentley's senior vice president of personnel and a score of legal eagles who were developing placement plans for executives who would not be retained in a new regime.

Ashleigh remained in the president's office after the meeting broke up and the last of her peers had filed out. "Charles is leaving the hospital this afternoon," she reported. "I need to be at his place by two o'clock." Because Charles had a medical directive on file with the hospital, Ashleigh did not have to produce a medical power of attorney to have him moved to his own home.

"He's come out of his coma?"

Ashleigh shook her head. "Not yet." There was no point in giving her rationale for having Charles moved to his own home. All her boss wanted to know was whether she planned to make a habit of leaving early. "With him at home, I won't have to conform to hospital hours any longer."

Jerome gave a reluctant nod. But an instant later, his eyebrows pinched together in consternation. "Where the break-in occurred?"

Again, she read between the lines. "There will be twenty-four-hour-a-day security at the house. And it's been thoroughly cleaned and repainted where necessary, so there's no sign of the violence that just took place."

CHAPTER
70

In a small conference room, on the last Thursday of April, an impressive and diverse crowd assembled at Sheldon and Arpel, Consolidated's law firm. Twelve board members had flown in from Cincinnati to meet early that afternoon. Ralph Learner, Consolidated's cantankerous CEO, was edgy and clearly out of sorts.

Murray Levich represented Philip Sloane as his private tactician. The impressive lineup presenting the case for the absentee buyer also included Lawrence Drew and James Kelsey from First Commercial and Sloane's M&A attorney, Howard Greenberg.

In the early stage of the negotiations, Levich left the room to make a phone call.

A yellow legal pad had been left beside one of the public telephones. Unable to resist, he glanced at the top sheet. He spotted a short list of familiar names—KKR, Denton, and others. He also noted equally familiar numbers alongside several of the names.

Levich surreptitiously jotted down the numbers. After quickly analyzing the data, he walked back into the conference room and made eye contact with Learner. "Something's come up, gentlemen" he said, looking at each of the board members in turn. "Give us about fifteen minutes, please." Levich then gestured to the Sloane contingent to join him in the corridor.

In a huddle, Levich told the team what he'd discovered. "Since the highest bid listed was $65, Sloane is sure to win the company at $68. Why else have we been invited?" Levich had not been convinced that the $67 bid Sloane had recently approved was going to fly. "Better to bump it up now and cut the risk. We don't want to come back to the bargaining table."

Back inside the conference room, they waded through myriad details until all parties appeared to be satisfied with the proposal. At $68 per share—all cash—the deal seemed imminent. All they needed was Sloane's approval.

At 4:00 p.m., Levich called Jules Ramsey to convey the news.

"It's a go at $68—all cash," Levich announced.

Silence.

"Jules. Did you hear me?"

"Yeah," he confirmed, "but we've got a problem."

"Now what?" Levich couldn't conceal his exasperation.

"We don't know where Phil is. The last we heard, he had taken off from Switzerland and was en route to Italy. He's been out of touch for more than twenty-four hours."

"Jesus!" Levich exploded. "It's one hell of a time for him to be incommunicado. Other than an oil company acquisition last year, this is the largest takeover in U.S. history. And here we are, stalled in the conference room while Sloane's out globe-trotting."

"Give me your number," Ramsey said.

The hands of the clock seemed loaded with lead. At 5:00 p.m., Levich had a paralegal who could speak Italian phone Sloane's villa. She was told Sloane was dining at Broginos, a local restaurant.

The paralegal finally contacted Sloane at the restaurant, but Levich took the phone the moment he came on the line and briefly explained the deal.

"Proceed," was Sloane's hasty response. "Now, if there's nothing more, it's going on midnight here. I'd like to get back to my dinner."

For a man about to pay nearly $7 billion for a corporation outside his field of expertise, he certainly seemed to lack interest in the details.

When news of Sloane's transatlantic approval trickled down the hallways at Sheldon and Arpel, the various factions returned to the conference room.

"We've agreed on all the major points, so there's no reason not to get the contracts drawn up and signed tonight," Levich insisted.

Learner stood up and said in a loud voice, "I won't be railroaded into this."

Levich continued to push for an immediate completion.

Learner stood his ground. "There are clauses to be written—details to be worked out. Monday is soon enough."

The board endorsed Learner's cautious approach. The meeting was concluded.

Levich hoped no new snags developed.

Ensconced in a secluded corner of Broginos with two of his would-be investors, Sloane waved for the telephone to be removed from their table. Viviana's heart pounded in anticipation.

"It's a done deal," he confirmed with a broad grin. He clinked his glass to hers.

Viviana felt giddy. She could hardly wait to see her former colleagues. For those who survived the buyout, Philip Sloane would be their boss, and she would be much more than the woman on his arm. She would be the person he'd rely on to translate retail trends and jargon. "To the number one negotiator on this planet," she said before flinging her arms around his neck and planting a slow penetrating kiss on his lips. She was squirming with desire.

Even in the dimly lit restaurant, she couldn't miss the instant glow of color that rose to Philip's cheeks. Gently unwinding her arms, he squeezed her hand. "Viviana is not one to hide her emotions." He then extracted the bottle of Dom Perignon from the ice bucket and refilled each of the glasses. "The buyout of the conglomerate we discussed earlier is a fait accompli," he said again, tapping Viviana's champagne flute, then, one-by-one, those of the two investors.

"Let's have a magnificent victory celebration at Carlingdon's," said Viviana. "I can take care of all the details." Surreptitiously, she had been planning the event for months and had her starring role all worked out. While the most influential men and women in the nation toasted her man, she too would have a chance to shine.

CHAPTER

72

Immediately following the exit of Murray Levich and the Sloane contingent, Ralph Learner, running on pure adrenaline, held court with the board. No matter how vile a taste the sale of his company to the absentee raider left in his mouth, he couldn't sidestep his responsibility. He must present the whole picture.

Learner took one last puff on his cigar before grinding it out in an overflowing ashtray. He immediately launched into a summary. "Sloane has proven he's no greenmailer. He's agreed to pay cash at $68 a share. He's lined up $1.5 billion in equity from creditable sources, he has Levich on his team, and First Commercial has committed to lending him more than a billion dollars of their own funds to tide him over if any of his lenders are slow to materialize. He has also managed to get a phenomenal price for the Babcock's division."

Then, leaning forward on his elbows, he made eye contact with each of the directors, who were also mandated by civil law to accept the best and highest offer for the shareholders. "That about sums up the positives.

"We can't refuse to sell the company to this real estate developer based on his lack of mental stability, the fact that he knows beans about the retail business, or even that he's borrowed too much money for his or the company's own good." He paused to take a breath. "But I'll be damned if I wouldn't rather gargle with lye than turn this company over to him. So, until he's officially engaged a commercial banker, we're under no obligation to sign anything he attempts to cram down our throats."

The entire weekend following the transatlantic call to Sloane, his lawyers and bankers popped in and out of the various conference rooms to work out the small print with Consolidated's lawyers.

Miraculously, Jordon's surfaced as a secret rival bidder over that same weekend. Learner summarily shelved the contracts Levich had tried to ram through the previous Friday.

Parallel meetings with Jordon's bankers and Sloane's group continued throughout the weekend. Consolidated's lawyers jumped from one conference room to another like busy politicians, keeping rival factions apart while tightening the commitment on both deals.

CHAPTER
73

Mark felt a glow of pride as he watched Paige glide across the floor with Franklin Nason, her head tossed back in amusement. He'd missed her sense of humor, her dry wit that always made him laugh. It seemed a long time since either of them had laughed, but tonight Paige was like her old self—the woman he'd married. Her expressive green eyes glinted in delight, and she seemed relaxed and at ease.

This was the third time Paige had joined Mark for dinner with prospective employers. And each time, he'd marveled at her ability to carry off the appearance of normality. It had taken all his energy to mask his emotions and get through the first two dinners.

Franklin Nason hosted the evening. Nason's was a nationally known group of quality department stores on a par with Bentleys Royale and Saks Fifth Avenue. After their top guns failed to capture Mark's commitment to become their next CEO, they'd enticed their former chairman of the board to fly to LA on their behalf.

Franklin Nason, one of the most admired and respected retailers in the nation, had guided the course of Nason's for more than fifty years. But like Charles Stuart, he was not one to rest on his laurels. Since retiring from day-to-day participation in the former family-owned retail empire, Nason had authored two books. The first, in Mark's opinion, was the definitive manual on retailing and should be required reading for any young person entering the world of business. His second focused on a theme close to Mark's heart—the pursuit of the *very finest quality*. While those who could afford the *very best* continued to be a small percentage of the total population, Mark wholeheartedly agreed with Nason's philosophy—the quality market would never die.

"You have a real treasure, Mark," Nason said as he pulled out Paige's chair. "A quality business such as ours could ask for no more elegant ambassadors."

"Thank you, Mr. Nason. We appreciate you coming to Los Angeles, and your offer is most flattering. However, I'm not prepared to make a commitment at this time. I plan on exploring a couple of options outside the retail arena."

"What a shame that would be," Nason said. "The world of retail would sorely miss the youth, vitality, and expertise you bring to the business."

Mark again thanked the elder Nason. "Like you, I'm energized by the challenges. And I'm not sure I'm ready to leave it all behind." Then, quickly shifting gears, he said, "The minute I've decided, I'll give you a call."

The maître d' approached their table. "Excuse me, Mr. Toddman," he said, "you have a phone call. Would you like me to bring the phone to the table, or would you prefer—"

"I'll take it in the lobby, thank you." Mark excused himself.

When Mark briefly touched Paige's hand before leaving the table, she felt that touch deep inside. And as she watched him leave, she realized the economy and simplicity of his movement paralleled the sense of directness that had catapulted him to center stage in business. He gave the impression he knew exactly where he was going and how to get there.

In Mark's absence, Paige steered the conversation away from the job offer to more general areas. A fairly easy feat since Franklin Nason loved discussing ideas for keying into the dreams of those who could afford the very best.

A short while later, Mark slipped back into his chair. He wore a broad smile on his face. "That was Conrad Taylor. Two new and somewhat surprising developments have surfaced. Number one, there's no evidence of any activity in Wainwright's camp. And number two, Jordon's is launching a bid for the whole of Consolidated."

"I understood their interests were confined to the West Coast divisions," Nason interjected.

"That's my understanding as well," Mark responded, "but Conrad tells me Cyril approached him soon after we folded, and they've lined up some impressive backers." Cyril Stein, CEO of Jordon's, was also a close friend of Consolidated's CEO, Ralph Learner.

"Have the wire services got it wrong?" Nason's brow furrowed. "Wasn't it a foregone conclusion that Consolidated would capitulate to Sloane?"

Mark shrugged. "Apparently, it's not over till it's over."

"Is Conrad backing Jordon's bid?" Paige asked.

Mark nodded. "Cyril spearheaded Jordon's management buyout a couple of years ago, so he's not new to the LBO phenomenon. Under him, Consolidated's key divisions will have a fighting chance for survival. But even if Jordon's is successful, the debt factor remains a major consideration. Conrad has only a small piece of the action."

Paige had not enjoyed an evening this much in a long time. She hadn't realized how much she'd missed the easy conversation and laughter that had been so much a part of her life with Mark. For the moment, her troubles seemed to melt away. Mark had also seemed in his element. He'd been charming and amusing, and his handsome features showed no sign of the strain of the past months.

In the euphoria of the evening, Paige allowed her hopes to soar. But once she and Mark had dropped off Franklin Nason at the Hermitage Hotel, an awkward silence fell between them.

In her heart, Paige knew Mark belonged to the world of retail. And while he was not yet ready to set his future in concrete, he had too much to contribute to that world to walk away. She ached to tell him how she felt, and yet, she no longer had that right.

Not able to endure the silence, Paige said, "Mark, I wish I knew what to do or what to say that would make things better between us."

As she waited for his reply, she prayed for control over her quick temper. She must listen without becoming defensive or allowing her words to turn into angry recriminations.

Mark's eyes locked with hers as he turned to face her. When he finally spoke, he was direct. "I'm fed up with this dating game. You're my wife.

I want you to come home tonight. We've always been a team. And we're damn good together."

Paige took a deep breath. They were right back where they'd started. Nothing had changed—nothing was resolved.

"I won't just roll over and promise to be somebody I'm not," he said. "The role of doting parents was never in our plan. I know you had no more intention of bringing a child into our lives than I did . . ."

She felt her body tense. Mark evidently noticed and held up his hand, warding off her response.

"I can't pretend to understand your sudden maternal instinct," he continued, "but I'm aware that to have you by my side, I must accept it."

He smiled. A smile that seemed unnatural and forced as his eyes shifted to the slight swelling in her abdomen. "I don't have to tell you—I'm not thrilled. But I'll accept the responsibility for a child as long as you agree not to allow it to dominate our lifestyle. Whether I go with Nason's or outside retail, maintaining our lifestyle must remain your number one priority. The child will be well taken care of and provided for . . ."

As Mark continued to speak, Paige felt the curtain close on their life together. "What you're saying," she broke in, "is that *our* child can have all the material advantages and perhaps, if she's lucky, visits from her parents when they have nothing better to do."

"Christ, Paige. We've been in perfect harmony about children—they're terrific as long as they're someone else's. Tonight you were in your element. There's no point in screwing up our own lives because of a freak accident."

Paige sighed, tears running unchecked down her cheeks. "I'm sorry. I can't help the way I feel. I never envisioned myself as a mother, but this baby is real and my love for her is just as real." She paused, her heart yearning for a way out of the inevitable choice she must make. "The feelings I have for our child are totally different from the kind of love we've shared."

Paige broke off abruptly—Mark's tense body formed an impenetrable wall between them. They'd reached an impasse. "I can't give up this child, nor can I bring her into a home where she is only tolerated." She swallowed past the lump in her throat and planted a smile on her face.

"I do want to continue to be your partner with prospective employers if you want me . . ."

He gave a firm shake of his head. "You've made your choice. There's no point in running it into the ground. I'm quite capable of entertaining or being entertained on my own." His voice was as cold as the eyes that bore into hers. "File for divorce whenever it suits you. I won't be stampeded into a lifestyle I find abhorrent, Paige. Nor will I continue to date my own wife. That's behind us. Headhunters and prospective employers aren't interested in my marital status. They're looking at what I can bring to their bottom line."

Paige nodded.

As Mark gunned the motor and pulled the car back on the road, she sat with her hands clenched in her lap. At the sight of her husband's face, she felt the color drain from her soul. It was not the face of the man she knew and loved. The face was cold and expressionless. The eyes had narrowed to horizontal slits, the mouth a hard, tight line. There was nothing left to say.

They rode in silence for what seemed an eternity. Mark brought the car to an abrupt stop behind Paige's rental car. He left the motor running while Paige rummaged through her handbag. The strumming of his fingers on the steering wheel unnerved her, but at last she pulled out the elusive keys.

"I'm so sorry," Paige said as she reached for the door handle. The words were inadequate, but her mind was blank. There was nothing left to be said.

Mark's face contorted with suppressed anger. His tone one of icy detachment, he stated, "You must move back into the house tomorrow. I'll be staying in town at the athletic club."

"I most certainly will not—"

"Listen to me," he said, cutting her off. "I've had about all I can take. With the company on the brink of disaster, and you doing a complete switch in values, the least you can do is get yourself and this unborn child out of harm's way. The very last thing I need is for you to be kidnapped."

"Don't be ridiculous. Who on earth would want to kidnap me?"

"I've no flare for melodrama." He reached into the inside pocket of his suit jacket, pulled out a folded piece of paper, and handed it to her.

The thin paper bore that day's date. It had been faxed to each member of Consolidated's "Big Five," which included the CEO, president, CFO, and two regional executive VPs—Mark Toddman and his counterpart. The message was direct. It stated that because their golden parachutes had been highly publicized, it was possible that a would-be ransom seeker might target them or members of their families.

Paige's vision blurred as she read past the warning to the suggested precautions. The impact of those few words cut into her like a sharp blade. Not because she feared being kidnapped; the likelihood of that was far too remote. Under Mark's unwavering gaze, she felt her control over her own destiny erode.

"Be right there," Paige shouted as she made her way from the bedroom. It sounded as if someone were kicking at the door rather than using the brass knocker she'd installed.

She looked through the wide-angle peephole and let out a spontaneous giggle as she pulled open the door. Below a pile of cardboard boxes was a familiar pair of Adidas tennis shoes. Above, a single tuft of unruly red hair.

"Sonny, let me help," offered Paige as the empty boxes tumbled to the floor.

"Aye, but it's good to hear you laugh."

"I feel wonderful," she said, no longer needing to pretend. "And you were absolutely right. Everything is working out."

"Are you the same troubled woman I chatted with only a few hours ago?" Sonny couldn't hide the delighted glint in his eyes below his quizzical brows.

Paige rose up on her tiptoes and kissed her trainer's raised brows. "No one could ask for a better friend. I've thought a lot about our conversation this morning. You were right about *almost* everything," she said. "I can easily commute to the shelter. I talked to the Rent-a-Dent attendant this morning, and he's agreed to switch me to their in-and-out garage."

At the sight of his pinched auburn brows, Paige said, "Having a chauffeur drop me off would be worse than driving the Jag. I'll use the garage as my in-between."

"In-between what?"

"Take that silly scowl off your face," she said. He sank down onto the overstuffed sofa, and she dropped onto the newly carpeted floor and made herself comfortable in her usual Indian style position. "I wouldn't want to embarrass my high and mighty husband, and I must admit that the Rent-a-Dent vehicle would be as much out of place in Hollywood Hills as the Jag is in this neighborhood. So, I'll pick up the rental at the garage in the morning and switch back when I return home in the evening."

"Aye. Flinging a wee bit of hostility at your thick-headed husband, are you?"

"I can't pretend it doesn't rear its ugly head from time to time. Things didn't have to turn out as they have, and sometimes I feel a whole kettle of resentment boiling up. Then I force myself to refocus. Mark has no more control over his feelings than I have over mine. When he's made up his mind, his convictions are as solid as Gibraltar.

"He is what he is. And I suppose if he'd been as flexible as I'd hoped about the baby, he wouldn't be as sought after in business. Maybe he'd have risen no higher than a buyer or general merchandise manager . . ." Her voice trailed off, and she changed course. "But enough of what might have been. A bad decision is better than no decision at all. Today, I want to dwell on the positives."

"What a fancy litany of blarney. Mark is far from the only inflexible Toddman."

She wanted to deny it, but she knew he spoke the truth. While she'd thought she was fairly flexible, she now realized that her flexibility was confined to matters about which she didn't feel strongly one way or the other. On important issues, she had the tenacity of a champion athlete; she'd never been able to give in—not on anything that really mattered. She shrugged and smiled. "Guilty as charged."

"Well, I'll rest easier once you're out of here and tucked in at your own lovely home."

"I'm afraid it's lost all its magic. I'll be there alone. Mark will be staying at the athletic club."

"Are you serious?" Sonny's voice rose with incredulity.

Nodding her head, Paige replied, "That's what he said. I'd think 78,000 square feet of living space would be enough to accommodate the two of us until we can get our lives settled, but . . ." She paused, again shifting her thoughts. "After Mark gets his career options settled, we'll put the house on the market, and I'll find something appropriate and comfortable for my new life with the baby."

"Paige. If you and Mark really can't set things right between you, I can understand why you don't want to rattle around in that lovely mansion with just a wee lassie and yourself. But as wonderful and precious a gift as this child may be, the wee one can hardly replace the life you've grown accustomed to. An intelligent woman such as you, with so much vitality, will be needin' more. Confinin' yourself to a life of baby talk is hardly—"

"You're beginning to sound like Mark. I'm not about to make a complete about-face in my lifestyle. There's too much about that life I adore. But for the time being, I want to satisfy another part of me. I love getting close to people with deep needs. Being a fund-raiser is important, but it doesn't give me the highs I experience seeing these people one-on-one and doing my small bit to help them."

Sonny raised his arms in a gesture of surrender. Then his eyes scanned the living room of the apartment and rested on the still empty boxes he'd dropped off earlier.

A smile curved her lips as Paige thought of all she'd accomplished since Sonny had left just a few hours before. And she again felt the giddy pleasure of having contributed to something really important. "I've been busy. After you left, I was so inspired that I couldn't put my mind to packing. In fact, I had just got back a few minutes before you arrived."

"Me inspiring you to forget about getting packed? Tell me what you've been up to."

"Remember Patti, the young woman I told you about? The one who came in during my first week?" When he looked at her blankly, she went on. "Come on, you must remember. She's the one with the five-year-old daughter named April who has enormous brown eyes."

Sonny nodded, his expression wary.

"Anyway, when you asked what I planned to do with the furniture, I began to think about Patti and April. I have no use for the furniture, and the rent is paid through the next six months, so I went back to my makeshift office and looked up Patti's address. This," she said, with an expansive gesture encompassing the apartment, "looks like a palace compared to their studio apartment. And there's an elementary school just down the block where April can go to kindergarten."

Paige felt a tear run down her cheek as another vision floated to the surface. She saw herself as a little girl looking out from a window high above a schoolyard, remembering the pain of not being allowed to attend school or play with the other children.

CHAPTER
75

Charles Stuart, locked in his own dark world, was not in pain, but he felt as if his eyes were glued shut and his limbs were made of cast iron.

From a distance, he heard Ashleigh's voice, soft and low. She was imploring him to open his eyes, to squeeze her hand, to let her know that he could hear her. Each time he became conscious, she was there beside him. But try as he might, he couldn't open his eyes; he couldn't even squeeze them tight as a signal that he heard every word. Every muscle in his body was locked up tight. He felt her hand wrapped around his, but his fingers were like limp noodles. They refused to respond to the messages his brain was sending.

His mind, in contrast to his body, seemed remarkably alert. He was not suffering memory loss. Every word the leather-jacketed hoodlum had said to him was etched sharply in his mind. He clearly remembered looking down the elongated barrel of a gun, hearing a car pull up in the driveway and praying it wasn't Ashleigh's.

He had understood Ashleigh when she'd told him he was now in his own home. What frustrated him most was the quaver of distress in Ashleigh's voice. He wanted to reach out to let her know he was in no great pain. To let her know that he heard her and knew she was beside him.

Charles Stuart had no fear of death. What he did fear was the loss of his independence through disablement, or being the recipient of compassion or pity from those he loved. He felt fairly certain that his brain had suffered no damage. Although he drifted in and out of sleep, he attributed that to the drugs that were most likely being pumped into his body. Most of the time his thoughts were clear. He would fight fiercely to regain his former quality of life. But if that was not to be, he wanted

Ashleigh to know that he'd lived a good life and that death was merciful in comparison to the alternatives.

The door chimes sounded.

"I'll be right back," Ashleigh said. He felt her withdraw her hand from his.

CHAPTER
76

Ashleigh descended the broad staircase quickly, hoping to ward off another series of the melodic chimes. As she was reaching for the door handle, she heard Pocino's husky voice.

"Hold it," he shouted as he strode to the foyer.

She stepped back from the door. "Sorry."

With an exaggerated raise of both brows, he said, "Yeah, yeah. But until we get the full skinny on the break-in here, you're not part of the reception committee."

"Got it," Ashleigh said with a sheepish grin.

The door chimes rang a second time, and Pocino withdrew his revolver and stepped in front of Ashleigh to glance through the leaded window-panes. Keeping the gun concealed, he swung open the door.

Morris Sandler heard the echo of chimes as he took in the Stuart property. This was the first time either he or Caroline had set foot in the Naples area of Long Beach. He liked what he saw. This estate was worth a pretty penny with its prime location, looking directly out on the bay, and its beautifully maintained grounds. Dollar signs flashed in his head.

Sandler had worked hard to overcome Caroline's resistance to coming face-to-face with her father. "I know it won't be easy," he'd told her, "but your father is a very old man, and you must pretend to forgive him, angel. It's up to you to prevent Ashleigh McDowell from taking your rightful inheritance." When the color drained from Caroline's pale face, he'd assured her, "I'll be by your side. That greedy bitch can't hurt you. Blood is thicker than whatever hold she has over the old man. Otherwise, she wouldn't have tried to manipulate you into signing a power of attorney."

When the door finally swung open, Caroline gripped his arm, and through the heavy wool of his Brooks Brothers suit jacket, he felt her tremble.

A burly six-footer in a rumpled shirt and pair of chinos opened the door. With a total lack of discretion and without a word, the ape stepped out onto the porch to scan the area around them, and then he turned to the attractive blonde behind him as he slipped something into his waistband.

The big man said something to the woman, who was undoubtedly Ashleigh McDowell, but Sandler didn't catch his words.

"Caroline!" the woman exclaimed. Her brown eyes were large and filled with apprehension. She stared first at his wife, then at him.

Stepping forward, Sandler offered his hand and introduced himself.

They were still standing outside the open door when Ashleigh introduced herself and the big man who hovered directly behind her.

The man she called Ross Pocino gripped Sandler's hand with the power of Mike Tyson. A grip that drained the color from his fingers and made them numb. The husky ape had to be a bodyguard.

"We'd like to come in," Sandler began, taking in the situation and adjusting his plans. A bodyguard wasn't something he'd counted on. He should have anticipated some added precautions since the break-in. Prepared that Ashleigh, still reeling from her treatment in Greenwich, might be reluctant to talk to them, he felt confident that he could prevail. But removing the bodyguard would be akin to moving a mountain.

Once inside the living room, Sandler made a quick estimate of the furnishings, particularly the art objects and paintings. The palms of his hands itched in anticipation of getting Ashleigh's signature on the papers Caroline had described.

Ashleigh gestured for them to be seated. He led his wife to the pastel print sofa with plump, comfortable-looking cushions. He sat beside her and held her hand to keep her calm.

"Ms. McDowell," he began as she lowered herself into the armchair across from them. "Caroline was so upset after your visit that she insisted on coming to spend time with her father."

Pocino pulled out a chair, plunked himself down, and leaned toward them, his elbows planted firmly on his knees.

Sandler kept a wary eye on the solidly built bodyguard but turned his attention to the young woman.

"He's still in a coma," Ashleigh explained. Her voice was so soft, Sandler had to strain to hear her.

"I understand," he said, "but Caroline would like to see him."

Ashleigh, clad in a white cashmere sweater and wool trousers, her hair pulled back in a loose ponytail, appeared much younger than Sandler had expected. He kept his eyes riveted on her as she stared down at her toes and thoughtfully pursed her lips. After a long silence, she looked up.

"Caroline, would you like to see him now?"

Caroline squeezed her husband's hand with surprising strength, and then she relaxed her grip. Her mood swung rapidly from fear to bravado. "First, show me to my room so I can freshen up."

"Your room?" Ashleigh repeated, her eyes filled with surprise.

Caroline glared at her. "This is *my* father's house, after all, and I intend . . ."

The bodyguard was on his feet, his gaze traveling between them as though he were a spectator at a tennis match.

Sandler put his arms around Caroline's shoulders and broke in. "Excuse me, angel," he said. "Ms. McDowell is not challenging your right to be here."

Ashleigh took in a silent breath and glanced at the bodyguard before responding. "I don't challenge your right to be here. However, I will make arrangements for you to stay at the Hyatt. It's less than a quarter mile from the house."

Again, Sandler broke in. "That won't be convenient for us, Ms. McDowell. There's plenty of room here."

Ashleigh shot to her feet, her voice losing its softness. "I'm sorry, but that won't be possible," she declared.

"Who the hell do you think you are? I have more right to be here than you do." Caroline's voice rose to a shriek as she jumped to her feet, knocking over the table lamp and looking as if she were ready to do physical battle.

Sandler grabbed her. He wished he could jerk her back down, but with her sudden mood swings, he didn't dare.

He met Ashleigh's eyes, which were now cold and expressionless. "I'm sorry, but my wife has been terribly upset since hearing the news of what happened to her father. She hasn't been herself since you left our home in Greenwich."

Caroline whirled on him, her eyes blazing. "Don't apologize for my behavior," she screamed. "*She's* the one who's out of line. Get her out of my father's house this very minute!"

Pocino stepped forward, his hand slipping to his waistband. "No, Mrs. Sandler. Ms. McDowell is not the one who's on her way out." Then, turning to Sandler, he said, "It's time you and your wife were on your way."

Caroline started to say something, but Sandler cut her off. "Let me handle this," he whispered, again squeezing her hand.

"I've no idea what role you have," he lied, turning to Pocino, "but my wife has every right to stay in her father's home."

"I'm afraid you got that wrong," Pocino said, withdrawing the gun.

"Ross, please put that away." Ashleigh closed the distance between them. Then, turning to address Caroline, she said, "If you'd like to see your father, I'll take you upstairs now."

Still gripping Caroline's hand firmly, Sandler answered for them. "Thank you."

Ashleigh didn't move. "I'm sorry, Mr. Sandler. Just one visitor is allowed at a time."

"This is a difficult time for my wife," he challenged. "She needs my support."

"The lady said one at a time," Pocino repeated, reluctantly pocketing his gun.

Sandler whispered in his wife's ear, "I'll be right outside the door." Then, turning to Ashleigh, he said, "I'd like to speak with you, Ms. McDowell, while Caroline visits with her father."

Pocino caught hold of Ashleigh's elbow as she turned to lead the Sandlers up the stairs. He whispered in her ear, "I don't like the way that clown looks at you. And I can only be in one place at a time."

Ashleigh furrowed her brow, remembering that Charles's nurse had gone to the Naples Pharmacy to pick up a prescription and had not yet returned. Caroline could not be left alone with her father, and Ashleigh had no intention of being alone with Morris Sandler.

"Mr. Sandler and I will talk in the dressing alcove," she said, keeping her voice low.

"Good idea," Pocino said. "Then I'll be able to keep an eye on both our unannounced visitors."

At the top of the staircase, Ashleigh led the small entourage down the corridor and into Charles Stuart's room. She walked over to his bedside.

Caroline's eyes narrowed, but Ashleigh gestured her over and said in a soft monotone, "You may stay as long as you like, Caroline. Your husband and I will be right across the room if you need anything."

Ashleigh's focus flashed to Pocino. She was relieved to know he was there. Leaning close to Charles Stuart's ear, she said, "Caroline has come to see you."

As they crossed the room to the alcove, deep lines creased Sandler's forehead. "Thought you told us he was still in a coma."

"He is," Ashleigh said without elaboration. She settled on the padded bench of the window seat and indicated he should sit in the armchair across from her.

Sandler apologized for his wife's behavior in Greenwich. "Please explain the offer you made to Caroline." But before giving her an opportunity to respond, he told Ashleigh what he'd been told. "I'm sure every-thing can be worked out to our mutual satisfaction. But if you were to be given Mr. Stuart's power of attorney, we would need to write in certain safeguards."

Wasting no words, Ashleigh asserted, "That won't be necessary. When I went to see your wife, I was not aware that my . . ." She was going to say "my grandfather" but stopped short. Sick and tired of searching for non-offensive nomenclature, she felt suppressed anger bubbling to the surface. "I already have Charles Stuart's power of attorney."

Sandler's lower jaw sagged. He took a deep breath before he chal-lenged her. "You can't get away with that. You have no blood ties. We'll take you to court and get any phony power of attorney overturned so fast it'll make your head spin."

"Take your filthy hands off me," Caroline's shrill voice rose from the other side of the room.

Ashleigh turned to see Pocino gripping Caroline's wrists and pulling her away from the hospital bed. Sandler was on his feet an instant before Ashleigh.

When they reached the bedside, Sandler took hold of his wife and silenced her by pushing his hand across her mouth. Muffled cries came from deep in her throat, and she began flailing her arms. Pocino and Sandler pushed, pulled, and half carried her from the room.

Ashleigh felt blood surge through her veins. Caroline had pulled the IV from Charles's arm. A thin trail of blood ran down his forearm and onto the sheets. Shaking, Ashleigh put her thumb over the source of the blood flow and pressed down.

She heard Pocino and the Sandlers outside the bedroom door, their voices raised in anger, Caroline's high-pitched voice louder than both men.

Ashleigh lifted Charles's hand to her lips and kissed it gently, telling him that everything was going to be all right. That's when she saw the deep indentations of fingernails on the back of his hand.

If Charles Stuart's nurse had been there, Ashleigh would have flown out of the room and asked Pocino to remove the Sandlers from the house any way he saw fit.

But unable to leave, she picked up a small square of gauze on the nightstand and placed it on the area where the IV had been ripped from his arm.

As Sandler strode back into the room, she glanced at her watch. The nurse should be back any minute. "Where's your wife?" she asked, unable to conceal the panic in her voice.

"In the next room. Out like a light," Pocino answered from the doorway.

Sandler dropped down in the chair beside her. "I appreciate all you've done for Caroline's father. I had no right say the things I did earlier. It's just that my wife's been under such a strain since learning of her father's misfortune, I'm afraid my concern for her clouded my judgment . . ."

When Ashleigh broke in, her anger was no longer bubbling, it was at full boil, and she didn't care if he knew it. Still, she kept her voice just above a whisper. "The problem is your wife. She isn't just upset, she's schizophrenic. And until Mr. Stuart has fully recovered, I'm getting a restraining order to keep both of you off the premises."

Laying his clammy hand on her wrist, Sandler said, "Please, Ms. McDowell, Caroline is no schizophrenic. That was a misdiagnosis. Otherwise she'd be hospitalized."

Ashleigh jerked her arm from his moist hand. His lie was feeble and transparent. Seeing that Pocino was no longer in the doorway, she called his name.

Instantly, he popped his head around the corner. "Yeah?" he answered.

"I just wanted to make sure you hadn't disappeared."

"Not a chance." Pocino grinned. "Just checking on Mrs. Sandler."

CHAPTER
78

Charles Stuart felt the tension in the air and directed his whole being into climbing out of the fog that imprisoned him. Things were beginning to take shape. Although he couldn't fully open his eyes, he could see through the tiny slits between his upper and lower lashes.

A hawk-like profile volleyed between Ashleigh and a husky male somewhere beyond her. "Ms. McDowell," he heard the "hawk's" familiar voice say, "I'll not beat around the bush. I'll soon be CEO of Consolidated as well as Amalgamated. I have no interest in Caroline's inheritance, but it is my duty to see to it that she gets what's rightfully hers."

Oh, my God, it's Morris Sandler. Charles hadn't been dreaming when he'd heard Caroline beside him. He hadn't imagined the foul accusations she'd hissed at him nor the pressure on the back of his hand.

"Hear me out," Sandler continued. "You offered to sign over any claims you might have to the Stuart estate, now or in the future, to Caroline if she would drop the lawsuit."

Charles felt the soft skin of Ashleigh's palm cross his forehead. His heart felt heavy. She was looking right at him but didn't know that he could see and hear her.

"Do not raise you voice, Mr. Sandler. Caroline's summary of my offer is essentially correct, but please give me credit for not being so naive as to believe that it is Caroline who initiated the lawsuit."

Sandler shrugged his shoulders. "Believe whatever you wish. All I want to know is this: if Caroline drops the suit, will you follow through with your offer?"

Charles couldn't believe what he was hearing. Blood or no blood, Ashleigh was his rightful heir. He had changed his will after learning that Sandler had remarried Caroline. With Caroline once again under Sandler's control, it was too dangerous to leave anything directly to her. And yet, she was his daughter. Having no doubt that when Sandler found out that Caroline was no longer his heir he would have her recommitted to a horrid mental institution, Charles had added a codicil to his will. The codicil provided for Caroline's care in a private institution. He also provided a fair allowance, which would be administered by Ashleigh.

Sandler said, "Now that the takeover is a fait accompli, I believe things can be handled without going to court."

"Meaning?" Ashleigh challenged.

Good girl, Charles thought.

"Meaning that Caroline is entitled to her mother's share of the Stuart wealth, which naturally includes Consolidated stock."

"Mr. Sandler," Ashleigh interjected, "that's not a foregone conclusion. That's what the lawsuit is all about, but I don't wish to discuss it here."

"Very well. Just one question." He paused, received her nod, and continued. "Do you still have the legal documents you presented to Caroline, which would relinquish your claim to her father's estate?"

Charles didn't hear Ashleigh's reply. It may have been a shake of her head or a nod, but he heard Sandler say, "I'm sure I can convince Caroline to settle for her share of the stock and leave the rest till after the old man's death."

"No!" Charles screamed. "Ashleigh, don't sign anything." But no one could hear the scream that echoed inside his head but Charles himself.

CHAPTER
79

Viviana De Mornay checked her reflection in the dressing table mirror in the elegant master bath of their Italian villa, and smiled. After close to an hour and the aid of hundreds of dollars' worth of cosmetics, she'd achieved a natural-looking youthful glow. She stepped out of her terry-cloth robe, ruffled her hair with a light touch to give it a slightly tousled appearance, and wrapped a bath towel around her slim body to create the illusion of having just stepped out of the shower. Her only accessories were high-heeled slippers, to slim her ankles, and a light dab of Joy beneath her breasts and at the top of each thigh.

Feeling very sexy and ready to once again celebrate being the first lady at Consolidated, she tiptoed back into the bedroom.

The circular king-sized bed had been abandoned. Viviana heard expletives booming from the office area.

Poking her head around the office doorway, she saw Philip Sloane, naked as a jaybird, standing with a portable phone tucked under his chin and a crumpled fax in his hand.

But what made Viviana catch her breath, and feel damp between her legs, stood at attention immediately below Philip's flat stomach. She wanted to get her hands around that marvelous erection before something happened to make it disappear. She was tempted to drop her towel and go straddle Philip, but the flash of fire in his eyes froze her in place. Perhaps it was just as well that he didn't know she was there.

Since early Monday morning, New York time, Sloane had been waiting for his aides to confirm his victory. By mid-morning, everything had been resolved and the board was about to ratify the sale. Not to Sloane, however—to Jordon's. News of the double-cross came over the financial wires, and Sloane's team phoned him posthaste, then faxed him the details.

Sloane's face was hot with fury as Murray Levich outlined their strategy. Sloane was beside himself over Jordon's sneaky eleventh-hour interference. Equally unsettling was Consolidated's duplicity in considering their offer.

He gripped the phone and listened as Levich explained. "This is not a deathblow. But it's imperative that we make your financing credible by signing up a commercial bank. If not, Consolidated's board won't give us a second thought."

"Then do it!" Sloane exploded.

"Hang on, Phil. I've got Jules Ramsey on the other line."

As Sloane paced, bare-assed and unabashed in front of the undraped window, he caught sight of Viviana wrapped in a mint-green bath towel and motioned her toward him. She looked good enough to eat. Jesus, how could he be thinking of sex at a time like this—his entire universe was crashing around his ears, and yet he felt himself growing hard.

Levich came back on the line. "Ramsey said that Bank of Pacific resurfaced after Jordon's announcement. They're angling for lead position again. But for the billions you require, I still favor First Commercial."

Viviana rubbed up against him, her towel dropping from her thin form, but Sloane was now miles away. His mind vacillated between the two commercial banks. He favored Bank of Pacific, as did his brain trust, particularly his CFO. But now he wasn't sure. Lawrence Drew at First Commercial was pushing to add more junk bonds to the deal, while Bank of Pacific wanted him to combine Amalgamated and Consolidated and sell off assets to avoid junk bonds.

Sloane felt the warmth of Viviana's lips as they traveled from his bare chest down past his navel. She was playing hell with his concentration. Feeling himself harden once again, he balanced the phone under his chin, reached down, and pulled Viviana to her feet.

"Work things out with my staff," he said. "And hold out for a deal where you can avoid junk bonds and don't have to sell assets."

"Come on, Phil, you're dreaming," Levich barked. "You know damn well no such deal exists."

"Just make it happen!" Philip shouted, banging down the phone. Business was no longer his top priority; Viviana was.

80

Mitchell Wainwright ground out his cigarette in the unused ashtray in Dr. Chang's reception room. He stared out the window overlooking downtown Long Beach and began to pace.

Christine rushed into the waiting room, out of breath as usual. "Sorry I'm late." She took a seat on one of the leather sofas and flipped opened her Chanel handbag.

"When I checked our answering machine, there were six messages. All about the Consolidated deal. Apparently, they're hoping you might change your mind."

Her husband shrugged. "Not a chance. But with the number of phone calls and faxes, it appears things are heating up. If I wasn't so damned worried about Mitch, I might get a kick out of my bird's-eye seat. From my position as an outsider, these last-minute gyrations seem almost comical."

Christine ripped a sheet from her notepad and handed it to him.

Wainwright glanced at his watch before scanning her list. Waiting for lab results was a nightmare. He'd tried to jump the gun with a direct call to Dr. Chang earlier, but the immunologist was still at the hospital, and no one at his office would confirm or deny whether the Wainwrights' son had leukemia.

Wainwright scanned the list of calls and times. "Cyril Stein. Well, I'll be damned. Things are getting down to the wire." Shaking his head, he added, almost to himself, "Two calls from Jordon's CEO in less than an hour."

"Still no interest, Mitchell?" Christine asked.

"Not the slightest. Toddman called first thing this morning. He and Learner would like nothing better than for Jordon's to snatch Sloane's so-called victory. The problem is, the winner of this LBO will lose in the long haul. Otherwise, Toddman wouldn't have folded."

"But you didn't agree. It's not like you to look at the glass as half empty," Christine countered.

"It's a lot more than half empty," he argued. He glared at his prim, proper wife, mentally condemning her for being such an unnatural mother. She should be worried to death, but for no valid reason, at least none he could fathom, she didn't appear overly concerned. "Doctors are obligated to paint the worst-case scenario," she had said. "What really worries me is that when you find out that Mitch is out of danger, you'll regret pulling out of the competition."

Well, she was dead wrong. "What I regret," he said, "is allowing my rivalry with Sloane to cloud my judgment." He looked off into the distance, doing his best to keep his mind from fixating on the mysterious world of medical diagnosis.

"I'd like to think I'd have pulled out without this personal crisis." Wainwright picked up his suit jacket from the back of the sofa and pulled out his cigarette case. "From where I sit, these buyout frenzies are headed for a fall. Before long the courts will be clogged with the aftermaths of the Philip Sloanes and their unrealistic number crunching. Everyone's ignoring the danger signs."

Withdrawing a cigarette, Wainwright tapped it on the case. After a long thoughtful drag, he continued, "Since going private, Jordon's has borrowed up the wazoo. They've paid off such a small percentage of debt, even their own board must be scratching their heads."

"But they're not pulling out," Christine observed.

"Apparently," he confirmed. "Consolidated has some terrific locations, and Stein's persuaded his board there's great opportunity. No doubt, he's counting on structuring the takeover so that Jordon's can turn around and go public again."

"Obviously, you see flaws in the plan, or you wouldn't be on the sidelines."

"The major flaw is price. Under Toddman's narrow parameters, he wasn't out of line calling a halt in the low 60s. Jordon's made an offer of $73.50 per share. That's nearly $500 million more than Sloane's last bump to $69. They're way over-leveraged."

"So, how high could it go?"

"Hard to predict. The Jordon's offer is only 80 percent cash, with the rest made up of stock and cram-down paper. The sideline analysts seriously doubt the Jordon's cash-and-paper bid measures up to Sloane's $69 pure cash. Still, Consolidated's board is leaning heavily toward Jordon's."

The receptionist called their names. All thoughts of the M&A games vanished.

At the first sight of Dr. Chang, Wainwright's rigid shoulders relaxed. The grave hopeless expression the doctor had worn at the hospital was gone. There was even a hint of a smile. The news couldn't be too bad; either that or the doctor was a fucking sadist.

As Wainwright and Christine slipped into the armchairs on the opposite side of the orderly desk, Dr. Chang began to speak. Wainwright's momentary relief disappeared.

"Hold it," he interrupted, his hands clenching into unconscious fists. "You're telling me my son has leukemia, but not to worry?"

"Let me finish," Dr. Chang said politely. "I'm not telling you that your son's illness is worry free. What I am telling you, however, is that we've made tremendous strides in the treatment of acute lymphocytic leukemia, or ALL." The doctor went on to explain the different types of childhood leukemia. Although Dr. Chang had gone through the same explanations that first night in the hospital, it had been Greek to Wainwright. Now he concentrated on every word and learned that his son *did not* have one of the forms of the disease that was essentially incurable.

"There's a risk from infection or blood loss, but modern treatment has greatly improved the survival rate. The outlook for your son's type of leukemia is far more promising for children than for adults."

"The treatment?" Wainwright asked. Christine sat silently, her expression blank.

"It includes transfusions of blood and platelets, and the use of anti-cancer drugs."

"Jesus, he's only four!" Wainwright leaned forward. "What are the side effects?"

"The drugs tend to make the patient more susceptible to infection, so powerful antibiotics may also be given." The doctor explained the entire treatment plan and concluded, "After the first transfusion, and some careful monitoring, we'll treat your son as an outpatient. I expect he'll be ready to go home by the end of the month."

Finally, Christine opened her mouth and asked whether Mitch would be confined to bed.

The doctor explained the initial precautions and told them that, in a rather short time frame, Mitch should be able to resume the normal activates of a four-year-old. "A state of remission is achieved when there is no evidence of leukemic cells in the blood or bone marrow. However, to prevent relapses, we generally continue the use of drugs for many weeks after remission."

"Give us your best- and worst-case scenarios," Wainwright said. Then, noticing an ashtray on his side of the desk, he withdrew his cigarette case and asked, "Do you mind?"

The doctor shook his head, and Wainwright lit up.

For a long moment the doctor glanced up to the ceiling, then he met Wainwright's eyes. "First, let me tell you, I feel that your son has every chance of a full recovery. The worst-case prediction is that he might experience repeated relapses and require a bone marrow transplant."

Even as the doctor explained that this was unlikely in Mitch's case, Wainwright's thoughts wandered to the article he'd read in the *Press Telegram* about a bone marrow transplant. When no match had been found, the young boy's mother conceived another child for the express purpose of providing that match. At the time, it seemed bizarre. At the time, Wainwright had no idea leukemia was curable. At the time, the victim was not *his* son.

As the bulky bodyguard helped him ease Caroline into the passenger seat of the rented Buick, Morris Sandler planned his next move.

Straight down Naples Plaza, a right turn onto Second Street, another right onto Marina Drive, and the Hyatt Hotel loomed in front of them. When they pulled into the parking lot, Caroline was still groggy from the tranquilizers he'd poured into her. "Wait here. I'll be right back," he told her, and then he slipped from behind the wheel.

Sandler dashed up the broad steps and entered the lobby. He signed in at the reception desk, requested that a pot of coffee be sent to their room, picked up the key, and was about to return to the car when Caroline stumbled through the lobby doors.

To his utter horror, he noted her rumpled clothing and her hair in total disarray. She was weaving as if she'd been on a drinking binge. *So much for keeping a low profile.* Sandler rushed to her side and quickly escorted her into the elevator. Hopefully, he could get her to the room before she made an even greater spectacle of herself. Luggage could wait.

Moments after the door clicked behind them, there was a knock at the door. *Not a moment too soon.* Sandler tipped the waiter, put the thermal pitcher of coffee and two steaming cups on the bedside table, and then arranged bed pillows so that Caroline could sit upright against the headboard.

He handed Caroline one of the cups. "Here, drink this."

A tense silence permeated the room as Caroline sipped the coffee.

"What the hell were you trying to do? If you'd actually killed your old man, you'd end up in jail and forfeit your entire inheritance." Sandler, his voice low, struggled to control the icy tone.

She banged the cup down on the nightstand, her eyes blazing in fury. "What are you talking about?"

Jesus, was she losing her memory as well as her mind? Ripping the IV out of the old man's arm wouldn't kill him, but it was damn stupid. He'd been a damned fool to insist on this trip.

When he didn't respond, Caroline continued, "I wasn't trying to kill him. I just wanted to hurt him like he's hurt me."

She sprung from the bed and turned on him. "Why are you blaming me? What happened wasn't my fault. When I went into that room and saw him lying on those white sheets with all those cords dangling from above his head, no longer strong and powerful, I wanted to make up with him. I wanted him to love me again. I told him I was sorry for my part in his losing control of his stores to Consolidated all those years ago. I even told him I forgave him for putting me in that mental institution, because I knew Ashleigh must have put him up to it."

"Why did you tear the IV from his arm?"

She folded her arms in front of her and said, as if it made perfect sense, "He wouldn't talk to me. His breathing was steady, and I knew he could hear me, but he wouldn't say anything. I squeezed on his hands real hard, but he just ignored me. Then I got mad."

"Caroline, your father's *in a coma*. He *couldn't* talk to you. You may have destroyed our chances of getting 100 percent of your father's estate."

"*Our* chances?" she parroted. "Sometimes I think you're only interested in my money."

Jaw clenched, Sandler nevertheless pulled Caroline down on his lap. "Angel, how can you think such a thing? I've always loved you," he lied, not giving her time to reflect. "I'm sorry I was impatient. I just want you to have what is rightfully yours. And if anything happens to your father, I don't want you to be blamed."

She took in a quick breath and expelled it on a broken sob. "*I'm* his daughter, but he loves Ashleigh. He's never loved me."

Sandler settled his wife back on the bed and brought a damp cloth to cover her eyes. While she lay still, Sandler opened the minibar and took out two small bottles of Drambuie. He poured the contents of one bottle into her coffee and slipped in one of the Valium capsules he kept unwrapped in his shirt pocket. Handing Caroline the coffee, he said consolingly, "I'm sure he loves you. Don't worry about Ashleigh McDowell; she isn't blood."

Ten minutes later Caroline slid back into another drug-induced sleep, and Sandler called his connection in the Bronx.

The phone was picked up on the first ring. Sandler's hand shook as he held the receiver, but mustering chutzpah he didn't feel, he said, "Just checking in to let you know you'll get your money, plus a bonus, but I need a little more time." Before the thug at the other end could respond or threaten, he pushed on. "I also need another referral. The last one blew the job. That's why I need more time."

CHAPTER
82

Ashleigh tossed and turned. In a kaleidoscope of flashing nightmares, she saw Sandler standing over Charles, a dagger poised above his heart, she herself grabbing for the blade. She stared at the blood dripping down her fingers and woke with a start. Each time she drifted back to sleep, Sandler reappeared. He was lighting a bomb directly under Charles's bed; he held a gun to his temple. A vision of Sandler, the ax he held descending toward Charles, was so vivid the blood pounded inside her head, waking her.

Charles had soft-peddled the man's immorality. Sociopath was the word that popped to mind after only moments in his company. Ashleigh was now convinced Sandler was behind the break-in, murder, and attempted murders.

She stared at the illuminated digital clock. Two a.m. Afraid to fall asleep, afraid to dream, she pushed herself up against the pillows and switched on the bedside lamp.

She longed to call Conrad, but resisted. The next best thing was distraction. Swinging her legs over the side of the bed, she attempted to shake the nightmares from her head and went in search of something to read.

Far too unfocused to get anything out of her most current books on management techniques, she picked up the novel she'd purchased that afternoon. The title, *A Suitable Vengeance*, had caught her eye as she'd scanned the shelves at Dodd's Bookstore. Apropos. She stopped short of imagining what hers might be, however, and climbed back into bed.

She heard a light tap on her door.

"Who is it?" she called out.

"Barbara," Charles's night nurse responded.

A stout woman with a round cheerful face aglow with excitement poked her head into her room. "I have wonderful news. Mr. Stuart is out of his coma! He's asking for you, Miss Ashleigh."

Ashleigh's foot caught in the covers as she sprang from the bed. She nearly fell face first onto the hardwood floor, but she quickly regained her balance and flew down the corridor.

"What's going on?" Pocino's voice boomed through the silence, stopping her abruptly in her tracks. He'd stepped from the shadow of the chiffonnier on the landing, his gun drawn.

In her haste, Ashleigh had forgotten all about him. "Put that thing away, Pocino," she demanded. Then, softening her voice, she said, "Sorry," and told him Barbara's news.

Ashleigh tiptoed into Charles's room and pulled a chair next to his bed. Only a dim light shone from the desk in the alcove, but she had no difficulty seeing his alert hazel eyes, wise and shrewd under wrinkled lids.

Her eyes filled with tears. There was so much she wanted to tell him—not about Consolidated, not about Caroline or her husband, not even about the man who had broken into the house. He was certainly not strong enough to be told of Mary's horrible and needless death. No, Ashleigh just wanted him to know how much he meant to her. But, if she tried to speak, her voice would surely crack.

Instead, she took hold of both of his hands and raised them to her lips. She felt a light pressure around her fingers and said with a counterfeit bravado, "It's about time you woke up."

His lips parted. She leaned close, but heard no sound. It seemed he was too weak to talk, too weak to even mouth the words she saw he was trying to form. And yet, hadn't the nurse told her that he had asked for her?

"Don't try to talk," Ashleigh implored.

Charles again attempted to tell her something.

"Please, wait till you're stronger, Charles."

She filled in the silence with idle chatter. The only thing of any significance she told him was that his daughter had come to see him. His eyes remained open and unblinking. Then, Charles seemed to open and close them in evenly spaced intervals. If his eye blinks conveyed any meaning, however, that meaning escaped Ashleigh.

His hand twitched in hers, and his lips parted. She placed her index finger gently across his lips. He most likely wanted to know more about his daughter. Not wanting to upset or deceive him, she searched for something positive to say, but to her relief, she saw he'd drifted off to sleep.

After kissing Charles gently on the forehead, Ashleigh tiptoed out of the room.

Later that same morning, Ashleigh went down the corridor to the guest room Pocino was staying in. She paused at the open door and heard nothing. Cautiously, she popped her head across the threshold and then jumped back. Pocino stared back at her. "My god!" she shrieked. "You scared me half to death!"

"What did you expect?"

Ashleigh took a few breaths. Her heartbeat began to slow. "Has Landes come up with anything on Sandler?"

"Affirmative," Pocino responded without clarification.

Ashleigh felt her anger quicken at Pocino's smug expression. "This is no time for cat and mouse."

The phone in the hallway rang, and Pocino said, "That must be Conrad."

Ashleigh snatched it from the hook, her eyes boring into Pocino's. "Stuart residence."

"My, how formal."

Ashleigh felt her body relax at the sound of Conrad's voice. But after a few brief words and his expression of delight upon hearing about Charles, Conrad rushed on to say, "Sweetheart, I miss you terribly, and I'll call soon as I can, but I need a quick word with Pocino."

Deflated, she handed the phone to Pocino, who glanced at her as if he expected her to give him privacy. She didn't budge. Rational or not, she would not be excluded.

She listened as Pocino spoke in a succession of monosyllables. "Right . . . Will do . . . Sure thing . . . Not a chance."

Unable to piece his responses together into any logical scenario, her frustration soared. When Pocino finally set the phone back in the cradle, she asked, "What was that all about?"

He hesitated, a look of resignation crossing his face. "Landes has enough on Morris Sandler to make him our number one suspect. The creep's up to his sweaty armpits in gambling debts with the kind of thugs that aren't interested in an installment plan. Seems he's past due, and if he doesn't pay up—and damn soon—he's history."

Which makes for a compelling motivation, Ashleigh deduced. "Why didn't Conrad tell me himself?" But then, with a dismissive motion, she asked, "So what are we waiting for? I don't intend to wait till Sandler makes another attempt on Charles's life. The Hyatt's only a quarter mile from here . . ." she rattled on as if Pocino were unaware of the facts.

"First, we need proof. Meanwhile, this house is well protected. Charles Stuart isn't going anywhere. You're the only loose cannon, and a hell of a lot more at risk. Like it or not, until this case is wrapped up, I'm going to stick to you like flypaper."

Ashleigh started to protest, but before she uttered a single word, Pocino's meaty hand jutted out. "Conrad's explicit orders."

"Ross, I have obligations at Bentleys Royale. As job security is becoming a faded memory, I've got executives bouncing off the walls. I can't stay here and wait for Sandler to come after me, and I want you here with Charles."

"This isn't a debate. I take my orders from the man who pays for my services. Two agents will be at the house at all times, plus the Naples police patrol will check the property as they make their rounds. But you, as I said, aren't going to be out of my sight."

No point in arguing. Ashleigh knew Pocino was every bit as hardheaded as she was, and the thought of Sandler so near made her blood turn to ice. "Okay, you win. But right now, I'm going to take a shower." She paused and then added, "*Alone*. As soon as we have another agent here, I'd like you to come with me to the Hyatt to pay a visit to Mr. Sandler."

"No way. Leave things in the hands of the professionals. Conrad wants you to stay clear of both the Sandlers," Pocino said, as if that should end the debate.

Ashleigh shook with anger. "Conrad is my fiancé, not my boss." She sounded childish, but she was too angry to care.

"Calm down. We've no proof tying Sandler to the hood who broke in here. You can't go off half-cocked making accusations."

"That's exactly what I intend to do. Proof or no proof, if Sandler knows he's a suspect, he'll be less likely to make another attempt on Charles's life. Besides, it's ludicrous to think that I'm in danger. After what happened here, killing me would be too risky. Besides, Sandler wouldn't benefit from my death as long as Charles remains alive. But something has to be done to get Caroline out of Sandler's hands and into the proper care."

Pocino sighed. "And just what do you intend to do about that?"

"I've no idea," she admitted. "My priority is to deal with Sandler. And from what you've told me, he's got to be desperate." Parroting Pocino's words, Ashleigh concluded, "This is not a debate, so unless you plan to tie me up and lock me in my room, I suggest you accompany me to the Hyatt, because that's where I'm going."

"You've got more guts than good sense," Pocino protested, reaching out and catching her by the elbow.

Ashleigh jerked herself free but didn't attempt to move down the hallway.

"Sorry, Ashleigh. Maybe you're not completely out in left field. Maybe Sandler should know he's not free of suspicion." Pocino scratched his head. "But there's a problem. Nobody who commits a crime expects to be caught. And this guy doesn't appear to be the type to do his own dirty work—probably plans to cover himself with a rock-solid alibi."

A shiver went up Ashleigh's spine. In her mind, Charles remained Sandler's target.

"I'll be ready to pay a visit to the Sandlers in about half an hour," she said, and continued down the corridor.

Pocino spun on his heels and muttered, "Goddamn skirts . . ."

Conrad Taylor felt a wave of relief when he spotted Dick Landes waiting at the bottom of the escalators at Kennedy Airport. "How's Ashleigh holding up?" Landes asked as they shook hands.

"Pocino says she's strung pretty tight. The meeting with Sandler and Stuart's daughter shook her more than she's willing to admit. Pocino's not letting Ashleigh out of his sight."

As the two men headed to the parking lot, Conrad sighed. "She claims Sandler scares her speechless, but now that Ashleigh's so sure he was behind the attempt on Stuart's life, she's oblivious to her own safety."

Landes nodded toward a dark blue Bronco and opened the door on the driver's side. Conrad jogged around to the passenger's side.

"I didn't tell her our plans for this evening, and I think she's ticked over my giving her short shrift over the telephone."

Landes shook his head. "Passive, she's not. As I recall, beneath that calm feminine exterior beats incredible strength and tenacity. I strongly recommend you tell her everything." He smiled and turned the key in the ignition, then added, "You can't protect her by keeping her in the dark. She's far too intelligent and perceptive. If she doesn't know our plans, I'm afraid she's likely to devise her own."

"Right," Conrad agreed. "I'll call later tonight and bring her up-to-date, if she hasn't already wangled it out of Pocino. Hopefully, we'll hit pay dirt at the Greenwich property and bring this drama to a close."

"Let's just pray that Mrs. Sandler's 'nurse' has gone with them to LA or is out on the town," Landes added. "Otherwise, we'll have to put Plan B into action."

In the lobby of the Hyatt Hotel, Ashleigh was acutely aware of Pocino and felt his disapproval as she asked at the reception desk to be put through to the Sandlers' room.

"Sorry, Miss," the desk clerk said, "Mr. and Mrs. Sandler checked out just a couple of hours after they checked in."

As Ashleigh tried to take it in, she heard Pocino ask, "Did they have a nurse with them?"

Puzzled, Ashleigh asked, "What difference does that make?"

Pocino raised his palm toward her as the man punched something into the computer and then replied, "They had a suite, but only Mr. and Mrs. Sandler were registered."

By the time they pulled into the driveway of the Stuart home, Ashleigh had forgotten all about Pocino's seemingly irrelevant question and asked, "Can you get your buddy to check the airlines to see if they're on their way home?"

Pocino heaved himself out of the car. "First, I've got to get Landes or Conrad on the horn."

Conrad kept one eye on the sketchy map he'd drawn from memory, the other on the heavily wooded area surrounding them.

"It's about a mile ahead," he said as they passed several Greenwich properties, all set back from the street and behind high brick walls or hedges. "It's a good hundred yards from the surface road and half again as far from the nearest neighbor."

Conrad spotted the entry gate to the Sandlers' once-magnificent estate. "Turn here," he said. The gate stood open and the kiosk empty, just as before.

As Landes eased the car along the gravel driveway, Conrad noticed the outside lights were on, and a few glowed from within the house.

"Could be an automatic timer, or someone's home," Landes said. He pulled the Bronco into the shadows beside the garage.

In silent communication, the two men checked their false IDs and cautiously moved from the garage toward the broad front steps. Landes rang the bell.

Conrad heard only the faint sound of chimes. Landes pressed the doorbell again, and again the chimes reverberated through the house. Still no approaching footsteps. For a brief moment Conrad thought they were in luck. But an instant later, he heard an echo of high heels pounding across what was most likely a tiled entry.

Landes visually cased the area before a woman in a short leather miniskirt pulled the door open a crack.

"FBI," Conrad said through the narrow opening. He flipped open his wallet and flashed the phony credentials.

"Mr. and Mrs. Sandler aren't home," she said, eyeing the men cautiously above the links of the safety chain.

"We know, Miss Lyndon," Landes said, flashing his credentials.

"How'd you know my name?" Genuine alarm rang in her voice.

"Mr. Sandler informed us," Landes lied. "We'd like to come in." His voice conveyed an air of authority.

The door closed momentarily, and there was a rattle of the safety chain before it reopened. The young woman stepped back, tucking in a flimsy, see-through blouse and straightening her untidy hair. Lipstick smears across the lower part of her face announced she hadn't been alone.

"Who else is here?" Conrad asked as they were led into a large sitting room.

"No one," Nikki lied.

Hearing muffled footfalls and the soft click of a side door, Conrad dashed across to the windows. Landes repeated the question, adding,

"We have a couple of men out back, so I'd suggest you answer truthfully."

"Don't tell Mr. Sandler," she pleaded. "Jeff's just a good friend," Nikki lied again.

Conrad pulled back the drapes from the paned window. A motorcycle roared to life, and he saw taillights disappearing into the darkness.

"I'll ask you again. Anyone else in the house?"

She shook her head, her eyes wide with fear.

"Cooperate, and there'll be no need to inform Mr. Sandler of your friend's visit. Mr. Gettie," Landes said, pointing to Conrad with his chin, "has a few questions."

Nikki blinked.

"Meanwhile, I'll pick up the papers your boss asked us to obtain." He paused. "Just direct me to his study."

If she had any suspicions, Nikki was beyond voicing them or offering resistance.

It took Conrad less than ten minutes to learn that Nikki's nursing qualifications were nonexistent and that her job most likely centered around keeping Sandler's wife drugged and Sandler sexually satisfied.

Nikki rattled on about some of her most intimate moments with Sandler as if she were being interviewed by a reporter from *True Confessions*. Her initial fear pushed aside, she seemed to relish the telling of each juicy detail.

For Conrad, it was about as exciting as having someone describe the plot of a porno film. He'd long since tuned her out when he heard the ping of gravel against metal and saw a beam of headlights flicker across the wall of the sitting room.

He shot to his feet, took hold of Nikki's elbow, and drew her upright. "Not a peep," he warned, drawing the unfamiliar gun from the equally unfamiliar shoulder holster. Pulling Nikki along, he went in search of Landes.

Landes was in the entry, his own gun drawn and a pair of handcuffs in his other hand. He gestured for Conrad to put them on Nikki.

Nikki opened her mouth as if to scream, then quickly shut it.

Landes pulled a handkerchief from his suit pocket and stuffed it in Nikki's gaping mouth. Conrad snapped on the cuffs.

"In the closet," Landes hissed, indicating the coat closet to Conrad's left. A surreal sensation settled in the pit of his stomach. "Just keep quiet, and you'll be all right," Conrad told Nikki. He adjusted the cloth in her mouth. She could easily dislodge the material with her tongue, so Landes must be counting on fear paralyzing her. Conrad left the door ajar to give her air.

A car door slammed, and loud voices rose above the crunch of gravel beneath swiftly approaching feet.

Landes took a position behind the front door and gestured with the butt of his gun toward the sitting room. Conrad stepped behind the door, out of sight.

There was the expected turn of the key in the lock, the groan of the door being pushed open, and then something everyone was totally unprepared for—the blare of Landes's pager shattering the silence.

"Tell me what's going on," Ashleigh demanded.

Pocino had his back to her, the phone pressed to his ear, when he erupted with a litany of expletives addressed to God.

The phone still pressed to his ear, he whirled around to face her, a deeply etched scowl on his round face.

When he didn't answer, she stepped up to the phone, looked down at the display screen, and recognized Landes's pager number. She repeated, "What's going on? And don't tell me it has nothing to do with me. I know better."

Pocino slammed the phone down and tossed his hands in the air. He told her about the clandestine mission to Greenwich. "But they wouldn't have rushed out to Greenwich if they hadn't thought Sandler and his manic wife were here in Long Beach."

Ashleigh didn't need to hear more. She sat down on the arm of the sofa, her mouth dry.

"Hey," Pocino said. "Get that look of doom off your pretty face. Landes is no novice; he can handle the unexpected."

"Don't placate me. If you were so sure, you wouldn't be so uptight. I'm no detective, but I'm hardly a novice, remember? I've been stalked, had my car blown up, had my house ransacked, been kidnapped, and, right outside this house, been assaulted." She gained momentum as she reeled off her contact with the world of crime.

When Ashleigh finally wound down, Pocino said, "Okay, Super Woman, if you're through spouting off, I'll repeat, Landes is a pro. A warning would only have given them an edge in revving up the search or taking off."

Pocino had a point. Still, Ashleigh had a fluttery feeling in the pit of her stomach. She rose slowly from the arm of the couch and concentrated on what was really bothering her. She couldn't tolerate being kept in the dark. "What do they expect to find in Greenwich? And why Conrad? Landes has no shortage of New York agents."

Pocino squinted his small eyes. "Seems you're not the only amateur detective that's signed on. At least Conrad can handle a gun if he needs to, and he isn't likely to get himself kidnapped."

Ashleigh glared.

"Sorry," he said, then answered her question. "They're looking for evidence to link Sandler with a known crime-for-hire crowd. Landes's agents are making simultaneous searches at Sandler's New York pad and his office at Amalgamated."

Philip Sloane had been swaggering in and out of one windowless conference room after another at First Commercial for hours. He'd started out being charming and agreeable, but after one of the younger bankers questioned his math, he'd thrown one of his legendary temper tantrums. "Who are you to question my numbers? I made my first million while your mother was still wiping your ass!" Sloane shouted.

Undaunted, the junior banker shouted back, "You've got to sell assets. You can't pile one debt on top of another. Eventually, the piper's got to be paid."

Murray Levich had attempted to keep the ball rolling, but since late afternoon, he'd been losing ground. He'd have liked to wash his hands of the egocentric madman but couldn't afford to lose the Consolidated game. If he did, Wall Street might wonder if he could do a deal without First Commercial. Equally as crucial for Lawrence Drew, Wall Street would surely question First Commercial's ability to do a deal without Levich if this one fell through.

The question was, could they afford to win? As the bids continued to escalate, the number crunchers scrambled back to their computers. In each new scenario more Consolidated divisions were to be put on the auction block, and more inventive measures were devised to enable the company's cash flow to cover added debt.

They were no closer to pulling the deal together today than the day before. In the morning, before the continental breakfast had been cleared from the tables, Sloane's CFO dropped his bombshell to Bank of Pacific. Jules Ramsey had sat down and calmly explained Sloane's decision to use Century as the lead commercial banker, with Pacific becoming a lesser partner in the deal.

The contingent from Bank of Pacific exploded. As a body of one, they had stood, left the conference room, and booked a flight back to California.

Levich and Drew had favored Century from day one, and Century was willing to fund Sloane's bid. But just as Levich thought they were on a roll, negotiations broke down again. Century demanded another $10-million fee, and Sloane issued a barrage of expletives and ordered his people not to pay.

As the hours wore on, Levich, Drew, and half a dozen bankers and lawyers, all blurry eyed, grew testier and testier.

Negotiations became hopelessly deadlocked. Sloane was nowhere to be found. "Where is he?" Levich shouted to Howard Greenfield, who was holding his own meeting with Jules Ramsey and Bob Talbert in Drew's private office. "We need him now."

The M&A attorney, along with Sloane's CFO and top adviser, looked up from a pile of legal documents. They looked worried.

Then, as if on cue, Sloane strolled in and announced he was returning to Italy the next morning. He looked fresh from a shower, clad in light-gray flannel trousers and a pink polo sweater, his hair still damp.

"Jesus, Phil!" Levich exploded. How a brilliant, savvy man of finance, as Sloane was rumored to be, could be so damn nonchalant over the purchase of a $7-plus-billion acquisition was beyond him. "Take off to the moon if you like," he continued, "but pay First Commercial's fee. It's no longer an option. We're losing our momentum, and Jordon's isn't showing any signs of going away."

Ignoring the protests of his top adviser and CFO, Sloane relented and instructed them to pay the $10 million and to call the minute the deal was final. He then turned on his heels and left the headquarter building and the country without knowing that Century had refused to sit back down at the bargaining table until his check cleared.

"I'm sorry," Morris Sandler said to his wife as he pushed his key in the lock. Then, taking a deep breath, he reigned in his temper and softened his tone. *God, I'm sick of having to apologize*, Morris thought to himself. "I didn't mean to hurt your feelings."

He slipped his arm around her narrow waist in a gesture of support. "I wouldn't sleep a wink if you were on your own in California," he said, nearly choking on the lie. He kissed her forehead and shoved open the door.

A high-pitched sound shrieked from beyond the open door. Just as suddenly, it stopped.

Sandler froze, shoved Caroline in front of him, and took a few steps back, dragging her along like a shield.

"What's going on?" Caroline hollered, confused. The piercing vibration had not been as loud as the alarm system, which would have gone off after thirty seconds if Nikki had left for the evening.

Sandler's voice caught in his throat.

"Freeze!" a deep voice demanded. A stocky, dark-suited man holding a gun in his two hands stepped into Sandler's field of vision.

Jesus! Sandler thought. Hadn't he made it clear that he was within a breath of getting his hands on some real money? Hadn't he earned a reprieve or at least a stay of execution?

"We need to t-talk," Sandler stammered. This goon had to be one of Vincent's men. He just hoped he wasn't trigger-happy.

Caroline struggled to free herself, twisted her head around, and shrilled, "Let go of me, Morris!"

"FBI," the man said. A second man, also armed, stepped into the entry. He was tall with thick, dark hair and an athletic build. He wore an Armani sweater and an expensive pair of slacks. He looked damn familiar, but Sandler couldn't place him.

The first man ordered, "Let go of the lady."

When Sandler released Caroline, she stumbled, then glared at him and smoothed down her skirt.

"Nick Cristanelli," the first man said. "My partner, Sheldon Gettie." He nodded his head in the direction of the other man. Transferring his gun to one hand, Landes flipped out credentials with the other. The other man also flashed his identification.

Taken aback, Sandler swallowed a knot of apprehension. His heart pounded like a sledgehammer. *FBI . . . FBI . . .* the word echoed in his skull. His legs turned to jelly. What did they know? What did they suspect? At least with Vincent's thugs, his life would be over in a heartbeat. With the FBI, his entire future could blow up in his face; the agony would drag on. And he'd never be allowed to forget that one day, quite unexpectedly, one of Vincent's men would bring his life to a violent end.

Caroline tapped his arm, ending his introspection, and he heard the man who called himself Cristanelli say, "I said, close the door and take a seat." He indicated the sitting room, his voice tough and authoritative.

Sandler did as he was told, seating himself in the leather armchair.

Unruffled, Caroline sauntered to the wet bar. "I could use a drink," she said. "Anyone care to join me?"

The two men declined, and Sandler, unable to risk a loose tongue, did as well. Caroline helped herself to a scotch on the rocks and sank into the corner of the leather couch, her wide eyes intent on the two visitors. She was enjoying the drama.

Sandler's eyes darted between his uninvited guests. He swallowed repeatedly to rid himself of the dryness in his throat. "I've no idea why you're here," he said, attempting to appear indignant.

"I believe you do," the stocky man corrected him as his partner disappeared into the entryway.

Sandler followed the other man with his eyes as he tried to think how to get rid of them without creating more suspicion.

At the sound of Nikki's high-pitched voice, his mind raced. How long had these G-men been inside his house? What had she told them?

When Nikki appeared, his heart sank even lower. Her hands were cuffed, and she looked like a two-bit hooker.

"Do you have a warrant?" he asked loudly, as if volume could add authority.

"Don't need one," the stocky agent said.

"You most certainly do," Sandler insisted. "Leave immediately."

"No," the stocky agent continued, "this is a friendly call to let you know that we're on to you. We're aware of your tremendous debts and your connections. We're giving you a chance—"

"Debt? What debts?" Caroline demanded as she pushed herself forward on the leather sofa. Her eyes scanned the faces of the two men before meeting her husband's gaze. "What are they talking about, Morris?"

But after a moment's hesitation, her eyes flashed across to where Nikki stood. "Get that little hussy out of my house!" she shrieked. And without warning, she picked up the old-fashioned glass that held the remains of her scotch and hurled it at the younger woman.

Nikki ducked. The glass hit the wall behind her.

After the melee that followed, Nikki was allowed to go upstairs to her room, but the agents refused to let Sandler take Caroline to hers.

Sandler felt he was between a boulder and a slab of steel. He didn't want Caroline to hear what the agents suspected. He also couldn't admit to them that she was mentally unbalanced and take a chance of her being unable to inherit. These guys had nothing on him or he'd be under arrest. And they'd never prove his connections with Vincent's thugs. He couldn't take the chance of the agents learning of Caroline's inheritance, however, or challenging the phony diagnosis of the psychiatrist who was to testify that she was of sound mind.

He dropped back into the armchair.

This time, the tall, dark-haired agent took the lead. "We know you were behind the break-in and attempted murder of Charles Stuart."

Sandler clamped his arms tightly across his chest. "You're barking up the wrong tree," he scoffed.

"You made a big mistake when you hired George Baker to make the hit. He was an amateur, but your connection with him will bring you down."

From the corner of his eye, Sandler saw that Caroline, far from sober, was listening to every word and attempting to assimilate it all.

"This is out-and-out intimidation, and I won't have it," Sandler said as he crossed the room and sat down on the sofa beside Caroline. Slipping his arm around her shoulders, he tried to calm her. "Don't listen to their preposterous shots in the dark, Caroline. There's not an ounce of truth in anything they've thrown out."

Then, turning to the agents, he said, "You're upsetting my wife. If you had a scrap of evidence, I'd be under arrest. The fact is you have none. And you're going to find none because there is none." He rose and was about to tell them to leave when he stopped short. "Hey. You're no FBI agent; you're the guy who ran Bentley's with Toddman and—"

"Right," Landes interrupted.

Sandler grabbed the phone and started to dial 9-1-1.

Landes seized the receiver and slammed it down.

Pointing his gun between Sandler's eyes, he nodded toward the other man. "Conrad Taylor, Ms. McDowell's fiancé." He paused to let his words sink in, and then he introduced himself.

Jesus, oh shit, Jesus Christ, oh shit Sandler's mind began to chant. His eyes darted to Caroline, whose head felt like dead weight against his shoulder. She'd passed out.

"You're right about one thing, and one thing only," Landes continued. "We don't *yet* have the physical proof, but we're damn close." With a heart-stopping click, he pulled back the hammer on his revolver.

Sandler squeezed his eyes shut and began to shake. "I'm innocent," he sputtered. "You've got to believe me. I'm a respected businessman. I'm about to become CEO of two major department store conglomerates. Why would I jeopardize all that for my wife's piddling inheritance?"

Conrad Taylor's eyes flitted from Sandler to Caroline and back. "It took a lot more than one scotch on the rocks to get your wife in that condition." He paused, shaking his head, and then fixed a blistering stare on Sandler. "You'd better pray Stuart pulls through and that not a single hair on Ashleigh McDowell's head is ruffled. If anything happens to either of them, you'll beg for one of Vincent's goons to take you out."

Sandler's breath caught in his throat. The cocked gun in Landes's hand ceased to intimidate. As had happened so many times in the past few months, his life flashed before him.

CHAPTER
87

Three weeks later, Morris Sandler paced the spacious reception area of Sheldon and Arpel, the prestigious law firm representing Consolidated. He sweated profusely as his focus darted around the lobby, the weight of dwindled options pressing down on him. What if Sloane failed to emerge as victor?

If he dwelt on the alternatives, his heart would come to a full stop. Fear and uncertainty tormented his every move; danger lurked around every turn. There remained no safe haven.

God, even his thoughts played like a melodrama. All his information was secondhand. Sloane had become increasingly noncommunicative. Sandler learned nearly as much from the wires as from Sloane or his team. The barrage of offers and counteroffers boggled his once rational mind. Still the bidding war raged on. The price had escalated to the point where any victor could retain only a few divisions, being forced to sell the rest to pay the mounting debt. It was no secret that both Sloane and Jordon's had already presold several divisions.

Sandler gaped at the wall clock, the steady sweep of the second hand. Although a confirmed atheist, believing only in what he could see with his own eyes, he found himself praying.

He prayed his recent pie-in-the-sky budget proposals and rationale for jacking up estimates on Consolidated assets would fly. He informed Sloane and his team, "If Consolidated wasn't worth every borrowed penny, Jordon's would have been blown away with our last jump."

Based on Sandler's revised models, First Commercial's number crunchers had dutifully produced one computer simulation after another to prove the deal still made sense. And miraculously, banks were setting their conservative natures aside, stepping forward, and offering to lend more. Even Levich, the First Commercial faction, and Sloane's CFO were caught up in the action; they had suspended their disbelief and were forging ahead.

Sandler prayed for a Sloane victory. Prayed even harder for a lightning fast close. And prayed most fervently for rapid access to its cash flow.

With teams of lawyers busy in various U.S. district courts battling over the validity of Consolidated's poison pill, it could go either way.

Nothing could stop Sloane from taking over the company if the pill was invalidated. But since Toddman's arrival on the scene, it seemed Consolidated's board was playing the auction to the hilt: pitting one rival against the other, yet doing their damnedest to avert a Sloane victory.

The door to the main conference room banged open. Sandler's heart quickened as he heard the thud of aggravated footsteps beating down the corridor.

Murray Levich's contorted face looked neither right nor left as he marched past. Sandler's gaze followed him as he crossed the lobby, gripping a cell phone in one hand and a haphazard pile of papers in the other. With shirttail hanging out the back of his trousers, Levich disappeared into the men's room.

Sandler sprinted after him. Stopping in front of the men's room, he cracked the door open.

"They've squeezed Jordon's offer another fifty cents, or fifty fucking million dollars," he heard Levich shouting. "And it looks like the goddamned board's about to accept their bid as final."

Sandler clung to the doorjamb, his knees watery and his heart beating as if in cardiac arrest. He took a series of short but deep breaths, squared his shoulders, and marched in.

Levich flipped the back of his hand in Sandler's direction and covered the phone. "Get the fuck out."

Sandler stared, his face growing hot. He stepped back a few steps but did not leave.

He heard the tread of more approaching footsteps and turned his head to see Mark Toddman striding through the door. The expression playing across Toddman's features left Sandler ill at ease, but Conrad

Taylor's appearance, a few steps behind Toddman, caused Sandler to break out in a cold sweat.

"That's not good enough!" Levich shouted. Holding the temples of his glasses between his thumb and forefinger, he spun them in agitated circles. "We need all the legal clout you can muster. Get Harry . . ." Levich cut off as Toddman and Taylor walked into the men's room. He covered the phone, and looked from one man to the other as if they'd just walked into his private office—unannounced and uninvited.

"You're needed back in conference room C," Toddman said.

"Be right there," Levich said, then stepped into a cubicle and closed the door.

Ignoring Taylor, Sandler greeted Toddman and received only a cool nod in return. Taylor's glare made the hairs on Sandler's arm stand up.

"I need five minutes of your time," Taylor said.

Sandler bristled. *The pompous prick just assumed I'd comply.* But seeing no way out, he pointedly glanced down at his watch and repeated, "Five minutes." Then, in an attempt to assert a degree of control, Sandler turned on his heels. With a fleeting glance over his shoulder, he demanded, "Meet me in the lobby."

Taylor nodded and turned back to Toddman at the far end of the row of urinals. Sandler heard the two men speaking in low voices as the door swung shut. Then it dawned on him that Taylor was no longer a principal of one of the Consolidated divisions. Nor was he a member of the board. The bastard must be here as an investment banker. He wasn't representing Sloane, so he must be working for Jordon's.

Conrad heard the door swish closed behind Sandler, but he was keenly aware Levich was still on his cell phone in a nearby cubicle. He and Toddman had been embroiled in meetings in separate conference rooms and had merely run into each other en route to the men's room. All the better for Sandler to think he was in collusion with Toddman and the Consolidated board, but Levich was another matter. Keeping his voice barely above a whisper, Conrad said, "Apparently the board's decided to give Sloane another go."

Toddman nodded, and in an equally low tone he added, "Our goal hasn't altered. We can't afford to loose the $1-billion windfall produced by the bidding war, and we're beyond hope of an eleventh-hour rescue." Glancing over to the closed door of Levich's cubicle, he called out, "The board's on hold and waiting in conference room C."

Wiping his hands on a paper towel, Toddman turned to Conrad. "Give Ashleigh and Charles my best."

At dinner the night before, Conrad had filled Mark in on Charles Stuart's condition, which improved daily. He'd also told him what he and Landes had uncovered on Sandler. Mark's reaction was the same as his own. "The very thought of Sandler getting his sticky fingers on any part of Consolidated makes my blood run cold."

Toddman crumpled the towel and tossed it in the wastebasket.

Toddman's regard for Ashleigh and Charles Stuart was genuine but could hardly equal his concern for Consolidated. Though he claimed to have come to terms with the fate of the company, he remained far from it—Consolidated was his alter ego. He would mourn a severed right arm no less. No matter which way the cards fell, there wasn't a flicker of hope the company could survive. In the worst-case scenario, Sloane would take over the conglomerate and spin off department store divisions to the highest bidders with no consideration as to the buyer's ability to manage them. If Sloane were victor, the best Toddman could hope for was to have his West Coast divisions scooped up by Jordon's.

Levich emerged from the cubicle and pushed down the antenna on his phone. "Sorry to keep you." He exchanged greetings with Conrad, who wished they'd had Levich in their corner. And yet, even this master negotiator had stretched beyond the limit any company could withstand.

As Toddman headed for the conference room with Levich, Conrad marveled at Mark's composure. The man was worth millions, but what good was it when he was losing everything he valued? And on the heels of losing the company, it appeared that he and Paige were going their separate ways.

Conrad spotted Sandler across the lobby in front of one of the leather couches, his arms folded in front of him.

Conrad approached, and both men remained standing.

"What is it, Taylor?" Sandler challenged.

Wasting no time on subtleties, Conrad stated, "Call off any arrangements for more 'accidents' at the Stuart estate pronto." He enunciated each syllable slowly and clearly, his eyes boring into Sandler's.

"What are you talking about?"

Conrad glared and waited a good thirty seconds before telling Sandler what he was sure he already knew. "That severed electrical cord that just happened to be placed beside the gas water heater was discovered before any damage could result. Stuart's place has been gone over from top to bottom, and the Long Beach police force is taking the matter very seriously. They know everything that Landes and I know. They've been given the complete lowdown on you—chapter and verse—including your motivation and unsavory ties."

Sandler's face blanched, and his eyes blinked spasmodically. But somehow he managed to lift his chin and square his shoulders.

"Remember," Conrad said, "things are closing in. Vincent's thugs aren't the only ones you've got to watch for around every corner and in your rearview mirror. From now on, you won't be able to take a piss without being observed."

CHAPTER
89

On Tuesday, March 29, Dean Zarkos, Sheldon and Arpel's lead attorney in the Consolidated negotiations, called for the auction to be shut down.

As the major players began to reassemble, Zarkos—fortified by a nap on one of the lobby couches and a glass of Bordeaux—did a silent roll call, unconsciously drumming his fingers on the tabletop while the men filed into the main conference room. Everyone, with the exception of Toddman, slid back into the seats they'd occupied earlier. Toddman remained standing at the far end of the table, away from the smokers, his ubiquitous jar of almonds close at hand.

Getting straight to the point, Zarkos emphasized the importance of immediate action to squelch the rampant rumors of back-channel negotiations between Jordon's and Sloane. He slowly made eye contact with each board member around the oblong conference table, then said, "If we don't take the initiative and negotiate a truce between the two factions, they may come to their senses and realize they can circumvent us and save $1 billion by pooling their resources. They could even divvy up the divisions and retract their current bids. We'd be left with a take-it-or-leave-it bid in the $60-plus range—our stockholders up in arms."

There was an uneasy silence. Bone-weary bankers, lawyers, board members, and advisers adjusted their positions around the table. Eventually, all eyes rested on Toddman.

With visible effort, Ralph Learner, who had been extremely vocal at the beginning of the negotiations, swallowed his pride and deferred to Toddman. Consolidated's CEO gestured for him to proceed.

"I agree," Toddman stated. "While a more realistic price might be healthier for the company in the long run, we can't risk the windfall our stockholders now expect. And, as Zarkos points out, we'd be in deep trouble if the competitors came together on their own."

With nods of agreement, the actual vote was a mere formality. Zarkos again outlined the terms of the truce. Sloane would acquire Consolidated at large. As a goodwill gesture, Consolidated would discount the price from Sloane's last all-cash bid from $75 a share to $73.50. Jordon's would buy the three West Coast divisions—Bentley's, Bentleys Royale, and P. G. Marshal's—for $1.1 billion and be given a going-away fee of $60 million in cash to pay their bankers and lawyers.

Toddman ducked out of the conference room as the various ramifications were discussed. He returned about ten minutes later. "I've just spoken to Lawrence Drew at First Commercial. It seems Sloane's spirits are at a low. He's concerned over the escalated price."

"Christ!" Learner blared. "We're down to the wire, and he's got cold feet?"

Toddman shook his head. "Sloane and his entourage are set to meet with Stein and the Jordon's team day after tomorrow. The last thing that Sloane's bankers want is for him to drop out. They're covering their bases. Drew dispatched his retail expert, Jim Sutton, to ride with Sloane on First Commercial's corporate jet from Melbourne back to New York. They can't afford to have this deal go down the tubes any more than we can."

CHAPTER

90

On the morning of April second, Paige Toddman sat cross-legged in front of the oversized TV in the exercise room of her Hollywood Hills home, her eyes glued to the CNN broadcast.

The fluttery feeling in the pit of her stomach had nothing to do with being pregnant. Philip Sloane's photo appeared in the window above the newscaster's head—the same damn picture that had flashed on the screen when this nightmare began.

"Paige." Sonny's disembodied voice filtered through her sense of déjà vu seconds before he appeared in the doorway.

She turned and looked up at the jaunty Irishman. "Top of the mornin'," he said, and dropped down beside her, his brows arched as if he was trying to judge her reaction to the Sloane victory.

"'Tis no surprise, lad," she said, forcing a smile to her lips.

He smiled at her imitation of his brogue.

"I've been getting a blow-by-blow update. Mark called the other night, and Helen Stein—the wife of Jordon's CEO—has kept in touch."

"Aye. The rundown you gave me a couple of days ago about how the pieces were about to fall was right on the money. So why are you staring at that tube as if in shock?"

"I guess I was," Paige broke in. "That photo just triggered a heap of emotional garbage." Not wanting to elaborate, she said, "But the stories behind today's news are a lot more interesting . . ." She cut off abruptly as footage of Mark and Sloane appeared on screen. Viviana De Mornay stood gazing at Sloane—a perfect imitation of Nancy Reagan's absorbed admiration for Ronnie.

A microphone was thrust toward Mark. His impromptu comments on the $7-billion takeover were smooth, polished, and noncommittal. Mark did a masterful job in concealing his heartache. He expressed none of his misgivings and appeared at ease and challenged by the opportunity to explore other vistas.

"What utter bullshit," Paige said and flipped off the TV.

"'Tis all part of the game. Politically speaking, your husband has no equal. A weaker chap would air his grievances."

"But it's so dishonest. Look what's happened to Amalgamated since Sloane got his hands on it. A well-respected retail empire has been torn asunder, and the rest is on a downward spiral. How can Wall Street sanction multibillion-dollar loans to a man who's had multiple nervous breakdowns over the past decade?"

"Since you ask, I think this whole LBO fever is about to bring Wall Street to its knees. And it seems fitting for Sloane's closing meeting to be held on the eve of April Fools' Day."

Paige nodded. It didn't matter what she thought of Sloane and the current folly on Wall Street—it was non-actionable and no longer had anything to do with her. "Okay, I'm ready to get started." Just past her first trimester, Paige had adapted readily to the milder exercise format Sonny had designed for her.

"Aye, colleen. It doesn't look like you've gained an ounce. And you've been talking a blue streak, trying to keep me from gettin' at what's troubling you."

She couldn't let him dig too deep. Her wall of pretense protected her, kept her from looking back, and propelled her forward. If that wall were to crumble, she'd be sure to follow. "Your imagination's working overtime, Sonny. I've adjusted, and I'm feeling great."

Sonny shook his head, locks of red hair falling on his forehead. "Don't give me that blarney. Your eyes tell the real tale."

When she didn't respond, Sonny continued. "You said Mark's been keeping you informed about the takeover. What else is going on between the two of you?"

"You mean, 'Has anything changed?'"

He nodded, his eyes holding hers.

How could she tell Sonny how nothing had changed yet everything had changed? She and Mark were like polite strangers. He had moved back home, but they passed in the hallways without touching. They talked about the takeover, about Paige's work at the shelter, about Mark's career options, about anything other than what was most significant.

She leaned over and kissed Sonny on the cheek. "I know you mean well, but I've come to terms with a future without Mark. To be true to ourselves, we must go our separate ways. Maybe this new start is exactly what we both need. I can't say I've stopped loving Mark or that we didn't have a wonderful life together. But with or without this baby, it was bound to explode in my face. I brought too many lies and too much emotional baggage into our relationship. Things could never be as they once were." She looked at Sonny's puckered brow and sad eyes. "I'm excited about my new life. Please don't worry. I'm not unhappy."

He gripped her two hands in his and said, "Aren't you the lassie who told me you were through with lies?" Giving her no opportunity to respond, he went on, "You are no more excited about a life without Mark than he pretends to be over his expanded career options. How two intelligent people can hide behind veils of pretense is beyond me. You may be able to fool others, but one day that veil will be lifted and you'll find pretense the most destructive of lies."

More than two hundred journalists, financial advisers, and a litany of other interested parties filed into the large conference room on the second floor of the Wellington Towers on the morning of April fifth.

Morris Sandler sat at the head table nervously gazing out at the sea of inquisitive faces duly assembled for the press conference. Where was Sloane? He was due back the night before, but he hadn't even shown up at this morning's public relations briefing.

Sandler's breath caught in his throat. In the fifth row, seated dead center and surrounded by journalists, sat Lucas Vincent and one of his thugs. Vincent smoothed his thick black hair, leaned forward, and planted his elbows on the straight-backed chair in front of him. Then he lifted his hands, cradled his chin on interlaced fingers, and fixed his eyes directly on Sandler.

Sandler's knee bobbed up and down uncontrollably as he noted the subtle shift of Vincent's eyes to the heavy-lidded hoodlum beside him. Caught in the glower of four unblinking eyes, fear surged through Sandler's bloodstream as if it were heroin. Then, from the corner of his eye, Sandler spotted Philip Sloane unhurriedly approaching the head table as if he hadn't a care in the world. Taking several deep breaths, Sandler willed his mind to concentrate on the business at hand and to block out the men in the fifth row.

First Commercial's CEO, Drew Lawrence, had made it clear that Sandler's presentation was key to the upcoming sale of Consolidated junk bonds and charged him with the responsibility of presenting a solid counterbalance to the dynamic, but flighty, Sloane. His mission was to reassure the financial analysts and bond market that he was a cost-conscious operator. He must also convince the doubters of his ability to cut budgets and teach Consolidated's fee-spending retailers how to run the company more profitably.

His most recent strategic plan, though excessively optimistic, might be doable if his budget cuts were strictly adhered to—if the flamboyant Australian didn't block his every move as he had at Amalgamated. But Sloane's perspective changed with the wind or, more aptly, with the most recently articulated option.

Sloane began to speak, but one of the reporters interrupted him to ask, "Is it true that you went to Austria for sheep-brain injections?"

Sandler groaned inwardly. They were here to talk about Consolidated, not Sloane's idiosyncrasies. Next, one of these reporters would ask for the name of Sloane's plastic surgeon for a write up in the *Ladies Home Journal*.

But Sandler needn't have worried. Sloane brushed the trivial question aside and embarked on an upbeat presentation. Before the journalists had a chance to challenge his $11-billion debt, Sloane said, "Don't believe everything you read. The fact is, we purchased Consolidated for a reasonable cost, far better than Amalgamated, and we plan to expand to our fullest . . ."

As Sloane rambled on, the article that had appeared on the front page of the business section of the *New York Times* the day before flashed through Sandler's mind. No way could they afford to build up to a hundred new regional malls anchored by Consolidated stores. Even by reducing their debt by selling eight divisions, for an estimated $5 billion, Sloane's claim of paying off debts from *greater cash flow* was pure pie in the sky.

"Job cuts in the Consolidated headquarters will be modest," Sloane falsely promised. He elaborated on what he would and would not do within the Consolidated and Amalgamated department stores, and then he introduced Sandler as his retail expert and CEO of both divisions.

Sloane had given his entire speech while seated at the table, but Sandler sought the security of the podium. As he stood and took his position behind it, he felt Lucas Vincent's eyes boring into him as fiercely as before the announcement. *Jesus, he never lets up.* Surely having Sloane confirm his appointment as CEO of both major retail conglomerates had bought him some time. If not, he'd come to the goddamned end of his rope.

A tremor traveled the length of Sandler's body. He looked down at the notes clenched in his hand. Miraculously, his hand was rock steady. Willing his mind to the task at hand, he prayed the audience didn't pick up the soprano tone that echoed in his head. "Together, we will turn the nineties into the decade of department stores . . ."

"What does that guy think he's doing?" Sloane muttered as Sandler lingered at the podium to answer questions.

By the time questions were redirected to Sloane, his mood had darkened. This was his show. Sandler had no right to center stage. Sloane responded testily to the analyst's unmitigated gall in challenging his projections and expansion plans.

"Is it true that the percentage of junk bonds in this deal has escalated beyond your original estimate?" a reporter from the *Boston Globe* asked.

"There are no junk bonds," Sloane lied. "I won't allow them."

CHAPTER
92

Conrad sat on the living room floor of the Stuart estate. With his back to the crackling fire and Ashleigh beside him, he felt more like himself than he had for months.

As animated and full of humor as ever, Charles sat in his familiar armchair facing them. His rapid recovery would have been remarkable at any age, but at eighty-eight and with the fall of Bentleys Royale, it was downright miraculous. Naturally, Charles had difficulty dealing with Mary's violent death and his inability to protect his daughter, but Conrad saw no sign of the depression Ashleigh described.

"Things seem to be falling into place quite nicely," Charles said.

Conrad nodded and squeezed Ashleigh's hand. "Dad's well on the road to recovery and eager to resume the helm."

Charles lifted a thick white brow. "And you think he'll be strong enough to take over in the next few weeks?" he asked.

Conrad nodded. "He's been involved for the past month. And while not totally at ease with some of the changes in the investment arena, he's adapting. Our current bottom line has opened his mind to new opportunities."

"And he's prepared for the inherent risk?"

"Not entirely. Nor am I. The risk ratio seems blown out of proportion. In my humble opinion, many investment firms are heading for a fall. On the other hand, we've been fairly conservative, and our bottom line for first quarter is impressive. We have a strong team of experienced investment banking talent." He paused momentarily. He had Charles's full attention, so went on. "Bob Hill, who was the lead M&A expert at First Commercial, is now heading our M&A division. He's top-notch, and I have no qualms in his wrapping up our portion of the Jordon's deal."

Slipping his arm around Ashleigh's shoulders, Conrad admitted, "Investment banking isn't my bailiwick, but I've enjoyed the challenge. Now I'm ready to move on. I have Dad's blessing. How he'll continue with the current modes of operation and his new team only time will tell."

At the sound of cups rattling on the lacquered tray, Ashleigh unfolded her legs and jumped up to clear the coffee table for Elizabeth, the combination nurse and housekeeper who now looked after Charles.

As the trim, gray-haired woman set the tray on the table, Conrad saw a dark expression flicker over the old man's face. It would take time for Charles to recover from the loss of Mary.

Charles quickly forced a smile to his lips, but Conrad now understood why Ashleigh had been adamant about the appearance of the woman who took Mary's role. "She must look nothing like Mary or my grandmother. The two of them looked enough alike to be sisters," Ashleigh had told him. Then pausing, she'd added, "It would be too painful for him if a new helper looked anything like either of the women he loved and lost."

"Thank you, Elizabeth," Charles said. Shifting his gaze to Ashleigh and Conrad, he gestured to the plate of cookies. "Bon appétit."

Conrad helped himself to a chocolate chip cookie, and Charles picked up where they'd left off. "I don't know what to make of the current shenanigans on Wall Street. How a man with Sloane's background, and a foreigner to boot, could finesse or, more aptly, coerce nearly $11 billion in loans is beyond my understanding."

"You're not alone," Conrad said. "And I'm sure his investors are scratching their heads over this morning's press conference. Disclaiming the presence of junk bonds contradicts everything the analysts have read in newspapers, press releases, and filings with the SEC. There's at least a billion dollars' worth of junk bonds in the deal. Last week's press conference should have given reassurance to the financial markets and paved the way for peddling their Consolidated junk."

As Charles shook his head, Ashleigh broke in. "Enough. You two will have plenty of time to talk about the mad Australian, Wall Street, and all the unorthodox antics surrounding the takeover while I'm holding the fort at Bentleys Royale." Her tone was one of utter exasperation, but there was a glint of amusement in her eyes as she set her cup on the coffee table.

Charles smiled and asked Conrad about the interviews he'd lined up for the week. "Are you sure Los Angeles provides the career opportunities you desire?" Charles challenged. "I wouldn't want you to confine your search to this area on my account."

Two weeks after the infamous press conference, Morris Sandler's life had gone straight down the toilet. Now, it was all but over.

His heart crashed mercilessly against his rib cage as he slammed the door to Sloane's office suite in Consolidated's New York complex.

He scanned the corridors and poked his head into the elevator before stepping inside. It was imperative to get in touch with Vincent before word got out.

Sandler cursed himself for not having tuned in to his gut instinct and made sure he was in on the meetings with Consolidated's division heads in Cincinnati. His head must have been up his ass. He should have predicted that in his absence, the "Majestic Seven" would take the opportunity to undermine him. Smug over their extravagant $28-million golden parachute package, they'd been expected to bail out immediately. To Sandler's detriment, the entire seven had stayed on a day too long during the transition. While sequestering himself in his office over the weekend to rework his master plan, they were busy and relentless, with Sloane the willing target of their lethal politicking.

When Sandler flew in on Friday to attend the celebration dinner in the banquet room of the Cincinnatian Hotel, he sensed an aura of hostility radiating from the seven. Amid ill-disguised whispers and eye shifts in his direction, he'd overheard one of the wives snicker about his jet-black toupee. Humiliated and ill at ease, he'd tried to keep a low profile. But he'd consoled himself with the fact they'd soon flee with their unjustified and grossly excessive parachutes.

Secure with a rock solid contract, he'd felt his long-awaited access to Consolidated funds was in the bag. At Consolidated his plan was one big hit-and-run. He had everything in place, including a new identity and a pad on Grand Cayman. Nothing could stop him.

But he was dead wrong. His grandstanding at the press conference made him vulnerable, and Sloane, who tended to listen to the last strong opinion, had been swayed.

Today, moments after he'd walked into Sloane's office, the roof fell in. "Your contract was written in good faith, but we must place a merchant in the CEO slot," Sloane said. In the next breath, he had the audacity to ask, "Will you stay on and help with the transition?"

Unable to take it all in, Sandler stammered, "A-a merchant has no conception of how t-t-to run a leveraged business. You appointed me, knowing I'm th-th-the man who can make the bold strategical moves and innovative cost cutting I've outlined. Don't let those weak management honchos lead you down the primrose path . . ."

Sloane's eyes narrowed, and Sandler knew he'd overstepped his bounds. By inferring that the volatile Australian was being manipulated, he'd made a fatal faux pas.

"Nonsense," Sloane countered, his voice unnervingly low and monotonic. "I already have the man for the job." Then he'd spelled out exactly how he would honor Sandler's contract.

Sandler's jaw tightened as he stormed back to his office, cleaned out his desk, and left instructions for the secretary to have his things expressed to his Greenwich home.

In the end, the Majestic Seven had won. Sandler, who'd worked round the clock for Sloane's victory, was the one who would not be donning a tux for tonight's victory party at Carlingdon's. He'd been used, then cruelly maneuvered out of the limelight and discarded. The fact that he was being paid the balance of his contract, a total of $3 million, didn't ease the pain. What it did was leave him vulnerable.

Sloane's lawyers had payoffs down to a fine art. But Sandler's problems were far from behind him. With the interest on his debt to Vincent compounding daily, it amounted to more than he'd net from the payoff, leaving him unemployed and bankrupt.

As Sandler hailed a cab in front of the Consolidated building, he spotted a burly, dark-haired gorilla he knew to be one of Vincent's goons. He was leaning against the wall of the building beside the corner newsstand, unconvincingly absorbed in the front page of the newspaper.

Sandler bolted into the first taxi to pull up before it had come to a full stop. Then, taking out his cell phone from his briefcase, he dialed Vincent's unlisted number.

CHAPTER
94

Viviana brushed back her hair to reveal the five-carat diamond earrings Philip Sloane had presented to her moments before.

"Well, what do you think?" she asked, swinging her head slowly from side to side to show off the pure radiance of each facet of the magnificent gems.

He was enormously proud of her; Viviana could see it in his eyes as he pressed her body to his. Feeling his erection through the thin fabric of her Versace gown, her eyes flashed to the crystal clock on the dressing table, then into the mirror. Looking at her smooth shiny hair, she reluctantly began to pull away.

"Not now, darling," she protested.

"I can't wait," he murmured in her ear as he rubbed the small of her back.

Viviana found her body responding, pushing forward to meet his. Her breath caught in her throat as she felt her gown being pushed up inch by inch, his fingers tickling her skin as he slipped them inside her panties. For a moment she wavered, torn between the urge to preserve her perfect image and her growing desire to do anything and everything he wanted.

"And I want you, but . . ." Her voice faded as she felt his palm on her stomach just above her pubic hair.

"Down here, you're hot. Incredibly hot," he said as his finger moved inside her, slowly and sensuously.

"Umm" was the only sound she could make. Momentarily adrift, Viviana felt a jolt of liquid pleasure. Oh, God, how she wanted him.

Making her eyes wide and forming her lips into a pout, she whispered, "How do you expect me to resist when you look even more dashing than usual in that tux?"

"Relax, and enjoy," he said, tugging her panties down over her hips.

It took every ounce of will to look over his shoulder and refocus her attention in the mirror. This strengthened her resolve. "No, we can't, Philip. We'd be terribly . . . terribly late. And tonight, of all nights, while you're the star, I can't walk into Carlingdon's with a Cheshire cat grin on my face. I want you to be proud of me."

Viviana's heart dropped to her toes when he abruptly pulled back and wordlessly adjusted his trousers. But then she caught the self-satisfied glint in his eye and knew he wasn't angry.

"Right you are," he said and swatted her behind.

As Philip fussed over his bow tie, Viviana surreptitiously opened her Judith Leiber evening bag. She withdrew the pillbox and, with her eyes fixed on Philip's back, she flicked open the top with her thumbnail. Pouring a tiny red pill into the palm of her right hand, she felt a tremor from somewhere deep inside as she stared down at the last of her amphetamines. She was also running low on quaaludes, so it was imperative she find another doctor on the East Coast to wheedle at least one more prescription. *Then I'll give them up for good*, she promised herself.

Lifting the water glass from the top of the dressing table, Viviana took another fleeting glance to make sure Philip was still engrossed in primping in front of the full-length mirror. She turned slightly, but before she could pop the pill into her mouth, she heard Philip's heavy footfalls across the polished wood floor.

"What do you think you're doing?" he roared.

Viviana jumped and dropped the pill. "It's not what you think," she lied as she bent down to pick up the pill.

But Philip caught hold of her wrist, pried the pill from her grasp, and then dropped her arm in disgust. "You told me you'd given up this crap. We've spent a bloody fortune getting ourselves in top shape, and this is the gratitude you show. You're becoming a goddamned junkie." His fist clenched, and he swung his right arm back. For a pulse-stopping moment, she thought he was going to hit her.

She stumbled back, bumping into the dressing table. Then, as spontaneously as it had begun, she saw him take several deep breaths and drop his arm to his side.

"Are you downright suicidal, Viviana? Amphetamines to get you going, quaaludes to get you to sleep."

"No, no, Philip. It's not like that. This is the first time in months I've even felt like I needed one."

"It only takes one time," he countered.

She shook her head. "You don't understand. They're not addictive; I've been taking them for years. I gave them up, but it's such a hectic time and I needed a little help. You had so many important things to worry about, I didn't want to add to them."

"Betty Ford said just about the same thing before she committed herself to her first clinic." Then shaking his head, Philip thrust out his open palm. The red pill rolled precariously on the surface as he moved his hand from side to side. "Jesus. Listen to yourself. 'They're not addictive. I've been taking them for years.'"

"I've had that one pill for months. I saved it in case of an emergency," she lied.

"So what's the emergency?" he challenged.

"Tonight's special. Carlingdon's will be filled with the most prestigious and influential people in the nation. I want to be my sparkling best—a real asset to you."

"Then stay away from the uppers, downers, and God knows what else."

"I will. I won't do it again. You've got to believe me," she pleaded.

Standing in front of the dressing table drawer that held her quaaludes, she watched in horror as he stormed across to the dressing room sink and washed the last red pill down the drain.

In a flash, her fear turned to searing anger. What *was* she doing? Her groveling tone echoed in her head, and she had to bite back the urge to strike out. Then, tilting her chin up, she said, "Philip, I'm sorry I'm not perfect. You're a lot stronger than I am."

She took a revitalizing breath and made her decision. The timing wasn't going to get any better. Win or lose, she had to make her play. "I wasn't cut out to be a mistress. I can't go on like this. If you don't intend to marry me, tell me now. I want to be able to rely on you . . ."

She cut off abruptly seeing something unsettling in his eyes. He thought she was bluffing. It started out to be just that, but now that she was on a roll, she realized it was the God's honest truth. This subservience was making her nuts.

Philip's eyes narrowed. "Are you giving me an ultimatum?"

Viviana kept her gaze steady and direct but didn't answer. Instead, with Sloane's victory party at Carlingdon's scheduled to commence in less than half an hour, she swung her hair to one side and began to remove the diamond earrings. Her heart beat a wild tattoo as the silence stretched to eternity.

CHAPTER
95

Sandler bolted down the front steps of his Greenwich home, a bulging suitcase clutched in each hand and his briefcase tucked under one arm.

Opening the trunk of the El Dorado, he heard the front door bang against the inside wall of the foyer and looked up to see Caroline flying down the front steps.

"Morris," she cried out, "where are you going?"

He'd hoped to avoid a confrontation, but what difference did it make now? He heaved the cases into the trunk and slammed it shut.

Caroline now stood leaning against the driver's door, her arms folded aggressively in front of her, demanding an answer.

"Zurich," he lied.

"Why didn't you tell me?"

"This is the end of the line, Caroline. You're on your own." *God, it felt good to drop the pretense.*

"What do you mean?" Her hands formed tight fists. "You can't leave me. We love each other."

"No, Caroline. I never loved you."

Her mouth fell open, and he saw fear trickle into her demented eyes.

"Do you think I'd have shackled myself to a sick, shallow bitch like you if you hadn't been Stuart's only daughter and supposedly his sole heir? But you even fucked that up."

She took in a quick breath and jammed a fist to her lips as if to suppress a sob. Her eyes clenched shut for a brief moment, and then they glinted with anger. "My father was right. You're evil."

"And you're insane. Now get out of my way."

Caroline stood her ground. "I'm not crazy. I know what you've done. You won't get away with it."

"You don't know shit. Besides, it's only a matter of time before you're back in the loony bin."

"I don't care what happens to me. You tried to kill my daddy, and I'm going to see that you're punished."

"You think so?" Even if the stupid bitch could get anyone to believe her, he'd be out of the country before anything could be pinned on him.

He swung his hand across his own body as if to backhand her.

Still she didn't move. She stood there, daring him to hit her.

"Move!" he hollered. When she didn't, he let loose, hitting her across the face with the back of his hand.

Caroline staggered and fell against the side of the car. When she raised her hand to her cheekbone, he grabbed her wrist and flung her to the ground.

Sliding beneath the steering wheel, Sandler patted his head to make sure his toupee was in place. For his parting shot he shouted, "You were a pretty good piece of ass at one time. Now, you're just a pathetic dried-up hag."

As he revved the engine, he saw Nikki gliding down the stairs toward the car. He thrust the car in gear and took off, leaving a spray of dirt and gravel.

Tiny stones pelted the fenders and underside of the car as he sped down the winding path to the main gates. Turning up the volume on the car radio, he checked his rearview mirror and let out a breath. Before picking his car up at First Commercial's parking garage where he'd left it earlier in the day, he'd ditched his tail in Manhattan with a series of stealthy taxi changes. He would be expected to remain in town for the victory party. Still, he wouldn't inhale a tension-free breath till the wheels of the 747 touched down in the Caymans.

In less than two hours, he'd no longer have to worry about buying more time with Vincent and his cutthroats. But, to play it safe, Sandler picked up his cell phone and pumped in the digits of the big man's private number.

After the third ring, Vincent's raspy voice crackled over the line. Sandler felt a wave of fear spiral to every nerve ending. It was as if the man were sitting beside him with a gun to his temple.

"This is Morris Sandler," he said, trying to dispel the image. Then swallowing hard, he pushed the practiced words through his throat. "Good news," he bluffed. "I knew you were anxious to get your dough, and I'm fed up to my back teeth with that slippery Australian, so I maneuvered him into paying off my contract. A cool $3 million. I wanted you to be the first to know."

"Too late," Vincent's voice broke in with icy detachment. "It hit the media a couple hours ago. And it sure don't look like you were in the driver's seat."

Before Sandler could say another word, Vincent said, "Shame on you, Morris. A man of your so-called intelligence cooking up that cock-and-bull story. It's a goddamned insult. Afraid your time's run out, old boy."

Sandler heard a click, then dead air. At the same moment, he felt the pressure of cold metal pushing into the back of his neck. "Turn here," a deep voice from the backseat demanded.

Sandler turned onto the deserted public road and caught the reflection of the gunman in the rearview mirror. It was Manny, Vincent's right-hand man. Now that he was sitting upright, Manny's head nearly scraped the headliner. *Christ, he must have been lying in wait at the house.*

Sandler had to get a grip. Slowly easing his head forward, he felt the gun barrel follow, pressing deeper into his flesh. "Hey, there's no shortage of money. Vincent will get every dime I owe him."

"That so?"

"Swear to God," Sandler lied, twisting his head over his shoulder.

"Keep your eyes on the road," the deep voice chided, and then he continued as if talking to a dull child. "Not smart. Lie to Vincent—and now to God."

"It's the truth," Sandler protested.

The gunman demanded that he pull up alongside a deserted stretch of land and stop the car. "You're a real unlikable SOB, Morris. It'll be my pleasure to watch you die."

Sandler decided to make a stab at working a deal with Manny. "Manny, I'll have the money for Vincent and a bonus for you. Just give me . . ."

Shaking his head, Manny said, "Get out of the car."

"What are you going to do?" Sandler heard the tinny tone of his voice, and then a thought occurred to him. "If you kill me, Vincent won't get his hands on a dime. Neither will you."

"Already been written off as a bad debt," he said. Then, tossing Sandler's briefcase to him, he said, "Give me your phony passport and whatever else of interest you've got in there."

Sandler's blood surged through his veins, thundered through his ear canals. How did they know about the passport? Shit, Vincent had his hand in every crooked deal in the Big Apple. There was nowhere to run, nowhere to hide. When he looked up at the gunman, his legs turn to mush. His last vision was that of the blacktop of the narrow road leaping up to meet his cheek.

Nikki Lyndon yanked the Louis Vuitton luggage Morris had bought her from the closet, and with a surge of self-loathing, haphazardly began throwing things into the large Pullman. That lying bastard dumped her and didn't even have the balls to tell her to her face. She thought of the price she'd paid for Sandler's false promises and, remembering the way she'd allowed his clammy hands to explore her body, a wave of nausea hit her. She'd feigned ecstasy, told him how handsome he was, and pretended not to be aware of his ludicrous toupee. All for nothing.

As she marched into the bathroom to gather her cosmetics, she heard Caroline's earsplitting wails from below. Raising herself on tiptoes, Nikki peered out the window. Caroline was still wallowing on the ground in the same spot where she'd been thrown before Sandler took off without a backward glance.

If that woman don't shut up, I'll go stark raving mad. Nikki swept her expensive cosmetics from the countertop into her small case. A bottle of Joy toppled to the floor. "Good-bye Joy, good-bye Europe," she said aloud.

She made no attempt to clean it up. Instead, she finished packing and hauled one case after the other downstairs.

"Oh, God," she said as she descended the front steps and saw Caroline's wild, disoriented eyes staring up at her. She couldn't just take off. Nikki would have to find someone to take care of the wretched thing.

"Mrs. Sandler!" Nikki hollered, attempting to be heard above Caroline's loud, repetitive sobs. Leaving her luggage on the porch, Nikki went directly to the deranged woman's side and attempted to pull her to her feet.

Caroline resisted with incredible strength. Nikki stepped back, and her stomach lurched as she looked into Caroline's swollen eyes and then noticed the tiny pebbles imbedded in the soft skin of her cheek.

"Please, Mrs. Sandler. Let me help you."

Like a balloon with a small leak, Caroline's resistance dissipated, and she allowed herself to be pulled to her feet. Her voice was like that of a small child. "I want Daddy."

It was nearly eight o'clock in the evening by the time Nikki got Caroline settled and made the call to the Stuart home. The phone was picked up on the third ring. Nikki recognized the voice. It was the pretty blond woman Caroline had locked in the drawing room. Nikki hesitated, but with nowhere else to turn, she plunged forward.

"Miss McDowell?" Nikki told her only what she thought she needed to know. Nikki was grateful the young woman didn't tell her to go to hell or hang up. She listened without interrupting and told Nikki she would handle the situation. Nikki didn't ask what she intended to do, and Ashleigh didn't say. She merely told Nikki she'd be on the next plane. Nikki reluctantly agreed to stay until she arrived.

CHAPTER
97

Ashleigh's conservative nature recoiled at the price of the impromptu airline tickets. But Nikki had made it clear that she'd stay in Greenwich no longer than twenty-four hours, so Ashleigh booked two round-trip flights, one for herself and one for a private nurse. She also arranged for a one-way ticket to Los Angeles for Caroline.

On Saturday afternoon, the sun was low on the horizon when the plane touched down at Kennedy Airport. A prearranged limo was outside the baggage area, and Ashleigh and Monica, the private nurse, made their way to Greenwich in record time.

As the rented limo pulled up in front of the dilapidated Sandler mansion, a flood of vivid memories danced through Ashleigh's mind. She was thankful that Charles had insisted she engage a private nurse to assist her in bringing Caroline to the West Coast.

Ashleigh took a deep breath and admitted to Monica, "I have no idea what to expect."

Unless Nikki's account of Caroline's behavior was greatly exaggerated, Caroline Stuart Sandler had been pushed over the edge—incoherent and out-of-touch with reality. How much the woman knew, or could even comprehend, was unknown.

"I don't want to do the wrong thing, so I'll rely on you to lead the way."

"No, problem," Monica said. "I've worked with all types. We'll create the script as we go."

Ashleigh smiled, stepped out of the limo, and held the door for Monica, who appeared well able to handle most any situation. The large-boned woman stood nearly six-feet tall and possessed a take-charge demeanor.

"We have a one o'clock flight tomorrow afternoon," Ashleigh informed the uniformed driver.

"One o'clock," the wizened driver repeated. "I'll pick you up at ten-thirty. That should be ample time."

Nikki appeared at the top of the front steps. She was in her coat, her handbag slung over her shoulder.

She blinked spasmodically. "Morris Sandler is dead."

Dead. The word echoed in Ashleigh's head. Sandler couldn't be dead. He was a major news item. Articles in major news sources across the nation told of his ouster as CEO of both retail empires and of his astronomical $3-million payoff.

"Did you hear what I said? He's dead," Nikki repeated, her voice shrill and rising.

"Are you sure?" Ashleigh paused. "Sorry. Of course you are. What happened?"

"He ran over the embankment on the surface road about three miles from here. The police say he must've fell asleep. But that's bullshit. He was wide-awake when he left and too damn hyper to fall asleep at the wheel."

"When did this happen?" Ashleigh asked.

"Sometime last night. They don't know for sure. But that's not all they don't know," Nikki said, with more than a hint of derision. "They've got their facts all screwed up. The cops say he was on his way home. But he took off from here like a bat out of hell about an hour before I called you. No way was he comin' back."

"Maybe he forgot something," Ashleigh offered.

"N-o-o-o way. He was damn sure fleeing the country." She adjusted the strap of her bag and instantly moved on. "Mrs. Sandler's been like a baby. Talking real crazy-like. Saying Morris was trying to kill her daddy. Couldn't make any sense out of what she said. She doesn't even want a drink. But I give her a couple of Valium in her OJ, and she's off to the land of nod. She won't bother you tonight."

Then, without taking a breath, Nikki continued. "Everything she needs for the trip is packed in the two suitcases by the front door." She gestured with a toss of her head, told them she had to go, and was down the steps and into her car before Ashleigh and Monica stepped into the entry of the cool, gloomy interior.

Once the two women chose their sleeping accommodations for the night, Monica went to check on Caroline. Ashleigh went into the drawing room and flipped on the TV to CNN.

She scanned the *New York Times* as she picked up on bits and pieces of the news—most of which she'd caught on earlier newscasts.

She caught a glimpse of Viviana De Mornay out of the corner of her eye. Setting the newspaper down, she focused her attention on the TV. As usual, Viviana was photographed with her eyes adoringly fixed on Philip Sloane.

> *Last night the nation's rich, famous, and influential gathered for a glamorous star-studded affair at Carlingdon's flagship store. The timing of Philip Sloane's takeover of Consolidated transformed the evening, originally planned exclusively for the benefit of AIDS, into a gala victory party for himself. The Australian real estate developer, who has acquired two of the country's largest department store empires through hostile takeovers, appeared rested and in top form. Unfortunately, his accolades to Americans for their contributions to free enterprise went over like the proverbial fingernail scrapping on a chalkboard, not only generating an uneasy hush over the audience but also calling attention to the fact that he is an outsider. However, he recouped some of the ground he'd lost when he introduced his American fiancée.*

So it's now official, Ashleigh mused. She wondered how the flamboyant Philip Sloane had managed to keep his divorce from his Australian wife from becoming front-page news.

She flipped off the TV. There was no point in attempting to adjust to the time change. She'd be back home tomorrow. But, taking in the cold, foreboding aura of the drawing room where she'd been so recently imprisoned, it seemed the least likely place to settle her nerves.

She turned off lights as she made her way to the staircase. She'd look in on Caroline and then try to make herself comfortable in the guest room. If possible, she'd immerse herself in the novel she'd tucked into her suitcase at the last minute and try not to think about what the following morning might bring.

CHAPTER
98

Mark Toddman ran a hand through his thick, sandy hair as he waited for his briefcase to pass through LAX security.

Could this hasty decision to take off on his own be a sign of a midlife crisis? Well, it sure wasn't by choice. There was nothing he'd have liked more than to have Paige beside him, going anywhere—it didn't matter where. Paige's words still echoed in his head. "I love you, Mark, but I can't bring our daughter into an environment where she is merely tolerated. I know what that's like and . . ."

What did she expect? He had told her he'd accepted the fact that they would share their lives with a child, but that wasn't good enough. He couldn't pretend to be excited about embarking on a completely different lifestyle, nor would she have believed him if he tried. These last few months had been the worst in his life. Perhaps there was more than a bit of truth in warnings about the effect of those pregnancy hormones.

What Mark wanted more than anything was to have the Paige he knew and loved return to him. Somehow he'd find a way to get through to her and show her that they belonged together. Maybe this time on his own would help put things in perspective and clear his head.

He sucked in a lung full of air, making a conscious effort to dispel the cloud of futility that he hadn't entirely shaken. Hopefully, things would look brighter once he left greater Los Angeles behind.

He strode down the corridor to gate 34B. There was plenty to do in San Francisco, he told himself. But now, thinking of what it would be like without Paige, it seemed pointless, and no act of will could lift his unfamiliar bout of depression.

Without Paige, he might as well have accepted Nason's offer and gone straight back to climbing the career ladder.

Toddman rechecked his airline ticket and slipped it back in the inside pocket of his Armani sports jacket. His mind drifted back to Paige's parting words. "Mark, I don't love this baby more than you, but you can take care of yourself. Our baby can't."

The vision of the unfamiliar tears clouding Paige's eyes when she'd stormed out of their bedroom, followed by the roar of the Jaguar's engine and the squeal of tires as she'd sped from their home, continued to replay in his head.

Mark heard the announcement for Flight 715 to San Francisco, reluctantly picked up his briefcase, and rose. He could always cut the trip short if he couldn't snap out of this funk. The line for first-class passengers moved so rapidly he'd barely had time to produce his ticket by the time he'd reached the uniformed attendant.

Handing her his ticket, he thought he heard his name over the loudspeaker. He paused and strained to listen. "Paging Mr. Mark Toddman," the raspy voice repeated. "Will Mr. Mark Toddman please come to the United Airlines information counter?"

"That's me," he said to the attendant.

"You have plenty of time," she said, and pointed to the counter.

It was probably Sloane with a new ploy, but just in case . . . He raced off to take the call.

Mark picked up the phone, making no attempt to conceal his impatience. "Toddman."

But it wasn't Sloane; it was Paige's personal secretary. He felt the blood drain from his body when Anna told him Paige's Jaguar had been sideswiped by a Texaco oil truck and flipped over on a soft shoulder on Mulholland Drive. She'd been rushed to the hospital.

"Christ. Is she hurt?" *Of course she was hurt.* "How badly is she hurt?" he asked. *Oh, God, please don't let anything happen to her.*

"She's listed in critical condition, Mark. I think you'd better get over here right away."

"What hospital?"

"Hollywood West."

"The one on La Brea?"

Anna gave him the address and asked him to meet her in the emergency room.

Mark gave a fleeting glance to the boarding area, and then he said to the girl behind the counter, "I won't be on Flight 715."

He had already turned away when he heard her ask, "How about your luggage?"

He paused. "Get it off, if possible." Taking out a business card, he jotted down his home number, handed her the card, and said, "Leave word when it can be picked up."

He again turned from the counter and sprinted across the waiting area and down the corridor to the escalators—his destination the Hertz counter. Luggage was the least of his problems. He wasn't even sure what he had packed. After Paige's abrupt departure, he'd just thrown things into his suitcase. As far as he could remember, he hadn't even packed any socks.

At the Hertz counter, Mark barged in front of the line. A burly man sporting a Stetson moved in as if to challenge him.

"Sorry," Mark said, "but my wife's been in a car accident. I've got to get to the hospital."

The time between Anna's phone call and Mark's arrival at Hollywood West was nothing but a blur. He felt like an outsider as he paced the sterile corridor in front of the curtained cubicle where Paige was being examined. He hadn't had so much as a glimpse of her since the accident. Anna told him that Dr. Gene had been called. He and another doctor were in with her now. He could hear nothing more than muffled voices.

Anna sat in a straight-backed chair in the hallway, her hands twisting restlessly in her lap. Knowing little, she'd told Mark only that Paige's condition was said to be critical.

Mark stared at the white curtain surrounding his wife and blamed only himself. He could no longer blame Paige. Nor could he justify his behavior or deny that his demand for 100 percent of Paige's love and attention had been unfair, unloving. Paige hit the target when she'd called him an egomaniac. She deserved better—a *lot* better.

The curtain opened. Dr. Gene and another doctor stepped into the hallway. Mark was vaguely aware of voices, but at the sight of his wife's pale, vulnerable form, his brain shut down. He took an unsteady breath and went to stand beside her. Paige's coloring blended into the stark white sheets, her dark hair and brows lending the only contrast. Mark stared at the mass of tubes and cords connecting her fragile body to overhead bottles of liquids and a small screen on which the rhythm of her heart registered in uneven, jagged peaks and valleys. He cursed himself for being an unfeeling SOB.

Taking her hand, he pulled it to his lips and whispered to Paige, "Forgive me. Don't leave me. I love you."

"Mark," Dr. Gene said, "Paige isn't conscious—"

"Is she in a coma?" Mark's concern turned to panic.

Dr. Gene shook his head. "No. It's just that we've given her something to relieve the pain. She's going to be all right." Then, gesturing to the man beside him, he said, "But we must talk to you." Dr. Gene introduced the consulting surgeon to Mark and said, "Paige's cervix has dilated."

Mark stared at him blankly, uncomprehending.

"She'll lose the baby unless we take immediate action to prevent it."

"What kind of action?" Mark demanded, his heart thudding erratically in his chest.

"The opening to her uterus has expanded," Dr. Gene explained. "Unless we suture the cervix to keep the baby in place until the lungs are further developed, the baby won't survive." The doctor hesitated, then said, his voice solemn, "We need your permission to proceed."

After checking to make sure the surgery presented no added risk to his wife, Mark said, "I'll sign whatever you want, just take care of Paige."

A moment later he scrawled his name on the authorization form. Pinching the bridge of his nose, he squeezed his eyes shut as he offered a silent prayer. And in this prayer, he found himself not only praying for Paige but for the life of their unborn daughter as well.

It seemed like an eternity before Paige was lifted from the emergency room bed onto a gurney and quickly wheeled down the long corridor through the double doors marked "Surgery." Mark stood for timeless moments outside those doors. He could not erase the image of Paige's wan face as they whisked her off to the operating room.

The hands of the clock moved as if loaded with lead weights. Minutes seemed like hours. For the umpteenth time he checked his Rolex. Paige had been in surgery for nearly two hours.

Every time the doors swung open, Mark looked up expectantly. But neither Dr. Gene nor the other doctor was among the army of green scrubs zipping in and out of the surgery area.

Spotting a copy of *USA Today* on one of the cushions of a nearby chair, Mark scanned the front page. Vaguely aware of the words dancing before his eyes, he flipped to the second page. There, in the upper left-hand column, was a photo of Philip Sloane and Viviana De Mornay, dressed in a pale peach Chanel suit and matching hat and veil. The caption read, "Raider retail king takes a bride." Mark tossed the paper aside, not bothering to read the article.

Mark stopped pacing when Dr. Gene materialized, his eyes cast downward as if studying the carpet.

Mark's heart felt as if it had come to a dead stop. "Oh, my God," he said aloud. Then closing his eyes, he visualized a stark white sheet being drawn over Paige's colorless, gamine face.

His legs felt like those of a cloth mannequin as he sank down into the nearest chair. He dropped his unshaven face into the palms of his hands, which shook like they'd never shaken before.

Dr. Gene's disembodied voice broke through his despair. Mark felt a gentle hand on his shoulder and looked up, his eyes burning with unshed tears. "I know you did your best, David." Then, the sea of words he couldn't quite comprehend swimming around in his head, he asked the doctor to repeat what he'd just said.

"I said, 'Paige is out of danger.'"

Mark met the doctor's eyes and murmured, "I've been such a damned fool." Then, not waiting for a response, he asked if he could see his wife and started to heave himself from the chair. But he felt a restraining hand on his shoulder and sank back into it. Before the doctor could say more, Mark knew.

"We weren't able to save the baby," Dr. Gene said. But as the doctor went on to tell him that Paige had begun to hemorrhage, he tuned out. All that mattered was that Paige was out of danger.

CHAPTER
99

Opening her eyes, Paige found herself staring at a cold ceiling and the white curtain that surrounded her firm narrow bed. A wave of claustrophobia overtook her.

She squeezed her eyes shut. Her hands traveled down her body, coming to rest on her flat stomach. A vision of the red and silver truck that seemed to have appeared from out of nowhere flashed before her. She felt her body tense as she remembered the tug of her seat belt and her Jaguar spinning onto a soft shoulder. She vaguely remembered fumbling with the buckle of the seat belt and pushing against the car door. Then she must have blacked out. She also remembered the sudden heaviness in her abdomen and the feeling of a fistful of needles making her double over in pain. Then, only darkness.

An anxious voice penetrated the cloud of haze surrounding her. When she looked up, she envisioned Mark beside her, reaching for her hand. But that wasn't possible.

"Paige," the voice said softly. She felt a strong, smooth hand wrap around her fingers. "You're going to be all right." A pause. "*We're* going to be all right."

It was Mark. He hadn't gone to San Francisco. He was here beside her. She ached to reach out and feel his arms around her, but something deep inside made her pull away.

"The baby?" she asked. But she already knew.

There was a catch in his voice when he told her that the doctors were unable to save their baby. Then he said, "I was wrong about so many things. Can you ever forgive me?" He'd never admitted he might have been wrong before, and yet Paige felt unable to forgive—unable to respond.

If this were a movie, Mark's words, spoken with such candor, would surely have sent her spiraling into his arms. But this was no movie. The wall between them was too thick to penetrate—she was not filled with forgiveness, only emptiness.

The unshakable trust that had held their marriage together was gone. And now Mark, the unsurpassed politician, could not turn the tide. The loss of a baby he'd neither wanted nor really accepted made things simple for him. But not for her. Unable to forget or forgive, Paige didn't blame Mark—he'd been honest and without pretense. She'd thrown him a bigger curve than he could handle.

His voice penetrated her veil of despair. "Let's begin again," he said. "We're too good together to let anything come between us."

Paige pushed herself onto her elbows. The effort sent hammers of pain through her body, causing her to wince. Not only could she find no forgiveness in her heart, she was not the woman he thought she was. She could not continue to live a lie. As her eyes met Mark's, she knew what she must do. And with that realization, she felt a far deeper and more permanent pain.

Charles had pulled himself from the car by the time Ashleigh dashed around to the passenger door.

"Do stop fussing," he chided. "I'm perfectly capable of hauling myself out of the car. Besides, with your constant hovering, I'm likely to become a helpless old bore."

"You, a bore? Never. But I will try to stop playing mother hen." Ashleigh smiled and slipped her arm through his as they headed across the driveway of his Naples home.

"You'll do a lot more than try, my dear." His smile belied the stern tone. But despite his bravado, Ashleigh knew the trip to the psychiatric hospital, which was now his daughter's home, had taken a lot out of him.

Elizabeth, who had obviously been awaiting their return, stood at the open kitchen door. "Just in time," she said. "I was about to make a pot of tea. How's Miss Caroline?"

When Charles did not answer immediately, Ashleigh said, "About the same. Still doesn't recognize us, but she's being well taken care of." *Oh, damn*, she thought. Why had she jumped in with a meaningless platitude without allowing Charles a chance to respond? But he hadn't seemed to notice.

Slipping out of his coat and heading for the staircase, Charles said, "I'll be down in about ten minutes."

Ashleigh watched his receding back but resisted the urge to follow him up the stairs. After all, he was quite steady on his feet and well aware of what he could and could not do on his own.

When he was out of earshot, Ashleigh told Elizabeth, "Despite his stiff upper lip, seeing his daughter in a catatonic state is terribly hard on him."

Elizabeth nodded. "Any hope that she'll come out of it?"

"There's hope, but it's slim." Drained of her usual energy, Ashleigh told Elizabeth she would join her in the living room after she changed.

Since the break-in, Ashleigh had sold her condo and moved into the Stuart household. When Conrad was in town, they stayed in his penthouse, but until he was free of his responsibilities at Taylor Commercial Investments and his career path was more certain, he wouldn't put it on the market.

Ashleigh took a quick shower and slipped into some casual clothes. She felt refreshed and ran down the stairs to the living room. Charles had not yet come back downstairs, nor had Elizabeth set out the tea.

With a few precious moments to herself, Ashleigh picked up the Sunday newspaper, which she'd given only a cursory glance that morning. A photo of Mitchell and Christine Wainwright on the front page of the Metro section caught her eye. They were pictured with their small son in front of the QE2, which had been docked at San Pedro Harbor. The caption read: "Innovative corporate raider Mitchell Wainwright shocks Wall Street with an unexpected and unprecedented about-face."

Puzzled, she read on. She scanned the portion detailing his abandonment of the battle for Consolidated and was about to set the article aside, but the next statement compelled her to read on. She could hardly believe her eyes. "Even more alarming," the reporter stated, "the West Coast guru of mergers and acquisitions has revealed that he's turned the reins of Wainwright Enterprises over to his CFO, Ron Dean, for an undisclosed period." The article went on to tell of young Mitch's battle with leukemia. It stated that he'd responded well to treatment and was now in remission. In a direct quote, Mitchell said, "This near tragedy has opened my eyes . . ." It certainly has, Ashleigh mused. She read on and discovered that when asked how long it might be before they returned, he'd said, "Maybe never."

Ashleigh glanced back to the photo and saw two uniformed nurses in the background and felt an involuntary shiver.

Moments later, when she heard the light banter of Charles and Elizabeth and the rattle of china cups, she tossed the paper aside and cleared the coffee table for tea.

CHAPTER
101

In the month since losing her baby, Paige had been on an emotional roller coaster. Though she'd thought of little else, she had no more idea of what lay ahead than she had before.

Nothing was the same. She'd made no attempt to resume her volunteer work, but she'd thrown herself back into her health and exercise regimen. Now in the exercise room of her Hollywood Hills home, Paige did her best to keep her mind focused. Sonny couldn't have been more supportive, but if she didn't pull herself together soon, he'd get as fed up with her as she was with herself.

From the corner of her eye, she noticed her trainer had halted his series of sit-ups. No longer keeping pace, he sat very still observing her.

"Am I doing something wrong?" she asked.

He shook his head. "You're a wee bit off, but that's not surprising."

"Ninety-nine, one hundred," she said aloud, hoping to bring a smile to his lips.

He cocked an auburn brow, but there was no smile on his freckled face.

She folded her legs Indian style. "Sorry," she said. "I'll soon get back in the routine."

Again, he shook his head. "Aye, colleen, but not till you make some decisions."

The knot in the pit of her stomach tightened.

"Remember when you told me," Sonny went on, "that not making a decision was a decision in itself?"

"Damn it, Sonny. Don't throw my words back at me. I hate being in limbo, but I honestly don't know which way to turn."

"Where's your spunk? You've come through a lot, and I've never known you to let circumstances keep you down." He pulled himself to his feet and looked down at her.

She wanted to run away, but Sonny was right. She was a fighter—not a coward. She had no respect for those who allowed themselves to become victims. It was up to her to take charge of her destiny. But how?

"You're absolutely right," she said, holding out her hand so he could pull her to her feet. "Let's call it a day and abandon our workout session. I'll get cleaned up and meet you in the living room for one of our good old-fashioned talkathons."

"Right you are," he said, and headed for the adjoining shower area. Paige picked up her towel and headed for her own room.

It took Paige less than twenty minutes to shower, slip into her jade-green jumpsuit, and arrange for coffee and a tray of fruit to be brought into the living room.

Sonny, donning a pair of chinos and crew neck sweater, was already stretched out on one of the plush white chairs, his feet resting on the ottoman and his coffee cup and saucer balanced on his thighs.

He looked up expectantly when Paige walked through the doorway.

Feeling self-conscious and unsure of herself, she picked up a handful of grapes. "Don't expect too much. I haven't anything profound to say, but . . ." She paused searching for the right words. "Why am I turning this into such a production? If I can't talk to you, I can't talk to anyone."

He gave her a disarming smile—totally nonjudgmental and filled with warmth.

She felt his support and acceptance. Her unease evaporated. "It seems I do my best thinking in the shower," she said. "Why I've kept myself in limbo all this time is pure procrastination. I've known what to do from the start, but I just haven't had the guts to tell Mark."

Sonny sighed. "Though you're talkin' in circles, I'm afraid you've given me your bottom line."

Paige nodded, but before she had a chance to slip in her rationale, Sonny leapt to his feet and spanned the distance between them. His face flushed, he stood towering over her. "Since when have you become a quitter?"

She opened her mouth in defense. But Sonny's words came out in a rush. "You'd walk out on Mark, now, when he needs you most? After twenty-two years of one of the most envied marriages in the country, you can't make allowances? You, of all people, know the incredible pressure your husband was under when you hit him with your life-altering news. He'd have come around if you'd set your stubborn pride aside and given him a bit of time. From all you've told me, Mark's done a damn good job of setting his ego aside, trying his damnedest to make amends. Why can't you put your differences behind you?"

After a quick intake of air, he sat down beside her, his voice softening. "Aye, colleen. Get back in touch with your loving nature. Remember your own reaction when the doctor gave you the news, and forgive him for not being able to adapt in your time frame."

Paige's throat constricted, and a tear slid down her cheek. She swallowed hard, hoping she could tell him what was in her heart. "I have forgiven him. It's me I can't forgive." Sensing her trainer was about to issue another platitude, she said, "Please, let me finish. When Dr. Gene told me Mark had given his consent to do what they could to save our baby, my resentment vanished. My love for Mark is stronger than ever."

"So?" Sonny's bushy red brows pinched together, making his forehead a mass of wiggly lines.

"Mark deserves a wife he can be proud of, not a fantasy created by piling one creative lie upon another." Allowing for no interruption, she continued. "As we speak, Mark is in Dallas working out the details of his contract as Nason's new CEO. I haven't told him I'd go with him—"

"But you haven't told him you wouldn't, have you?"

Shaking her head, she said, "No, but I can't. Once I tell him the truth, and admit to all the stories I've fabricated about my early life, he won't even want me. Mark loves an illusion. He doesn't know who I really am—if he did, he'd stop loving me. I'm so ashamed," she said, thinking of the litany of lies she'd heaped on him.

"Paige," he said, tipping her chin up so that her eyes met his, "you're spouting pure blarney. So what if you stretched the truth a wee bit?"

She wasn't buying it. She spread her arms out wide to indicate the enormity of her fabrications.

"Paige." His voice rose. "Take a good look in the mirror. Look beyond the surface. Mark is not living with the child you once were. The so-called illusion that captured Mark's heart is the woman you had become. She's no illusion."

Fresh tears sprang to Paige's eyes. Before she could say anymore, however, she heard an echo of rapidly approaching heels in the corridor, which abruptly died as Anna stepped onto the thick white carpet. "Sorry to disturb you, Mrs. Toddman, but there's a little girl on the line who says she has to talk to you right away. She was sobbing pretty hard, but I think she said her name is April."

CHAPTER
102

Mark Toddman hit the front steps of his Hollywood Hills home like a contender for the fifty-yard dash. If his spirits were any higher, his feet wouldn't have hit the ground.

"Paige," he called out from the doorway, "where are you?"

"In the library," she called back.

When Mark strode into the library, Paige was sitting at her antique desk and crumpling a piece of writing paper.

The image of another goddamned note flashed though his mind, but he pushed it away. He was about to launch into his news about Nason's when Paige said, "Mark, before you tell me about your trip, we have to talk."

His antennae went up. Her tone was deadly serious, and there was no sparkle in her eyes. If he didn't know her better, he'd have sworn she'd been crying.

"Please sit down," she said.

"Hang on," he said, "how about a drink to celebrate—"

"No, thank you," she said.

Walking across to the wet bar, he said, "Be right with you." He poured himself a stiff scotch and soda.

The first words from his wife's lips confirmed his worst fear. With no lead-in, Paige began, "I can't go to Dallas with you. I'm not who you think I am . . ."

He blinked, trying to make sense of her words, but they made no sense. His apprehension turned to anger. "If you're not who I think you are, who in the hell are you?"

"Please, just listen, Mark. God, this is so hard . . ."

The damn nerve in his left eyelid began a steady twitch, but he reined in his temper. He was observing a side of Paige he'd never seen before. She stared down at a wad of Kleenex clenched in her hand, and he saw tears flow down her cheeks, unchecked and real.

But when he drew up a chair to sit beside her, she turned away.

"Let me finish." Then, she proceeded to confess what she labeled her "pack of lies."

Mark's tension vanished. She hadn't told him anything he didn't already know. He felt so relieved that it took every ounce of will to let her get it all out.

When she finally wound down, he said, "Is that all? I thought you were going to tell me something shocking."

Wide-eyed, she stared at him. The look of incredulity etched on her face filled his heart with love. "Paige, I love you. I always have, and I always will," he said. "You haven't told me anything I didn't already know."

"I don't understand," she said. "How could you have known?" Then, answering her own question, she said, "Consolidated." Apparently, it had never before occurred to her that a background check had been run on her before Mark's first CEO appointment at Consolidated's Atlanta division. "Why didn't you tell me?"

"It didn't matter. I figured if and when you wanted to talk about it, you would. Besides, if you'd lived in that picture-perfect world you painted for yourself as a child, you'd never have grown into the woman you are today—the only woman I've ever loved—the woman who has shared my dreams."

"I can't believe you could find out that I had fabricated my entire life before we met and just dismiss it." She glared at him. "You hate lies and liars. If only you'd told me—"

"Paige, I loved the person you'd become, the person you were with me. By the time I was presented with your background check, it was ancient history. I saw no point in digging into the past, and quite honestly, I forgot all about it. After all, we've always been focused on the future. So what if you fabricated an ideal past to protect yourself. That little foster child who was shuffled from one household to another is not the woman you are today."

She didn't respond. Instead, she pressed her face into his shoulder. Her entire body shook. Then abruptly, she pulled away, wiped her eyes with the back of her hand, and sat upright.

There was more. He saw it in the determined set of her chin and uneasy motion of her eyes. Steeling himself, he said, "Okay, tell me."

"What I have to tell you will change everything."

He saw her reluctance, but his patience was waning. Why didn't she just get on with it? "Paige, I can hardly comment on what I don't know. By now you must know I'm beyond being shocked or blown-away by anything you might tell me."

"Yes, but please let me tell you the whole story before you ask any questions."

He nodded. *Just get to the bottom line so we can map out our future.*

"Remember the young woman and her daughter who moved into the apartment I had rented?"

Again, he nodded, but couldn't conjure up much interest or enthusiasm. It had nothing to do with them. But as Paige brought the story to a rapid conclusion, telling him a drug-crazed john had killed the young mother, he realized it most likely had everything to do with them. "If you found a legitimate job for her, why would she—"

"I don't know," Paige cut in, "but the fact is, Patti's dead, and April is being placed in a foster home."

Placing his finger over his wife's lips, he smiled. "So, I take it, we'll have a ready-made daughter?"

Excitement surged through Viviana's veins. The subtle elegance of Rodeo Drive in Beverly Hills had faded for her. Manhattan was where she belonged. She stopped in front of the magnificent storefront confident it had no equal on Fifth Avenue.

When Glenn Nelson, the impeccably groomed man at her side, made no comment, she couldn't resist prompting him. "Well, what's the verdict?"

She so wanted the creative young buyer to be impressed. She'd admired his finely honed talents since their early days at Bentleys Royale, and now she needed him desperately.

Attempting to conceal her anxiety, she stood back as Glenn paced the length of the marble frontage, stroking his angular jaw. Dressed in a pale-blue shirt and paisley tie beneath a gray wool blazer, he was so damned handsome he looked like he belonged on the cover of *GQ*. Viviana, irrationally, felt a surge of desire. Her libido had not been quenched since she'd become Philip's lawfully wedded wife—an age-old problem. She turned her mind back to business.

Viviana's self-confidence dwindled as the silence stretched between them.

"Nice," he finally said. Then, with a noncommittal shrug, he took in the total structure, top-to-bottom, his eyes resting for a moment on the distinctive lettering above the door. "De Mornay's," he mouthed as if testing how it rolled off the tongue. "Not bad."

"Not bad?" Viviana parroted in disbelief.

One sandy brow raised a fraction, but he made no further comment. Instead, he asked, "How about a tour of the interior?"

Viviana fumbled for the keys while Glenn peered through one of the floor-to-ceiling bay windows. While confident her store was the most elegant in Manhattan and her merchandise unsurpassed, business hadn't taken off as she'd expected. She'd thrown her energy, her heart, and her soul into the essence of De Mornay's, and her ego demanded that it become the epitome of shopping in Manhattan and a financial success as well. Certain that this young man held the key to that success, she wanted him to see the store's potential.

Glenn was as much a perfectionist as she was. He was obviously considering what he had to gain by leaving Bergdorf's to work with her. She intended to make him an offer he couldn't refuse, even if it meant giving him a sizable piece of the business.

Viviana could hardly wait for Glenn to see the interior. At great expense, she had taken the very best of Bentleys Royale and added her unique creativity. The building was meticulously modeled in the image of the Los Angeles icon.

Glenn came to an abrupt stop just inside the front doors of her miniature couture cathedral, and then he slowly moved forward. He circled the elegant fixtures, studying the merchandise, and was most likely evaluating the presentation. She watched his gaze move over every inch. What Viviana didn't see was the admiration she had hoped for. His scrutiny appeared judgmental, if not downright critical.

Viviana pressed her lips together. What could he be seeing that she had missed? She was just about to ask when he picked up one of her very own designs. "Nice," he repeated, a smile widening across his chiseled features.

"Nice," she snapped. "Is that the extent of your vocabulary?"

"Take it easy. Your designs are tastefully superb."

"But?" she challenged.

"No buts, my bitchy friend," he said, flashing her a boyish smile. Then, waving the full-skirted silk dress gracefully in front of him, he said, "Seriously, this fluid simplicity is bound to be a winner."

Pleased, but still waiting for the other shoe to drop, Viviana asked, "Any suggestions?" Then she impulsively added, "Pity you were out of the country during our grand opening. I'm sure you read all about it."

Glenn nodded, still gazing around.

"It was truly a star-studded affair." She knew she shouldn't oversell, but pride demanded she drop just a few names. She rambled on, "Cher wore one of her outrageous see-through numbers, and Barbra Streisand ordered a Donna Karan and two of my own designs. Nancy Reagan also showed a lot of interest in my label. Even Henry Kravis . . ." Viviana caught the impatient roll of Glenn's eyes and aborted her monologue. "Sorry. Guess I got carried away."

When Glenn failed to respond, Viviana said, "Well, now that you've seen every nook and cranny, what do you think?"

"No pussy-footing around?"

Viviana nodded, her teeth involuntarily clamping together.

"Your merchandise selection is top drawer."

Again, she nodded, knowing damn well it was superb, as was her presentation. "I thought we agreed, no pussy-footing around. If you see a problem, give it to me straight." Leaning against one of the marble pillars, it took all her willpower to stop the toe of her right pump from tapping.

He moved his eyes up and down and from side to side, taking in the complete backdrop. "The problem is this austere ambiance."

She felt her body stiffen. "It's been open just two months, but it's already won two prestigious architectural prizes, and it's being featured in *Architectural Digest* next month."

"Terrific," Glenn said, "but this is a store, not a goddamned museum." Then, putting his arm around her shoulders, he said, "Sorry, but you asked me to give it to you straight. You've done a lot more right than wrong, but if you want to sell high-ticket, quality merchandise, you must provide more than elegance. You must provide entertainment. De Mornay's should be the most exciting Fifth Avenue boutique in Manhattan—*not* a miniature Bentleys Royale."

Heat surged to her cheeks.

Leading Viviana to the brocade sofa, he pulled her down beside him. "There's nothing that can't be fixed, but while unquestionably elegant, De Mornay's lacks warmth. It has a cold, unfriendly aura." His eyes locked on hers. "That's why, after the big hurrah and flourish of satisfying their curiosity, the rich and famous aren't coming back."

She stiffened. "What makes you think people aren't—"

"Cut the bullshit, Viviana. I know."

Tears brimming in her eyes, she said, "It was great for the first month, but lately . . ." Her voice faded. She couldn't let him know she was barely covering overhead. She didn't want anyone to know, not Glenn, and not her husband, who'd been so damned proud of her.

"Look, Viviana. There are few secrets in the retail world. Buyers, manufacturers, reps, what have you—at the end of a hard day, they talk. As effective as CNN, we all know what the next guy's up to. If you're serious about getting together in this venture, don't hold back."

Viviana took in a big breath, recalling how talkative merchants grew after a few drinks. "How about talking over dinner? Philip is tied up this evening, and I've booked a table at Twenty-One."

"Dinner sounds great, but—"

"But what? You have a hot date?"

He raised his brows. "Not tonight. What I need to know before we go forward in this venture is whether the financing for De Mornay's is tied to Sloane's other retail ventures."

Puzzled, Viviana wondered what he was getting at. Glenn's dazzling eyes bore into hers, and she momentarily lamented the fact that Glenn, like so many of the handsome, desirable men she dealt with, was gay. "Odd question," she remarked, "but since we're laying all our cards on the table, the answer is no. De Mornay's is all mine."

"Great. Before I'd consider jumping ship from Bergdorf's, I'd need to know there's no novice retailer second-guessing our decisions, and De Mornay's won't be swept into Chapter 11 along with Consolidated."

Chapter 11 . . . Chapter 11 . . . Chapter 11. The words rang in her ear. She must have heard him wrong. She *hoped* she'd heard him wrong.

CHAPTER

104

There was no end of headhunters contacting Conrad with opportunities in the retail and investment banking arenas for him to consider. For the past couple of months, he had explored many lucrative positions from coast to coast. He had not narrowed his prospects strictly to the West Coast, but, all things being equal, that was his preference. Now, after a series of interviews and being wined and dined by a multitude of firms, he'd made his choice to sign on with the O'Leary Financial Corporation in West LA.

Sure that Ashleigh would be delighted that the most appealing and lucrative offer was on the West Coast, he was utterly blown-away when she looked him straight in the eye and asked him a couple of unexpected and soul-searching questions.

"I can't tell you I wasn't tempted when Toddman offered me the presidency at Nason's," he said. "The opportunity to work in a quality retail environment again in tandem with Mark is incredibly appealing, but other offers on the table are far more lucrative. And the position at O'Leary's is in LA."

They were in front of the circular fireplace in his Long Beach penthouse. Ashleigh was curled up beside him on the black leather sofa. Slowly, she uncurled her legs, took hold of both his hands, and coaxed him to his feet. "Love, when you talk about O'Leary's, the attraction is mainly financial. And being the CEO of a major financial company is nothing to sneeze at—it's a worthy goal," she said, gently leading him to the large mirror in the entry "But when you talk about Nason's, your eyes light up. Just look in that mirror. Do I need to tell you where your heart lies, or what you really want to do?"

She was incredible. She'd opened the door, and the truth hit him like a Mack truck. "You're absolutely right, Ashleigh. I'll call Mark in the morning and tell him I'm signing on."

The next morning, after he had talked to Toddman, Conrad sank down on the leather couch with Ashleigh and took her in his arms. "Mark's agreed to give me three weeks to tie up loose ends. And he and Paige said they look forward to introducing us to Dallas."

She kissed him on the forehead, then leaned back until her eyes met his. "How are they?"

"All I can tell you is that when Paige answered the phone, there were sounds of laughter in the background."

"Will they be able to take the little girl into their home?"

"Apparently. But I assume it will take awhile to get all the legalities taken care of."

He pulled Ashleigh close and said, "But let's talk about *our* future." Before she could respond, he said, "I've been rethinking our time schedule and realize it's not fair to rush your move to Dallas, which means we'll need to postpone . . ."

Shaking her head, she said, "My outplacement counseling will be wrapped up within the next month."

Rather than let her continue he said, " Being away from you is unbearable, but I want to begin our lives together with balance."

Her brow furrowed, and she opened her mouth to speak, then she quickly closed it as he went on. "Knowing my track record, this first year in a new job will leave me little time for anything but work . . ."

Ashleigh, who had been the one responsible for delaying their wedding plans time after time, felt a sinking feeling in the pit of her stomach. What was he trying to tell her? Had she put too many other responsibilities ahead of him? Did he want to start his new life without her?

Aborting her inner dialogue, Ashleigh felt two strong hands squeeze her upper arms. "Ashleigh, I love you. I want you beside me forever. I'm not dictating we postpone our wedding. I just thought it would be better to wait until I get settled—"

"Of course," she said, "that makes a lot of sense."

Before she could elaborate, Conrad said, "Dallas isn't far. We'll be together as much as possible. I'm earmarking a portion of my severance package as our kitty for weekly flights between LA and Dallas. I want you with me every free minute."

CHAPTER
105

Viviana's spirits plummeted the instant she stepped across the threshold of their Wellington Towers suite. Abandoned briefcases, computer printouts, and miscellaneous stacks of paper littered every flat surface in the spacious living room. There were even torn and wadded scraps of paper floating in half-filled cups of cold, stale coffee.

This was bound to be another all-nighter. She pushed on her lower abdomen and imagined stress eating into her raw ulcer. It would be a miracle if it weren't bleeding.

Although she wasn't ignorant of the financial problems Sloane's corporations faced, the idea of Chapter 11 had never occurred to her. It just wasn't possible. Philip would hardly file for Chapter 11 without saying a goddamned word to her. Or would he?

His retail empires were leveraged to the hilt, and the unrealistic expense cuts Sandler suggested up front had proven unproductive. It seemed Sloane's bankers and financial advisers were inept as well. Glancing around the room, she prayed Philip would bring this meeting to a quick conclusion so she could get to the bottom of the rumor Glenn had sprung on her. As Sloane's wife, she must know everything that might affect her and her lifestyle.

With effort, she shifted her mind back to the bargain she'd reached with Glenn. Though promising him 40 percent of the profits felt scary, it proved he believed in De Mornay's. Trusting him completely, she felt certain they could turn the business around. She shifted her focus to the fact that 60 percent of a thriving business was a lot better than 100 percent of a faltering one.

Inevitably, her thoughts flipped back to the present lifestyle she wasn't willing to lose. At the image of Philip Sloane without power or, God forbid, without money, her thought processes broke down.

She pressed on her temples, searching deep into her heart. Power and money—was that all Philip was to her? Was she really that shallow?

No, no, no, a silent scream echoed in her head. She truly cared about Philip. She was good to him and for him. Philip Sloane had been everything she had desired. And yet, he had not taken possession of her heart and soul. No one would ever get that close again.

Impulsively straightening piles of paper and picking up dirty ashtrays, she heard the sound of a key turning in the lock.

At first she saw only Philip, not the entourage at his heels. The others came into focus when he spoke her name. For the very first time, Viviana noticed that Philip was by far the shortest man in the room.

In stocking feet, but still pristine in her Chanel suit, Viviana looked up and paused in the middle of the living room. Looking around the untidy suite, Philip smiled, his heart filled with pride. She was such a perfectionist. "Don't bother, kitten," he said. "I'll have housekeeping come in first thing in the morning."

His attention had turned to the small group of men surrounding him. Somehow the importance of his presence in the next phase of the meeting vanished. He was paying a fortune, and he might as well let his advisers earn it by handling the blooming details. He checked the time; it was after 3:00 a.m. "Write up your recommendations, and we'll meet back here at 8:00," he said.

The men retrieved their briefcases and piles of paper before saying their good-byes. When the door closed behind them, Philip asked, "What's troubling you, kitten?"

Her arms wound around his neck, and after giving him a long, passionate kiss, Viviana threw her head back. "These damn rumors about the stores going into Chapter 11 are so unnerving."

"Don't worry." he said. "I can't tell you this retail deal is running smoothly—you know damn well it's not—but Chapter 11 isn't an option." No major retail division had ever recovered after Chapter 11. It would be like a death sentence, and he had far too much to lose.

"You're not just trying to protect me?" Viviana asked, her eyes wide with apprehension.

"No," he reassured her. He pulled her to him and began unbuttoning her suit jacket. "More divisions need to be sold. But let's not belabor the fates. This too shall pass." Taking her hand, he led her to the bedroom for some much-needed distraction.

CHAPTER

106

Time passed in a whirl of activity once Conrad assumed the presidency of Nason's. As his fiancée, Ashleigh was caught up in glamorous black-tie affairs and promotions.

Nason's could not fully fill the void left in Ashleigh's heart by the deterioration of Bentleys Royale. And yet, her spirits soared upon discovering how Conrad and Mark continued to embrace the high standards and love of quality she'd grown up with, and how they'd validated the power of those inbred standards by producing an impressive bottom line.

Her burgeoning friendship with Paige Toddman became an unexpected bonus. And Ashleigh found that Paige's knowledge of the area, and her quirky sense of humor, made the ordeal of house hunting fun.

Other than her brief stint at the University of Washington, Long Beach had been Ashleigh's home since birth. But in Dallas, Paige made her feel as if she belonged. From day one, Ashleigh had been totally captivated by April, the shy, withdrawn child the Toddmans had taken into their home. Always candid, Paige put on no airs. She'd told Ashleigh of the changes April continued to make in her life, and she admitted, "What I don't know about motherhood could fill an entire university. It's an uphill battle, but I'm adjusting."

Then, shaking her head, and with a mirthful glint in her eye, she said, "It's a lot harder for Mark, but April's brought a lot of laughter back into our lives. And whether he admits it or not, she's winning over his heart. Of course, he's impatient at times, and I have to remind him that it's hard on April too. Also, I don't let him forget he didn't have to put up with a pregnant wife or a ton of smelly diapers. We have a lot to be thankful for."

Ashleigh had a great deal to be thankful for too. Conrad personified everything Ashleigh valued—he was decisive, a fabulous listener, and sensitive to her needs. He never failed to set time aside for quiet candlelight dinners and evenings alone. Their conversation invariably centered on their hopes and dreams for the future. The weekend before he had asked, "What do you think of starting a family on our wedding night?" They'd giggled like teenagers and chose names for their fictional children.

In LA, Ashleigh had been far too busy to be miserable over time away from Conrad. Her greatest challenge had been keeping Charles's spirits up, as well as her own, as they painfully watched the deterioration of Bentleys Royale.

David Jerome, clearly committed to the high standards set by Charles, left with the first wave of the grand exodus of top management. The next blow was Jordon's decision to combine the two specialty store divisions they'd acquired in the Consolidated spin-off. Bentleys Royale was no longer a separate entity. It was now under the supervision of P. G. Marshal's, headquartered in San Francisco. Morale among the remaining employees sank to a new low once they no longer had the prestige of their own president.

Many of the Royale's buyers had been given incentives to remain, but soon the majority disappeared. It was not profitable to have staff in San Francisco and Los Angeles buying essentially the same lines. The top buyers had been asked to relocate to San Francisco or lose their positions; others were asked to become department managers. Several did so, but most either joined the competition or took early retirement. Only the cosmetics, fine jewelry, and bridal buyers remained in their original positions. They became responsible for the P. G. Marshal's stores in Southern California as well.

An up-and-coming female executive from P. G. Marshal's replaced David Jerome. Though highly intelligent, the new general manager lacked an appreciation for the standards that had set Bentleys Royale apart. When Ms. Rose Ellis arrived in the flagship store in a rumpled pantsuit to address the loyal sales associates, they were shaken. Within days, the dress code was revised. Dresses and skirts were no longer the standard for female sales associates. The mature, tenured sales associates stuck to their former standards, while others, particularly the younger associates, adapted to the new standards, donning increasingly casual outfits. Morale plummeted another notch.

But the deterioration of the dress code was minor in comparison to what followed. The Bentleys Royale insignia was to be replaced by P. G. Marshal's. The associates were not alone in their dismay. A cry was heard from far and near at the very thought of the legendary icon being stripped of its identity. So great was the outcry, spearheaded by the California Heritage Society, that Jordon's did not remove the insignia from the flagship store after all. Instead, P.G. Marshal's was added, and the phones were answered using both names.

As rumors circulated that Jordon's, as well as Consolidated, faced an imminent financial collapse, morale sank even lower. Ashleigh attempted to turn a blind eye to the declining housekeeping standards and a multitude of other things she was powerless to change. Instead, she made a point of pasting an optimistic expression on her face when she walked through the store.

CHAPTER
107

For nine months, in between impromptu trips to Europe for sheep-brain injections and to Bermuda to check the expansion plans for his cliff-top villa, Philip Sloane worked around the clock with his own staff, bankers, lawyers, and accountants. Recently, he and Viviana had resorted to leaving notes for one another. When he was not embroiled in negotiations or working his way through legalized mumbo jumbo, Viviana was invariably dashing off to take care of some mini-crisis for her tiny empire. But that would all change quite soon.

For the moment, he must not shift his focus. Deliveries to his retail locations had slowed or been cut off entirely by various suppliers who were up in arms about not being paid for goods on time. Why couldn't they get it? By cutting his stores off, they were cutting their own throats. Without fresh merchandise, he couldn't generate the cash flow to pay them. The vicious circle could not be broken, so alternatives needed to be found.

Through his own last-minute interventions, many of Amalgamated's remaining divisions had been sold for more than a billion dollars. By playing an active role in the actual sales of several divisions, he'd managed to wheedle an extra $40 to $50 million out of various buyers. Had he left the decision making to First Commercial, they'd have accepted the original low-ball bids on his behalf. Viewing their high-priced advice as utterly useless, he refused to pay for it.

Sloane's lack of respect and continuous jabs at First Commercial made mortgage lenders uneasy. When challenged, Sloane would shrug off the fact that three of the department store divisions that he sold for inflated values had already fallen into Chapter 11.

With the collapse of the foolhardy endeavors of the big deals, the bankruptcy courts were now clogged. Sloane and his lenders had ignored the danger signs. Through their wishful number crunching, he now faced disaster. In this era of debt barons, banks had showered billions of dollars on all kinds of creative speculation from native sons like Donald Trump to foreign entrepreneurs such as himself. The fact that Sloane was not alone did not help one iota. He planned to use the full capacity of his creative mind to limit his personal damage. After all, he had been a newcomer on Wall Street and had paid *top-dollar* for *top-notch* advice, which should have garnered an equal ratio of protection. But Chapter 11 had become a familiar refrain, and it was now clear that he was about to face the inevitable comeuppance.

Rumors of the trouble on Wall Street and the inescapable demise of the dinosaurs called department stores had circulated for months. He could no longer deny the unraveling of his empire. Now was the time to break the news to Viviana, before it leaked. He looked at his wristwatch; it was after midnight. Where was she?

CHAPTER
108

Paige felt a pair of eyes on her. "Hold on," she said, tucking the receiver beneath her chin and holding her arms out to April. "I won't be long, love," she whispered in the child's ear. "It's Grandma Martha."

Knowing she'd get no peace until her daughter talked to the woman she called grandma, Paige smiled and handed her the phone. After a few words, April said good-bye and was about to hang up. Paige rescued the receiver before it disconnected.

"Mark is probably in the stores," she explained with a sigh.

"No doubt," Martha agreed. "Walter always taught him, 'No matter how sophisticated the statistical data, the heart of the business is in the stores.'"

"I'll have him call when he gets home," Paige said before terminating the call. Then she turned her attention to April. As they assembled the ingredients for the cookies she'd promised to help April make for her dance class, she found her mind returning to Martha Winslow.

Walter Winslow had succumbed to a malignant tumor shortly after Sloane's hostile takeover of his family legacy, and Martha had taken his seat on Consolidated's board of directors. Walter had not been around to see his department store divisions torn apart, one after another, or sold to the highest bidder. But Martha had. Paige shared Martha's pain. No matter the victories or successes she and Mark enjoyed at Nason's, they felt each blow inflicted on Consolidated. The weight of its dismantling and impending bankruptcy clearly registered in Mark's disposition.

The Toddmans kept in touch with Martha, but over the past few months as rumors of Consolidated's peril filled the media, Martha was the one who made the calls. And, it was Mark she wanted to talk to.

These talks invariably left Mark depressed. "Consolidated is no longer the same company," he lamented. "The board must think I'm a bloody magician. Not a single major retailer has pulled itself out of Chapter 11. Besides, I have a commitment to Nason's."

If it weren't for Mark's $9-million contract with Nason's, Paige would have joined Martha Winslow's plea for Mark to return to Consolidated. The past months at Nason's had been terrific. She and Mark had again become a team, easily integrating into the Dallas community as proud representatives of the prestigious stores. Mark's imagination and know-how had brought excitement and greater profitability to the stores. But Paige sensed the arena was growing too small; Mark would soon need greater challenges. If he didn't take a shot at rescuing his former retail empire, she feared it would leave an impenetrable void in their lives. She also sensed Mark was the only man who could pull it off.

"Mommy. Will Ashleigh come to my dance show?"

April's tug at her pant leg pulled Paige's thoughts to the upcoming wedding. Paige was to be Ashleigh's matron of honor, and April her flower girl.

CHAPTER
109

A bundle of nerves, Viviana set her briefcase on the Lalique coffee table. It was obvious that Philip was agitated and had been waiting for her return.

"May I pour you a drink?" she asked as she sauntered to the wet bar. He shook his head and pointed to the half-filled tumbler on the end table. Before she had a chance to pour herself a drink, he began pacing.

Viviana finished pouring her martini, kicked off her shoes, and sank down onto the sofa.

Philip did not stop pacing until she was settled. A few weeks earlier, when he'd told her of his plans to sell Carlingdon's, she was shocked and dismayed. Now, after hearing his first few words, Viviana felt as if the blood had stopped circulating through her veins. Curling her legs beneath her, she tried to concentrate. A hundred questions buzzed through her head.

Before she could ask a single one, he said, "Please, Viviana. Just listen. If we were to sell Carlingdon's, we'd have a heavy capital-gains tax. The same is true of the junk bonds we thought about buying back at the discounted price. It's turning out to be a catch-22. No matter which way we turn, we end up reducing the funds available to pay off debts. Tax laws give breaks for entering into LBOs, but they tie our hands with huge tax disadvantages when we run into a snag . . ."

As Philip explained the so-called reality of the present world of finance and his own situation, Viviana's throat felt dry. She ran her tongue along the roof of her mouth, attempting to create enough moisture to swallow back her fear. Then, as his words washed over her and she realized that Chapter 11 was no longer a rumor but about to become a reality, she downed the martini and returned to the bar.

On the afternoon of Friday, May 24, Philip Sloane emerged from the courthouse with his team of attorneys. News instantly spread across the nation—Amalgamated and Consolidated were officially in Chapter 11.

In the master bedroom of their suite, Viviana downed another Valium. She no longer made any effort to conceal her dependency. In the past week, she'd flaunted it. And Philip no longer attempted to stop her.

Now, pointing to the TV, she repeated, "Please turn it off." If she had to hear Philip called "the flamboyant Australian entrepreneur" one more time, or hear about the debt-free status and faultless fifty-year record for paying bills on time of the two department store enterprises before Sloane's arrival on Wall Street again, she would not be up to facing the throng of reporters who lurked just beyond their door.

"Pull yourself together, Viv." Philip clicked off the TV.

Viviana's body stiffened. Philip never called her Viv.

Though he quickly apologized, Viviana remained unsettled.

That afternoon, outside the Wellington Towers, reporters bombarded Viviana and Sloane as they hurried toward the limo. Sloane ducked his head as microphones were thrust in his direction. Not even the customary "No comment" passed his lips.

"Is it true," Viviana heard one reporter say, "that your checks to suppliers bounced if deposited after Friday morning?" Many of the resources for her boutique had complained to Viviana that they were not paid for deliveries to Consolidated and had no way to recover their merchandise. But this was the first she'd heard about bounced checks.

As the door to the limousine opened, Viviana paused and turned to her husband. A sudden flash of light exploded in her face. Temporarily blinded, she heard the click, click, click of the camera shutter. Flashbulbs were going off in every direction. *Get a grip*, she told herself, and did so. Slipping her arm through Philip's, she smiled and posed for the photographers.

CHAPTER
110

"There she is!" April cried out as Paige pulled up to the curb in front of the baggage claim area. Unbuckling her seat belt, she pointed to the doorway as Ashleigh emerged, wheeling a small suitcase behind her. Then, before Paige could stop or even caution her, April pushed open the car door and ran to meet Ashleigh.

Paige did not take her eyes off the little girl until she saw Ashleigh throw her arms around her. April's adoption was now final, but Paige could not dispel her fears of having her taken from them. With all the things that could, and did, happen to young children, it took great effort for Paige not to worry. Though still adjusting to her new role, it seemed as if April had always been a part of their lives. She tried hard not to be overprotective or to stifle April's independent spirit, which was just beginning to unfold.

Paige hit the release button for the trunk and ran around the back of the Jaguar to welcome Ashleigh to Dallas and help her with her luggage. The young woman had become far more than an acquaintance; she'd become the first female friend Paige had had since leaving New York. She also treasured Ashleigh's unreserved enthusiasm and easy rapport with April.

Ashleigh's light blond hair glimmered in the sun. She looked fabulous—as good as any of the professional models whose faces she'd seen on the covers of major bridal magazines. Before she had a chance to comment, Ashleigh said to Paige, "You look great."

While Paige made her way to the driver's side, Ashleigh handed April a small package and opened the rear car door. The child climbed in the back seat, fastened her safety belt, and began unwrapping her gift.

Ashleigh slid in beside Paige. "She's really blossoming," Ashleigh whispered.

Paige nodded. "She's quite a handful, but I love it. I learn something new every day." She paused as she turned onto the freeway. "Don't postpone having a family, Ashleigh. Your instincts are far superior to mine, and youth definitely has its advantages. I'm often tempted to ask Sloane to sign Mark and me up for those injections he gets in Europe. But enough about my newfound philosophy of life. You have a lot more important things on your mind."

The two women talked nonstop from the airport to Highland Park. Their main focus was the upcoming wedding. "I thought Charles might be with you," Paige said. "He *will* be giving the bride away, won't he?"

"You know he will. But he's tied up this afternoon, attending his daughter's art exhibit. I'm picking him up at the airport Saturday afternoon."

Paige frowned. The last she'd heard, Charles Stuart's daughter was in a mental institution. Did he have another? "You mean the one who was married to Morris Sandler?"

Ashleigh nodded. "She's taken up oil painting and is quite good. Her work is being shown in a local art gallery, and Charles is escorting her to the exhibit."

"Obviously, she's no longer catatonic."

"No," Ashleigh said and then frowned. "I can hardly believe I left that chapter out. Although the progress has been slow, and Caroline will most likely spend the rest of her life in the institution, she's doing much better. At least she and Charles can now talk to each other, and he won't be alone."

As they pulled into the circular drive, in front of the house Ashleigh and Conrad were soon to share, Ashleigh felt overwhelmed. The gracious estates of the Highland Park area were nothing like the casual ones she'd grown accustomed to in Southern California. Though not nearly as large as the Toddmans' home, the lovely colonial house, situated on three-quarters of an acre, seemed quite grand to Ashleigh. Past the graceful sloped lawn leading to the wide front porch, an image of what lie beyond the broad double doors crystallized in her head. It was perfect, and she and Conrad would have such fun turning this house into a home.

Involuntarily, Ashleigh's mind reviewed all that was in store for them in the coming week, and she fought a wave of apprehension. Saturday night, a week before their wedding, Paige was throwing a gala event in her own home and had invited the Dallas elite—the city's wealthy benefactors who supported the museums, theaters, symphony, opera, ballet, and colleges and universities. She and Conrad were to be the guests of honor. Already thinking of herself as the wife of Nason's president, she wanted to make a favorable impression. Small talk had never come easily, but for Conrad's sake she would overcome her fears and master that art.

Breaking into her thoughts, Paige asked, "Would you like us to give you a hand?"

"Thanks," Ashleigh said, "I can manage. The furniture arrived a couple of weeks ago, and most of my personal things won't be here until tomorrow." She and Paige would have plenty of time to get caught up, but right now Ashleigh was too excited to make conversation. She wanted time to add her touches to the house before Conrad stepped through the door.

Paige and April helped her take the luggage from the trunk to the porch. Stopping in front of the wide double doors, April presented Ashleigh with a long white box. Ashleigh quickly took off the top. "How wonderful," she said, admiring the array of brightly colored fresh flowers. She thanked Paige and gave April a warm squeeze.

After waving her good-byes, Ashleigh turned the key in the lock, pushed open the door, and felt as if she had finally come home.

Paige did a final walk-through with the head caterer as four tuxedo-clad men and two young women in long black gowns arranged their chairs and instruments in the area beside a three-tiered fountain.

"Those centerpieces look skimpy. Add two more red roses and a bit more baby's breath to each," Paige instructed. Then, noticing a missing champagne glass, she said, "And please recheck each place setting."

Next, she straightened tablecloths, which were already perfectly straight, and consulted with the orchestra leader about his selections, rechecking to be sure he knew the exact moment to play "It's a Wonderful World."

Throughout the day, Paige fussed over every detail. This long-awaited occasion must be truly memorable. Gazing around, she began to relax. The setting was picture perfect. But as she spotted the caterer scurrying from table to table, shouting orders to various members of his staff, it occurred to her that she'd probably wounded his artistic soul with her nitpicking.

"Leonard," she called out, shortening the distance between them. "Everything looks lovely. Please forgive me for being such a tyrant." She could almost see the tension evaporate from his shoulders as he told her she had nothing to apologize for.

Giving the outdoor gardens a final inspection, Paige set off to find Mark.

"It looks spectacular. Just like a fairyland."

Paige whirled around to see Ashleigh smiling down at her from the top terrace. She wore a simple peach Donna Karan sheath dress with a double strand of pearls. There was a rare delicacy and beauty in her face, and her huge brown eyes seemed to radiate from within.

"I'm so glad you're early." Paige dashed up the spiral stone steps to meet her. She was about to ask about Conrad, when she saw him. What a stunning couple they made.

Conrad's deep-set blue eyes approvingly took in the surroundings, the elaborately set tables, the garlands of live flowers lining the rails of the terraced patios, the host of catering staff and musicians. "I didn't think it possible, but somehow you've even outdone yourself," Conrad said. He gave Paige a brotherly hug, then stepped back and slipped his arm around Ashleigh's slender waist.

"Let's have a toast to the bride and groom," Mark said as he and Charles Stuart strode through the tall French doors.

Charles added his accolades as Mark fixed drinks for the entire party. They had barely finished their toast to the bride and groom before the guests began to trickle in.

"Time to get acquainted with the local color," Paige said, grinning at Ashleigh. She quickly arranged the party in a semiformal receiving line.

Ashleigh felt a tiny somersault in the pit of her stomach. Paige seemed to sense her unease and changed places with Mark to stand beside her. Conrad was on her other side and Charles beside him. As guests approached, Paige whispered interesting personal tidbits about several of the Dallas elite before introducing them. Her revelations often brought a smile to Ashleigh's lips, and in a few cases she had to quell an urge to laugh out loud over Paige's unreserved candor. Soon she found herself relaxed and beginning to have a good time.

Finally, Mark said, "That's most of them. Let's mingle. I believe we've earned our freedom."

In the next hour or so, Ashleigh lost track of the number of people she talked with. Many seemed to go out of their way to make her feel welcome. Her anxiety quickly melted away.

"Oh, there you are," Paige said, walking into the circle surrounding Ashleigh. Excusing herself for the interruption, Paige took Ashleigh aside. "I'm afraid my headstrong daughter is refusing to go to sleep until . . ."

Ashleigh glanced at her watch and cut Paige off. "Sorry. I didn't real-ize it was so late. I promised I'd pop in to see her before bedtime."

As Ashleigh followed Paige up the steps, they heard Philip Sloane's name being bandied about. Snippets of conversation filtered through her state of bliss. "Fifty-thousand unpaid creditors" . . . "fall of the junk bond market . . ."

The laundry list of economic woes she'd read about in *Barron's* en route to Dallas briefly crossed her mind—unemployed retailers unable to buy new cars, stricken investment bankers selling their collectibles and Park Avenue apartments, deal makers no longer indulging in $150 lunches. They had all been artfully interlaced with Sloane's acquisition of the Amalgamated and Consolidated retail empires. Sloane had been a force, Ashleigh thought as they walked through the large commercial-sized kitchen, but to blame the fall of Wall Street on any single individual was a bit far-fetched.

As they climbed the spiral staircase, Ashleigh pushed thoughts of Sloane and other power-mongers from her head. " By the way, Paige, how was your trip to Manhattan?"

Pausing in front of her daughter's room, Paige gave her a mischievous grin. Before she could answer, though, April called out to them.

"Mom, I can't sleep. Can I come back to the party? Please?" April looked to Ashleigh for support.

"How would you like to have me read one of those?" Paige said, gesturing to the new books Ashleigh had given her that April had spread across the top of her comforter.

April's eyes focused on Ashleigh. "You look just like this fairy prin-cess." Her eyes traveled from Ashleigh to the doll beside her, and back again. Then the pint-sized politician asked, "Would it be okay if Ash-leigh read to me?"

Ashleigh got no farther than the second page before the little girl's eyes fluttered closed for the last time, and she was sound asleep.

They closed the bedroom door and headed for the stairs. Paige said, "I didn't realize how much I missed Manhattan until last weekend. The theater, the bright lights, even the hustle and bustle of people on the sidewalks. The heartbeat of Manhattan is like no other. Love it or hate it, no one is blasé. That's where I met Mark, and the crackle of romance in the air seems even stronger . . . ."

As Paige rattled on enthusiastically, Ashleigh thought of the Toddmans' thwarted dreams of a home in Greenwich with a condo in the heart of Manhattan. She wondered if Paige was as content in Dallas as she appeared to be. Was it merely a facade?

"When Mark was tied up with business," Paige continued, "the first thing I did was stroll down Fifth Avenue on my own for a firsthand peek inside De Mornay's. It was great to chat with Glenn Nelson. And what a dramatic change his presentation skills have made. He's brought the store to life."

"I'm not surprised," Ashleigh admitted. "It was a real blow when Bergdorf's lured him from Bentleys Royale. His loyalty had kept him from accepting several lucrative offers, but we couldn't compete with the opportunity to be with such a quality specialty store headquartered in Manhattan." Ashleigh smiled as they reached the bottom of the spiral staircase. "Like yours, his heart never left New York."

"I'd hoped to run into Viviana, but Glenn told me her appearances were unpredictable since Sloane plunged what was left of two great retail empires into Chapter 11. Apparently, she's standing by Sloane, at least for the time being, and at least in public. But I'd be willing to bet Sloane will be history when the money runs out."

Ashleigh shrugged. They quickly melded into the throng of guests, but her mind lingered on Viviana De Mornay-Sloane. Viviana was much stronger and less shallow than most people assumed. Sloane had made and lost fortunes before. And, if rumors were to be believed, he'd protected most of his real estate holdings. Money wouldn't be the main issue. The real question was, could Viviana's marriage survive her husband's loss of power?

Conrad retrieved the key from the lock of their new home and literally swept Ashleigh off her feet to carry her over the threshold.

Ashleigh laughed and threw her arms around his neck. "Isn't this a bit premature?"

He flipped on the entry light and set her gently down on the marble tiles. "Just practicing. I don't want to blow it on Sunday." She looked so damn beautiful. His heart filled with love and desire, but he took a deep breath and resisted the urge to take her straight upstairs. Now, with their weekend visits behind them, he could wait. Soon she would be his forever. Loosening his tie, he led her to the sofa facing the fireplace.

She kicked off her shoes, her eyes shining with delight.

He pushed a strand of glistening hair from her cheek and ran a finger across her smooth skin.

In the reflected light from their entry hall, he saw an expression of amusement cross her face, further peaking his curiosity. "The grand party is behind us. You have my undivided attention, so please let me in on the mystery." He smiled, thoroughly enjoying the drama.

Her lips curved into a mischievous smile, and she said, "I just want you to know that we may be flying separately in about eight months."

It took a moment for the significance to sink in. "Oh, Ashleigh," was all he managed to say before crushing her to him.

"So," she whispered into his shoulder, "the doctor was wrong. It seems you delivered this little miracle the first weekend we disposed of my pills. I'm afraid you'll have to marry me."

He stood looking at her, joy and elation coursing though him. He was a lucky man. "What a wonderful gift," he said.

She looked so young and so very happy. As he reached to undo the buttons in the back of her dress, she wound her arms around his neck and asked, "Me, or the baby?"

In Manhattan, Viviana clenched and unclenched her long pale fingers, her eyes locked on her husband as he stormed to the closet to retrieve another suitcase. His eyes did not meet hers as he tossed his three-suiter on the bed. His face was crimson, and she feared he might have a stroke. "Please, Philip. It doesn't have to be like this. I never said I wanted a divorce."

He shot a malevolent look in her direction and silently continued to haphazardly empty the contents of the mahogany chiffonnier into the bag.

Viviana clutched her stomach and felt her knees go limp and spongy. She gingerly eased herself onto the love seat. She was about to try again when he wheeled around to face her. "Cut the theatrics. If you really cared about me, and our marriage, you wouldn't be obsessed with maintaining your own identity. I've given you everything." Now standing squarely in front on her, he said, "Even, it seems, the means to get along without me."

She felt trapped with him hovering above her. But desperate to make him understand, she patted the seat beside her. "Please."

Instead, Philip backed up and sat on the edge of the bed, his arms folded in front of him.

She leaned toward him, propping her elbows on her knees, and said, "I love you, Philip." That was nearly the truth. She was grateful, and she did care for him. But, she was unwilling to give up her own identity.

"We can work things out. But I can't move to Bermuda. I'm proud to be your wife, but I also need to be my own person. The bankruptcy hasn't changed my feelings for you," she lied.

Although his eyes did not leave her face, his expression told her that he didn't believe her. Still she went on. "I promise to come to Bermuda as often as possible and—"

"No, Viviana." He shook his head sadly, a pained expression on his face. "What you suggest is no kind of marriage for me. I won't take a backseat to your career. Apparently, I'm not enough. I guess I never have been. If so, you wouldn't have to prove yourself to the rest of the world, over and over again."

Viviana studied her cuticles for a long moment and then looked up with tears in her eyes. Slowly, she rose to her feet, knowing this was a battle she wouldn't win. "I'm so sorry," she said, wishing with all her heart he'd take her in his arms, make love to her the way he used to, and tell her he understood.

"So am I," he said. "There's plenty of time to discuss divorce proceedings. At present, I have other priorities."

Feeling the sting of his acceptance of a life without her, Viviana lifted her chin and left the room. She stepped into the sitting room and stood lost in thought, staring at the second hand of the Tiffany clock as it slowly circled inside the gold-leaf frame. Money was no longer a major issue. The best of what she and Philip had together was basking in the glory of his power. She loved to see him on the evening news, loved to open the morning paper and see his face staring up at her as she sipped her first cup of coffee. A stab of pain shot though her chest. She was not alone in her need to feel important and in control of her destiny. Over the past weeks as his power diminished, age had taken its toll on Philip's now-pale face.

She felt a tear slide down her check, then heard his footsteps behind her and turned. She'd wanted to reach out to him, but when she saw his head held high, and the look of authority and superiority on his face, she felt the gulf between them widen. The face looking back at her was filled with malice, cynicism, and greed. This man didn't give a damn about her or anyone else. All he cared about was himself. Viviana cared about many of those same things. She loved beauty and quality in the world that surrounded her, but, even though she did not always show it, she cared deeply about people and their feelings. Philip would survive.

Face to face with that reality, she turned her mind from thoughts of being alone to survival and independence. And, with that turn, she felt an unexpected surge of exhilaration.

CHAPTER
114

Pushing herself up on her elbows, Paige untangled her legs from Mark's and from the smooth cotton sheets. With a contented smile, she ran the palm of her hand across his unshaven cheek and said, "Now I understand that expression."

Mark raised a brow. "What expression?"

She leaned over and whispered in his ear, "*You* most definitely are *not* growing older—just better."

"Is that so?" His tousled hair gave him a youthful look, and the grin on his face could be called nothing but rakish.

"Stop fishing. I just told you so. Now, let's get April and open your gifts."

"I think this morning's gift from you and April would be impossible to beat."

"April?"

"Sure. She wasn't up at the crack of dawn."

By the time they slipped into their robes, they heard a tap on the bedroom door. April burst in with two birthday gifts balanced precariously in her small arms.

"How old are you?" she asked as the packages tumbled onto the king-sized bed.

Bending down to her level, he smiled and asked, "How old do you think I am?"

Her forehead crinkled, and she rolled her tongue around the inside of her cheek, deep in thought. "Twenty?"

Mark laughed. "Close." He gave her a squeeze. Actually, forty-eight didn't feel too bad. He reached out to take the handmade card and package that April eagerly thrust at him. His only fleeting regret was not starting a family in their youth. But as he watched Paige, her impish green eyes mirroring delight as she pulled their adopted daughter onto her lap, he felt luck had played its role. They were enough—more than enough.

Then he opened the gift from Martha Winslow. When it had arrived in his office, he hadn't opened it. Somehow he sensed it was a gift to be opened with his family.

Mark ripped off the gold-leaf paper. As it fell to the floor, revealing a gray-hinged watch box, Paige felt a little flip in the pit of her stomach. The x of the distinguished Rolex emblem was worn off. Paige's curiosity had peaked earlier in the week when Martha called to see if Mark had opened her gift. Now, knowing the significance, she studied Mark's expression.

Mark's hand trembled as he lifted the lid and took the familiar Rolex from the box. It had belonged to Walter Winslow, his mentor and surrogate father. His eyes met his wife's for a brief moment.

"Why did Grandma Martha give Daddy an old watch?"

Paige explained, and then she reminded April it was the day of Ashleigh and Conrad's wedding.

"Can I put on my flower girl dress now?"

"It's already in the car, so it won't be wrinkled before we get to the church," Paige said, watching Mark from the corner of her eye. "Now run along and ask Becky to run your bath."

Mark unfolded the paper enclosed with Martha's gift and began pacing back and forth.

As April skipped out of their room, Paige turned back to Mark. "Darling, please stop."

He didn't stop; instead, he handed her two small pieces of paper. She immediately began reading. Instantly, she understood his silence.

> Dearest Mark,
> The very happiest of birthdays.
> Walter would want you to have this. Forgive me for taking so long—it comes to you with no strings attached.
> Love,
> Martha

The second page was also written in Martha's familiar hand.

> On behalf of the Board and myself, I am making a final appeal for you to come back "home" and save our company.
>
> With Chapter 11 consuming what is left of Consolidated, you are our one-and-only hope. The Board feels so strongly about you and your ability, they negotiated the compensation package I outlined and sent to you and, in addition, have agreed to cover any expense related to you breaking your contract with Nason's.
>
> Please take time to consider this offer. Not another soul possesses your degree of expertise in business and merchandising, nor has gained your sterling credibility with Consolidated's creditors, with Wall Street, and with the business community as a whole.
>
> If you follow your heart and it does not lead you back to Consolidated, I will be surprised.
>
> All my love (whatever you decide),
> Martha

Paige looked up from the note and saw that Mark had stopped pacing. His eyes were riveted on her face as if attempting to read her thoughts.

Her spirits soared, and she smiled. "Looks like we're going home."

He shook his head. "Not so fast. It would take a bloody magician to pull this off." He paused, glancing up at the ceiling. "But I've given it a lot of thought over the last few weeks."

"You have?" Somehow Paige had missed the signals. "But I thought—"

"It's a tremendous risk," he continued, "and before we decide to take it, certain safeguards and incentives must be written into the employment contract. But I think I've come up with a plan that just might work. The thing preventing most companies from climbing out of bankruptcy is the demands to pay for goods up front," he explained. "Without the usual 30-60-90-day billing, the cash flow . . ."

Paige wasn't tuned into the details of his master plan. If anyone was up to the challenge, it was Mark. What she was tuned into was his unbridled enthusiasm. He hadn't been this animated since Philip Sloane first set his sights on Consolidated in January 1988.

When Mark began talking about the implications of breaking his contract with Nason's, she stopped him mid-stride and wound her arms tightly around his neck. "Bullshit," she whispered in his ear. "Nason's is adequately covered."

He grinned and nodded. "Right," he said, as if it hadn't already occurred to him. "Taylor's more than ready to fill my shoes. And probably as ready for a new challenge as we are."

"Get ready, Manhattan, here we come!" Paige squealed.

He pushed the strand of hair from his forehead as he closed their bedroom door. He turned the key in the lock before slipping Paige's robe off her shoulders, the best birthday gift of all.

Questions regarding our vanishing department stores continue to echo from coast to coast, while their future is still being written upon the American scene.

The rise of department stores in the mid-1850s was a major phenomenon, not only for business but also for society. They emerged as a result of mass urbanization. Established vendors and shop owners feared being driven out of business—and many were.

The first notable department store in the world was Le Bon Marché in Paris. In 1852 it began to display a wide variety of goods, each at a fixed price, in various departments under one roof. A "money-back guarantee" was offered that allowed exchanges and refunds. Employing up to 4,000 personnel and with daily sales of $300,000, Le Bon Marché became the anchor of downtown urban centers in the nineteenth century.

In 1858 Rowland Hussey Macy, a Nantucket Quaker and whaler who had failed several times as a store owner, founded a "fancy dry goods" store in New York City on 6th Avenue near 14th Street. There he began selling at fixed prices for cash. He offered discounts and advertised his merchandise. He was the first to employ women executives, and he owned eleven buildings at the time of his death in 1887.

Isidor Straus and his brother Nathan bought full control of Macy's in 1898 and moved the store to Herald Square. In 1902 a new Macy's store that was proclaimed to be "the largest store on earth" was built on that site. It was nine stories tall, featured thirty-three elevators and four escalators, and had a pneumatic tube system. This structure grew to thirty stories and covered an entire city block by 1924. Macy's Thanksgiving Day Parade, which began in the 1920s, drew crowds of more than a million by the mid-1930s.

Just before the 1900s, Dime Stores (also known as Five-and-Dimes) came into prominence and competed for department store clientele. But by the turn of the twentieth century, millions of people shopped in department stores, and the term *downtown* entered daily conversation. In fact, the department store was a contributing factor to the creation of modern skyscrapers. Eight Chicago department stores dominated that city's skyline and commercial life, commanding nearly 90 percent of the retail business. Stores mushroomed in other cities as well, nearly tripling in number between 1909 and 1929.

Many historians credit the department store for liberating women by creating jobs and opening new career opportunities for them. Department stores changed society's values, making it acceptable for women to shop on their own. Department stores provided a window on the world and a valuable meeting space for women.

During the Roaring Twenties, many downtown stores were remodeled as modern pleasure palaces, with high ceilings, wide cathedral-like columns, marble floors, and Art Deco façades. Some included tearooms, restaurants, and concert halls. Department stores added such amenities as air-conditioning and electric lighting that were not yet available in most American households.

With war rationing and supply problems in the 1940s, buyers were cut off from the fashion houses of Paris. They met that challenge by keeping stocks low, selling goods quickly, and convincing customers that they wanted what was offered for sale. At the same time, they began aggressively promoting American designers and turning to Hollywood for inspiration. Casual dressing was introduced. By 1945, business again boomed.

Consumer demands skyrocketed with the postwar baby boom, but as families moved to the suburbs, traffic clogged city streets and people preferred to shop closer to home. Parking in the cities was an overwhelming problem. Downtown business stalled, then declined. As the consumer demographics changed, department store branches opened in the suburban shopping malls, keeping their corporate parents afloat in the 1960s. The three biggest U.S. department stores in the mid-1960s were Macy's, Hudson's, and Marshall Field, in that order, with matching sales volumes.

By the late 1970s and early 1980s, many reputable, established department store conglomerates began to go under—unable to compete with fellow retailers who were doing anything and everything to capture and retain customers. During this period, midnight sales, early morning sales, and all sorts of new sales were initiated. Merchants cut the prices on new merchandise that had not yet hit the sales floors of competitors. No longer did customers line up outside their favorite department store for the "after Christmas" sale. Sales had become year-round events or, perhaps, non-events.

By the early 1980s, department stores faced the strongest adversary of all—other competitive department store merchants. Larger department store conglomerates began to acquire stand-alone department stores, and entire department store conglomerates fell victim to hostile takeovers.

Since the late 1980s to the present, we have seen more and more of our favorite department stores disappear. Today, successful department store conglomerates are focusing on consolidation and branding. There are fewer and fewer department stores. Many regional department store icons have been stripped of their identities, their names replaced by nationally known brands. Is that a positive or a negative? It depends on your perspective. The bottom line is: only time will tell.